THE CHASE

STEEL PACK ALPHAS: BOOK 1

REECE BARDEN

Copyright © 2022, Reece Barden
First electronic publication: October 2022
www.reecebarden.com
All rights are reserved. No part of this book may be used or reproduced in any manner whatsoever without written permission, except in the case of brief quotations embodied in critical articles or reviews. The unauthorised reproduction or distribution of this copyrighted work is illegal. No part of this book may be scanned, uploaded, or distributed via the Internet or any other means, electronic or print, without the author's permission.

NOTE FROM THE AUTHOR

This book is a work of fiction. The names, characters, places, and incidents are products of the writer's imagination or have been used fictitiously and are not to be construed as real. Any resemblance to persons, living or dead, actual events, locale, or organisations is entirely coincidental. The author does not have any control over and does not assume any responsibility for third-party websites or their content.
Due to adult language, violence, and steamy scenes this book is recommended for 18+

CHAPTER 1

BLAKE

Pressing my shaking fingers to the cool glass of my office window, I stare out at the inky sky. The moon is full and bright, rising high and bathing the land below in silver shards of light. The sounds of laughter and music filter in on the breeze.

Everyone else is celebrating.

They're excited for the pack run, where all the wolves in my territory gather to run free through the secluded forest that is our home. It's a chance to reconnect with friends and with nature, to feel free and go wild, and enjoy what we are.

Normally, I live for this night. No matter how busy I am, I make sure I get home to join in and bond with the wolves I don't always get to see day to day.

But not tonight. And I haven't really felt like myself for the last year if I'm honest. As the Alpha of this pack, that's not a good thing. And as the Alpha over all the packs in the region, it's a distinctly bad thing.

I rub my sweaty palm across the back of my neck and try to calm my racing heart. Adrenaline courses through my veins as I struggle to catch my breath. It's been days since I've had more than a couple of hours of sleep. Insomnia forces me to walk the floorboards or return to my office at some godforsaken time of night to distract myself.

There's something seriously wrong with me and it's getting harder to hide it. I blink away the bright spots in front of my eyes, shaking my head to clear the sluggishness from my brain. Given it's getting progressively worse and comes back at each pack run, it's obvious what it is.

Moon madness.

"Is it bad?" Max asks from behind me. I didn't even sense him coming, providing yet more evidence that I'm slipping.

I nod without turning, unable to face my beta, and see the sympathy and worry that I know are etched on his face. We're like brothers, and I've watched him become increasingly anxious as he witnesses me falling apart before his very eyes. To the outside world, they might not yet have noticed, but I can't get anything past Max. He knows my calm demeanor is all a facade at this point. There's no use in pretending. I need his help.

"They'll know I'm sick if I run. I won't be able to control my wolf. Can you make up something, a council meeting or whatever? I'll go to the cabin for a couple of days until it passes."

"*Will it pass?*" he asks, not questioning my decision to abstain from the pack run for the first time. That tells me I'm further gone than even I thought. My trusted friend isn't trying to convince me I should stay and ride it out, because he knows I'm past that point. If anyone gets a whiff of this, my position will become untenable and the questions will be endless.

I sigh and turn slowly, flexing my hands out in front of me, concentrating on stopping the trembling, but it doesn't work. He leans casually in the doorway, head tilted to one side as he observes me. Max's eyes fix on my twitching fingers and his lips press together tightly. When he meets my gaze, I can't maintain focus, and my eyes wander around the room. I glance back at Max and it's the first time in all the years we've known each other that I've seen him genuinely scared. And we've been through some dangerous situations together.

"You just have to do it," he says simply. "I know you don't want to hear it, Blake. I really am sorry. I know it's not what you want, but this has gone on for too long."

Max watches me expectantly, tattooed arms folded over his chest, waiting for me to relent and agree. I remain silent and turn back toward the window, looking out over the dark forest that surrounds the packhouse. She's out there somewhere, waiting for me to come to her... and she's close, so close I can feel it. Taste it. I can't bring myself to give up on her when I know she's near.

Then again, maybe that's the madness talking and my mind is playing more tricks on me.

"Goddamn it, you stubborn bastard," he spits out, exasperated. "Blake, there'll be no coming back if you let this go on for too long. And I'll be the one who has to deal with the fallout." Max clamps his big hand on my shoulder, forcing me to turn and face him. To see his anguish. To hear the truth in his words.

If anyone else grabbed me that way, I'd rip his arm off. But he's right to be upset. Cruelly, it would be up to my best friend and beta to put me down before I become a real danger to my pack or the public.

Of course, there's a simple solution for a mateless Alpha in their late thirties: Give up on my fated mate and take a chosen one instead. It's the only surefire way to save my sanity and my life. But at what cost? It would be different if I had someone I loved to choose as my mate. That's not the case. It would have to be a mating of convenience, and I'm not sure I could live with that.

Ducking into the walk-in closet off to the side of my office, I grab an overnight bag and shove a couple of changes of clothes inside. Coming back out, I add some bottles of water from the fridge and one of the best bottles of whiskey I own from the collection on my shelf. There doesn't seem any point in keeping these for a special occasion anymore.

"Tell Jenna where she can reach me if she really needs to get in touch, but make it clear that I want privacy."

Max's jaw clenches as I pass him on my way out the door. For a second, I think he's going to stop me and make me talk about it again. The words he's biting back hang heavily in the air between us. He thinks I'm making the wrong decision. We've spoken about it before, many times, but that was when it was a hypothetical scenario and seemed way down the line. Not with the threat of moon madness breathing down my neck.

He called me old-fashioned and a sappy romantic for wanting to wait for my mate. The names he would call me now are probably a little less complimentary.

Max has always been open to the idea of taking a chosen mate and feels he could do so without dwelling on what might have been. I wish I could be like that, but I've seen the fated mate bond, seen the magic, the intensity, and the joy… and I want that. I long for it.

I still have hope. It might be just a glimmer, but I won't give up. What kind of mate would I be if I did?

I'll roll the dice one more time, one more moon, and hopefully, it's not Max who has to pay the price for my gamble.

CHAPTER 2

ZOE

Sliding out of the red vinyl booth with an enormous sigh, I rub a hand over my belly and groan. It's so swollen I can barely breathe. I drop the receipt back onto the table, along with a few notes from my pocket, and stretch. My aching muscles protest. They had been hoping they could finally give up for the evening and rest at last, but we still have to make it back home.

"Earl, what are you trying to do to me?!" I moan while flashing him a big grin as he comes out of the kitchen to stand at the counter. He rests his large hands flat on the pale grey surface as he admires his handiwork. This man loves nothing more than to fill people to bursting. I was on my way back from a call out to assist with a foaling mare when the flashing lights of Earl's diner called out to my rumbling stomach and lured me in. Dinner and two pieces of pie later, I'm thinking I would have been better off with the boring sandwich I had originally planned to inhale before falling into bed. I'm so full I can barely move.

"Zoe, I bet you haven't eaten since breakfast," he comments, like a stern parent, drumming his fingers on the counter as he waits for an answer. He rolls his eyes when I have to pause and think about that. I can't even remember whether I ate any breakfast, but I know that I've survived on coffee and adrenaline since.

"My cousin is a veterinarian, and he never stops to sit and eat a meal either. So, if I get the chance, you bet I'm going to take good care of you. Someone needs to." Earl continues, clearly very proud of the amount of food he's tempted me into eating.

I hop onto the foot rail that runs around the outside of the counter. Leaning over as far as I can, I press a kiss to his waiting cheek, where he taps his finger pointedly. Sly old dog. Earl might have been happily married for the last forty years, but I bet he was quite the charmer in his day.

"You're a god among men, Earl," I praise as I toss some change into the tip jar and wave at Mandy, my server, before walking out into the crisp evening air.

It's already dark outside and the town is all but deserted. As I glance back toward the white-painted diner and spot Earl bustling around inside, I realise there's a strong chance he stayed open just for me. It's eerily quiet. He might have closed up and let Mandy go home if I hadn't waltzed in. There isn't another person to be seen. Which is probably a good thing, considering how I look. I zip up my fleece and look down at my worn boots and mud-stained jeans.

At least I hope it's mud. In this job, it could be anything. It's better not to think about it.

"Milk, bread, cereal," I mutter to myself as I push into the tiny store next door to the diner, remembering the reason I was driving home this way in the first place. My fridge at home is practically empty. I need to grab some essential supplies if I want to get through to the end of the week without having to go grocery shopping. I definitely don't have time for that.

Loading my arms with bread, milk, and a box of cereal that probably has more sugar in it than a bar of chocolate, I head to the till and pay. The gangly teenager scans my purchases and accepts my card without once looking up from the screen of his phone. It would be impressive if it wasn't so rude.

"Thank you!" I say brightly, wondering if my overly cheery tone will be enough to get his full attention, but no dice. He's so engrossed in whatever he is watching that I don't think he even hears me. With my arms full, I use my hip to shove the door open and push my way out into the night.

Balancing everything on one arm, I manage to open the car door without dropping anything, and I toss my purchases across the console. The passenger seat is already cluttered with other junk, and I watch in disgust as the milk topples off the pile and onto the floor, squishing the bread.

Wonderful. Too tired to even care, I climb in and turn the engine on.

Glancing in the rearview mirror, I sigh as I pull a bit of straw out of my messy blonde bun and try to ignore the dark circles under my eyes. I look awful.

There's a brief flash of light that catches my eye and I turn to see where it came from. Another car is parked at the far end of the lot, tucked in under the trees and well out of the way. An amber flame glows in the darkness where a cigarette has been lit. It burns even brighter for a second as the smoker takes a deep pull. Whoever it is appears to be looking straight at me.

Propping my groceries back right side up, I reverse my brother's big, old black Land Rover Defender out of the parking lot in a wide arc and set off for home. I'm mentally calculating how much sleep I can still get if I'm home and back in bed within half an hour. It won't be very much.

A loud yawn escapes me and my eyes water. I'm bone tired and even taking a shower when I get home seems like a monumental task. But I need to. I must stink. While a soak in a hot bath sounds much more appealing, I'm afraid I'd fall asleep in the tub. Living alone means nobody to rescue you from drowning.

Shaking my head hard to ward off the drowsiness creeping in, I turn up the radio and roll down the window. My hair whips around my face in the breeze as I sing along to a pop song that

I'm probably far too old to be enjoying. I sit up straighter and blink hard, concentrating on staying awake long enough to get home and crawl in the door.

Relief washes over me as I turn onto my long driveway. Nearly there.

The wide-open pastures around me dance and sway in the breeze. The odd silver light is invigorating. It feels magical, like the energy in the air after a thunderstorm. I suck in a deep breath of fresh air and just enjoy the moment. The peace is why I bought this place after all. I didn't want to be in a city clinic treating caged hamsters and rabbits all day. I wanted the great outdoors. Big skies and open spaces. That and the fact it was all that I could afford within a reasonable drive back to my parents'.

The Land Rover bounces and rolls over the uneven surface of the driveway I need to get fixed. Eventually. It's on the to-do list, but it's way down the order of priority. Hiring someone to help me manage the place is number one before I run myself into the ground. I only took over the practice a year ago and things are going well, but I've spread myself too thin. It's all well and good winning new business, but there just aren't enough hours in the day for me to do it all. Much as it pains me to admit it, I need help.

I'm contemplating where I might advertise for a part-time manager and new veterinary nurse when the glint of something behind me catches my eye in the rear-view mirror. There's a car stopping at the end of my driveway, but with its headlights turned off. If it wasn't for the full moon and the light reflecting off the chrome trim, I never would have seen it. My heart hammers in my chest as I slow down and watch it closely, praying for it to just pull off and go on its merry way.

I curse as it moves again, but not in the direction I want. Instead, it slowly rolls forward and turns into the driveway behind me, lights still off. Sometimes I get late-night calls, but normally they need me to go to them; if it was an emergency patient, surely I'd have a call on my phone. And they definitely wouldn't be driving in the dark with their lights turned off.

My older brother Chase is a military man, protective by nature. With three younger sisters constantly getting into mischief, he always worried about us. Chase drilled into us to trust our intuition when we were out and about and to always be aware of our surroundings. If something didn't feel right, to never worry about looking foolish, just get the hell out of there as fast as we could.

And right now my instincts are screaming at me that something is very wrong, to run. Except I can't. That car, the one that doesn't want me to know it's following close behind, is blocking my only way back to the road.

I'm trapped.

CHAPTER 3

BLAKE

My wolf gradually calms down the farther I get from the packhouse. With the pack run going on without us, he should be itching to get back and run alongside his friends. I try not to dwell on what that might mean as I drive, turning the radio up and enjoying a rare moment of solitude. Being Alpha of a pack of rowdy wolves and living in the main packhouse means I am never truly alone. Since taking over as the head Alpha for the region, things have gotten significantly more hectic. With ten packs under my watch, there is always something that needs to be done.

I love it. It's what I wanted. I worked so hard to get the position and I remember the satisfaction I felt when I found out that the council had chosen me. But there's always a price to pay for success, and that price is privacy. Even when I'm locked in my office or my living quarters, there is always someone or something waiting for me, work to be finished. I haven't had a day off since I started.

The cabin is the only place I ever get to be on my own. It's where I know there isn't anyone right outside the door about to demand my time or attention. There's nobody there that I need to impress, or who'll judge me if I let my guard down and just relax.

I'd like to spend more time there, even if I'm still working on my laptop, but I won't find my mate locked away in the middle of nowhere. I sigh and rub a hand over my stubbled jaw.

Maybe that is the true price of my success. Not having the luxury of time to travel to other packs looking for her. Look where it's gotten me, hiding from my pack in case they figure out I'm losing my mind. Lonely and unmated. If this is what success looks like, I'm not sure I want it anymore.

My phone ringing interrupts my thoughts. I grit my teeth and force a smile onto my face before answering so my frustration doesn't come across in my voice. My patience is not what it should be, but that's not Jenna's fault.

"Hi, Jenna," I answer, knowing exactly what she's going to say before she says it. I can picture the panic in her pale blue eyes when she realized I was gone. To say that Jenna doesn't like surprises would be an understatement.

"Max told us you had to leave, but, Blake, I haven't had time to prepare the cabin. If you're going to stay up there for a few days, I need to get some supplies in. You should have warned me."

She sounds out of breath, and I can hear the chatter of the rest of the pack in the background. They must be finished with the run. I can picture everyone tucking into the food Jenna arranges for when we return, before having a few beers and catching up. Their Alpha should be there with them. I swear I can feel their unease from here.

"It's fine, Jenna. It was a last-minute thing. I'll sort it," I state, not wanting her to fuss or get drawn into the details. Jenna is sharp. We've known each other since we were pups and she knows something is off about this. She knows my schedule better than I do.

"Don't be silly. I'll grab some stuff from here and follow you down. I can stay and help while you're working, like I normally do, and…" she presses, continuing to ramble on, making plans to join me at the cabin. Ignoring what I just said.

"*No!*" I shout, before grimacing when there is stunned silence on the other end of the line. "I'm sorry for snapping. I'm just exhausted. Please, don't worry. I'll stop and pick up some stuff. It's just going to be me, so there's no need to go to any trouble. Don't follow me."

"Fine," she mutters sulkily and I roll my eyes. It's clearly not one bit fine. She's angry I didn't invite along her, but she knows better than to push me when I've made up my mind about something. I'm just about to hang up when she continues.

"But, Blake. I saw your hands shaking earlier. I know what's going on and I'm worried. Talk to me," she pleads softly. I can hear the genuine concern in her voice. The soft click of a door closing and the gradual fading away of the background chatter tells me she's moved somewhere more private. Rather than being relieved to have someone other than Max to talk to about this, I'm annoyed at the intrusion. It's my personal business. Mine and my mate's. An Alpha does not like to admit any weakness, and I certainly don't want the pack talking about it.

"It's fine, Jenna. I'm going up here to work and clear my head. I'm not as old as you seem to think I am. There is still plenty of time for me to find someone who'll put up with me."

I try to sound light-hearted and make a joke of it, but I can tell by the long pause that follows that she's not buying it. We work closely with each other every day. Jenna knows me better than most, and how stubborn I've been about waiting to find my mate.

"You mean you'll consider a chosen mate?" she asks with a note of hopefulness in her voice that's impossible to miss. She doesn't want me to suffer. We've spoken many times over the years about what we'd do if we never found our mates. Jenna is younger than me though, and she's not of Alpha bloodline, so the urgency for her isn't as great. She regularly tries to set me up with females from other packs, but I always refuse.

"Maybe. Look, I need to go, another call is coming through," I lie, guilt gnawing at me. I don't like to fib, but I need to get off this call.

"Okay. Drive safe."

She sounds disappointed by my abrupt end to the conversation, but I ignore it. Jenna is my friend, she works hard for the pack as the manager of the pack house, but my love life is my own. I need to have something for myself.

When the line goes dead, I exhale loudly and thump my head back against the leather headrest. Since when did who I date, or don't date, become a topic of discussion for everyone? I need to shut it down now or the next month is going to be even more painful than the last.

Ahead of me, a red neon sign for Earl's Diner blinks in the darkness. It has a small gas station with a convenience store tucked in beside it. It's late and practically deserted, with just two vehicles parked in the wide lot. I need to pick up some food, anyway. It may as well be here since my wolf is twitchy and suddenly seems desperate to get some fresh air.

As I stop and step out, the faint scent of something delightful tickles my senses. My wolf lunges forward, and it becomes clear exactly why he's so riled up. She was here, and recently.

My wolf howls in my head and claws at my insides, desperate to get out and track the delicious scent. I breathe deep and savour it, the most tantalising smell I have ever come across. I scan up and down the road, but can't see any taillights disappearing from view. Hopefully, someone can point me in the right direction. I stride with purpose toward the tiny store and a bell jingles as I push it open. A scrawny kid looks up at me nervously from his phone when he sees me make a beeline straight for him.

Every cell in my body is on fire, and adrenaline floods my veins.

My mate. I've finally found her.

CHAPTER 4

BLAKE

Even though I know she's not here, I can't help scanning the aisles of the store as I enter, searching for her. My heart is pounding hard in my chest, and I can hear my blood rushing in my ears. Her scent is setting my body on fire. Every cell tingles in anticipation of meeting her, and the hair stands up on the back of my neck.

I shake out my hands, trying to ease the tension firing through me. *She's not here*, I silently repeat to myself. If I don't calm down, I'll miss something that might tell me who or where she is. When I reach the counter, the kid has his wide-eyed gaze fixed firmly on me and is clinging to the counter with such a tight grip that his knuckles are white. If he has an alarm under there, he's about two seconds away from pressing it.

My angry alpha vibes are making him nervous, so I try to rein in my emotions as best I can. Using one hand, I smooth down the front of my shirt, drawing his attention to the expensive suit I'm wearing and the watch on my wrist. He seems to register my clothes, eyes narrowing as he looks outside and spots my luxury SUV. Realisation dawns on his face that while I might be worked up about something, I'm not here to rob him. His shoulders relax and he meets my gaze for the first time, swallowing hard.

"Good evening," I say evenly, using my reassuring alpha voice and hoping to ease his nerves further. "I'm hoping you can help me with something." I raise an eyebrow in question, and he nods cautiously.

"Sure, I'll try anyway. What's up?" He tries to sound unaffected by my presence, but the slight wobble in his voice gives his anxiousness away.

"Well, I'm late to meet a friend and her phone has gone dead. I think she might have popped in here before taking off. Did you see which direction she went? She's quite a catch. I don't want to miss my shot."

I smile my most charming smile, trying to make him feel like we're buddies and he'd be doing me a solid. He slowly smiles back, giving me hope he might have some useful information for me, but his mouth quickly drops into a frown. I can see the disappointment in his eyes that he doesn't know.

"Jeez, dude, I wish I could help. There was a hot chick in here, but I didn't see where she went," he apologises, reaching up to scratch at his thin, patchy beard. I grit my teeth at the disrespectful words he uses to describe my mate. The future mother of my children. I should snap his skinny neck.

Focus.

"Shit," I curse, balling my fists and turning to go back outside. I jog for the door, but just as I push out into the night, he calls out behind me.

"Hey, mister! Check the diner. Earl doesn't miss much, especially when it's this quiet."

My gaze shoots towards the white building next door and I veer towards it, sniffing the air as I go. She was definitely here too, but even earlier. Her scent is very faint now, but I can still follow it to a booth along one wall. No other scents linger nearby. At least she was alone.

I can't believe she was sitting here, probably less than half an hour ago, but now she is gone. Only a hint of her scent remains, like a ghost of her presence.

I can't let her slip through my fingers. Bending down to pick up a receipt from the seat, I bring it to my nose. She touched this and held it in her hand. I close my eyes and breathe deeply, needing her scent to keep my head as all sorts of horrible scenarios flit through my brain.

What if she was just passing through on business? What if she lives on the other side of the country, and this was the last stop on her way out of town?

An older gentleman watches me with curiosity from behind the immaculate counter, which he has been pretending to wipe down since I walked through the door. Shoving the receipt into the inside pocket of my jacket, I walk confidently over to him and extend a hand. He looks at it for a second, then back up to my face, before reluctantly reaching over to shake it, staring me straight in the eye as he does. I don't miss the extra little squeeze he gives my fingers before he releases me.

"I'm looking for the woman who was in here a while ago, sitting there." I point over to the booth and the man I am assuming is Earl doesn't follow my finger. He knows exactly who I'm talking about. There aren't many fresh scents in here. Things must have been really quiet this evening. Earl stands back to his full height, and despite his age, he's tall and well-built. This man is no pushover, and he doesn't seem to like me.

"You the FBI?" he asks, looking up and down derisively at my dark navy suit, a hint of a smirk playing at one corner of his mouth. He's mocking me. I bristle, not used to anyone questioning me, especially in such a dismissive manner.

"No," I admit, "but-" Earl cuts me off by raising his hand up and shaking his head as if to say *don't even bother*.

"Then tell me why I should tell a stranger, a suit like you, who's clearly not from around here, anything about one of my customers? And a woman, no less." He raises an eyebrow at me and rage courses through my veins like hot lava.

This is wasting precious time. She's getting further away from me every minute I stand here talking, but I respect what he's saying and what he's doing. I could be a creep. Sniffing the receipt probably didn't help.

Taking a deep breath, I pause before I say something that I might regret. A quick glance around tells me this is a well-run place. Everything is immaculate. There are numerous framed awards and recommendations on the walls. While it's not busy tonight, it's safe to assume it usually is, and I bet Earl is here every single night. He knows everyone and everything that goes on in this place.

Maybe honesty is the best tactic because bullshitting him definitely won't get me anywhere.

"Because she's the love of my life and I'm going to marry her," I say, with a completely straight face. "If she'll have me, of course."

He lets out a booming laugh at that and slaps a hand to his thigh as he doubles over. That wasn't what he expected.

"*You?*" He bursts out laughing once more, as though this is the funniest thing he's ever heard and looks me up and down again, stopping for a second to take in my shiny dress shoes. Assessing me, and clearly finding me lacking. Good. I'm not worthy of my mate. I already know that. He doesn't have to find it so hilarious, though. Wiping a tear from his cheek, he meets my gaze again, and I tilt my head in question.

"Oh, Lord, you're actually serious. I guess we're really having this conversation," he says, shaking his head as he comes back to the counter. "Then tell me, Loverboy, why have I never seen her with you before?"

Jackpot.

She's not some stranger drifting through town, she's a regular. Which is why he's so protective of her.

"It's a recent development," I answer smoothly, and he raises his eyebrows, sensing no deceit in my answer.

"Then why don't you know where to find her? I'm sure as hell not going to tell you where she lives if she hasn't herself," he scoffs, eyeing me dubiously.

"I was supposed to meet her, but I'm late and missed my chance. If I mess this up, I'll never forgive myself," I say honestly because, technically, I was meant to meet her. It's destiny. If I mess this up, I'm doomed, because after knowing what it's like to find my mate, to feel these urges… I know what it would be to give this up. I can't even fathom doing that now that I've had a taste. There's no going back. If I wasn't already feeling the effects of the madness, I could wait. I could come here every day until she reappeared. But the one thing I don't have is time. I need to find her now.

"Sorry, buddy. I feel for you, I do. She's a wonderful gal, and I'm sure she'll give you a second chance, but I just can't give out her personal information. It's not right."

He's right, of course, but *fuck!*

It's a crushing blow after being so close. So fucking close.

My skin itches with the need to see her right now, to touch her, to hold her. I'm already trying to figure out how much time I can take off work to come down here and stake the place out when someone clears their throat from the entrance to the kitchen.

"Blake Steel, isn't it?" a soft feminine voice asks.

Whipping my head up, my gaze connects with the big brown eyes of a female wolf. Not one of mine. Not one of any pack. A rogue. She holds my gaze for a second and I see a glimmer of knowing sympathy in them before she turns to Earl and walks over to him, placing a hand gently on his arm.

"It's okay. Zoe mentioned him."

Zoe.

"Zoe." My mate's name sounds perfect as it rolls off my tongue. "Zoe."

Earl glances at me as though I'm not of sound mind as I repeat her name again.

"He doesn't seem like her type," he quips, tipping his head toward me again. The mere suggestion that she has a type, that she has any male in her life other than me, causes my heart to constrict. My chest rises and falls rapidly as my breathing quickens. The brunette gives me a warning look as she aims a disarming smile up at Earl. If I don't behave myself, I won't find out anymore tonight. I need to keep it together.

"And how would you know? She's never brought anyone in here," she says kindly, for my benefit, and Earl huffs, still eyeing me warily.

"I'll vouch for him, Earl. He's a good guy. I know his friends and the charity work they do. They're great people. You never know, he and Zoe could be soulmates. Take pity on the man." She laughs as she looks toward me and I blink slowly at her, a silent thank you for having my back. Earl rolls his eyes, but they crinkle with the small smile that crosses his face. He's an old romantic at heart, I can just tell.

"You sure about this, Mandy?" he asks her, looking at me appraisingly again. I try to make myself look as harmless as possible.

"Absolutely," she replies, giving him an assuring nod. Earl's shoulders drop as he relents. The soulmate's part got to him in the end.

"Fine. You'll find her at the Shady Pines Veterinary Clinic, but you leave her alone till the morning."

He points a finger right in my face, a stern expression fixed there. He's unaffected by my broad grin as I nod vigorously in response. I can't believe it. I'll get to see my mate tomorrow.

"Thank you, sir." I shake both his hands in mine and mouth another thank you to my saviour standing at his side. I owe this little wolf big time.

"If you mess with her, you'll regret it. She's an angel," Earl warns in a brusque tone. Mandy nods along beside him. She meets my gaze with a cool stare, something that's unusual for any wolf, especially a packless one, to do with an Alpha. She doesn't seem to have a submissive bone in her body. A smile plays on her lips as she turns back to Earl and chuckles.

"Anyway, if he does anything wrong, Zoe's used to castrating dogs."

CHAPTER 5

ZOE

My mind races as I run through all my options. There aren't many.

Maybe because I'm driving his Land Rover, I try to think about what my brother would do. He wouldn't just meekly wait to see what the creepy driver wants, that's for sure, but I'm no fighter. I need to get myself somewhere safe, but my nearest neighbours are too far away to run for it.

Fuck it.

With only a half-baked idea in the back of my head, I press my foot to the floor, grateful for the sudden acceleration driving a manual allows, and take off, bouncing over the pothole-filled laneway. I have no elaborate plan other than to get inside, lock the door, and call the police. And pray that they happen to be nearby.

A quick glance in my mirror tells me I've caught whoever it is off guard. Any lingering hope I had that this is a customer and that they're going to think I'm nuts for driving like a crazy woman is dashed when I see them rapidly pick up speed. I've extended the distance between us. Not by much, but hopefully, it's enough. I skid to a stop next to the side door and leap out, keys and phone in hand. Without shutting the car door behind me, I race to the door and key in the code with trembling hands.

By some miracle, I get it right, even though I'm shaking like a leaf. I wrench the door open just as the sound of screeching tyres behind me sends a chill up my spine. This is no innocent late-night call-out. Resisting the urge to look over my shoulder and see exactly where they are, I dart inside. The second I'm in, I use all of my strength to slam the door shut behind me. Wiping my clammy hands on my thighs, I edge back and press myself against the far wall, as far away as I can get.

Think, think, think.

We use this entrance for deliveries, so the supply room is the closest door. I rush inside, flicking on the light as I pass and scan the shelves for anything useful. Shoving a few random items in my pockets before grabbing what I really came in here for, I creep back outside. I can just about make out two deep voices on the other side of the door. My blood runs cold when I see the handle move. I choke back a cry when it rattles as someone shakes it violently before they slam their fist against the metal door in frustration. I can't believe this is happening.

As quietly as I can, I move to my office and lock the door behind me. Tossing my keys onto the desk, I log in, my fingers racing over the keyboard as I fire up the computer. My screen fills with the feed from the CCTV cameras. My brother forced me to install a decent system when he found out there had been a robbery here a few months before I bought the place. The footage is crisp, and I always suspected that he spent way more than he let on when his buddies installed it. It's clear enough for me to make out two men circling the premises in opposite directions, hoods up, looking for an easy way in.

They were waiting for me instead of just breaking in while I was out. They need something from me. My eyes drift to the set of keys sitting on my desk, which I am guessing are what they're after. There's no cash kept on site, as they discovered the last time. I have plenty of expensive equipment, but it's not stuff that would be easy to sell for a petty criminal.

Drugs are the only thing that makes sense.

That's what the previous owner thought they were looking for when he was robbed. Except they couldn't get into his strong cabinet without his keys, so they left empty-handed, but it seems they've come back.

If they want my keys, they can have them. It'll buy me some time. Another look at the cameras shows them testing the rear door, but some loud barking from my overnight guests makes them think again and they tip their heads toward the front of the building.

Tiptoeing out of my office to the front of the building, my heart thumping in my chest, I toss my keys into the tray on the reception desk and sprint back. I click the door shut just as a violent bang rattles the front door. I nearly jump out of my skin when the jarring sound fills the air again as I settle into my chair. Flexing my fingers and taking some deep breaths to calm my jitters, I load my rifle carefully and watch the feed.

One man takes two steps back before aiming a well-placed kick at the door. The whole thing shakes, and I swallow hard. His friend hands him a crowbar and my stomach plummets. It won't keep them out for long.

Lifting the phone to my ear, I call the police, whispering my address and that a break-in is in progress. The operator assures me that someone will be here as soon as they can, but that's little comfort when you live in the middle of nowhere.

I watch with dread as the mangled front door gives way and swings wide open. As the first man strolls inside, he lifts his face to the camera, shoves back his hood, and blows me a kiss. With a wink that makes my blood run cold, he heads straight for the front desk and starts rummaging through the drawers while his friend opens and closes every cabinet, searching. They know what they're looking for.

Standing straight with a triumphant look on his face, he grabs my keys and dangles them from his fingers. With a shout that I hear from my office, he and his partner split up to search for the locked cabinet where the controlled substances are kept. My time is almost up.

I squeeze my eyes shut and drag in a deep breath. There is no way the police are going to get here in time to help me. The door to my left, the second door into this room, leads to the kennels for dogs being kept here for treatment. If I leave that way, the animals will bark and they'll hear me, but maybe I could still make it around to the Land Rover in time.

There's a chance they won't even care that I'm running away and will just continue their search.

A furious roar from the supply room tells me that's not going to happen. A quick glance at my screen shows the guy who seems in charge, tip over one of the free-standing shelves in anger, raining gloves and face masks down all over the floor.

"You fucking bitch!" he shouts, kicking something out of the way and stomping for the door. "You'll be begging to give me the code when I'm done with you. I'm going to enjoy teaching you a lesson."

He's found the cabinet, which I replaced as soon as I arrived with a stronger one. One that needs a combination, not a key. Clearly, he's unimpressed. If I'm going to escape, it's now or never. I have no intention of letting that man teach me anything.

With my back pressed flat to the door, I reach behind me and twist the handle, stepping back into the long corridor. I keep my eyes fixed firmly on the locked office door that is all that remains between me and the burglars. Slipping through quietly, I gently close it, wincing at the soft click it makes. I don't switch on any lights, afraid of alerting them to where I am. Not that it'll take them long to figure it out once they get into my office.

The silence is deafening, and goosebumps dance across my skin. Why aren't the dogs barking? Something is off.

Slowly, I turn around. It's not just the expected four sets of eyes from the dogs that greet me, but a man. A third man. No, no, no.

How did he get in without getting caught on the cameras? Why did the animals not alert when he broke through the back door? Why are they all just lying flat in their crates?

The man doesn't move a muscle. He doesn't say a word. He's big and broad and even in the near pitch black, I can tell he's breathing hard and staring straight at me. My body goes rigid and my mouth is dry. I'm cornered. I've nowhere left to go.

We stare at each other for what seems like an eternity, but in reality, is only a couple of seconds. The air crackles with tension and I wait to see what he'll do, my feet rooted to the spot in terror while I suck in deep breaths. A hint of spicy aftershave hits me, alluring and masculine, and it seems at odds with the terrifying situation that I even notice it. I ignore it though, as I keep my gaze firmly on his. They seem to glow silver in the darkness and I'm transfixed. I have to fight the urge to move closer to him to get a better look.

What the hell is wrong with me?

Suddenly, a low growl breaks the spell, and he lunges toward me. I can't help the small scream that escapes me. He moves so fast it startles me and, without thinking, I fire the gun. It clatters to the floor with a loud bang as I throw it away from me, raising my hands to my face in shock that I've done it.

Pressing a hand to his side, he bends over to look at the weapon lying on the tiles beside him. He slowly raises his gaze to mine and prowls forward into the one shard of moonlight sneaking in through a narrow window. I can see him clearly now, a white dress shirt tucked in a pair of navy suit trousers, a belt, and smart shoes. His shirt sleeves are rolled up to his elbows, revealing tanned, toned forearms.

This is a man that takes care of himself. This is no common thief.

Confusion is written all over his handsome face as he stalks forward silently, following me as I skirt away. He's seemingly unfazed by what had just happened. My legs hit a cabinet stretching along one wall, and I grip the edge behind me tightly. I have nowhere left to go as he leans close, never taking his eyes off mine, and whispers.

"You shot me?"

CHAPTER 6

BLAKE

Normally, I'm a man of my word. Tonight, however, I leave Earl's diner and drive straight to the vet practice that Zoe owns, fully intending to go back on the promise I just made. I won't try to see her tonight. I want our first meeting to be special, but there is absolutely no way I can drive back to the cabin without at least seeing where she lives.

Zoe, my mate. I love how that sounds. It's heaven to finally know her name. The woman who already owns me, heart, body, and soul.

Grinning to myself, I whistle and drum my fingers on the steering wheel to some imaginary tune as I follow the winding road out of town. I'm perfectly content, or in all honesty, excited, about the prospect of sleeping in my car tonight, once I'm able to be close to her. Cooper, one of the Alphas under my command, once told me how he used to sleep in the woods outside his mate Hayley's house when they first met, just to keep his wolf calm. It never made sense to me before, but it does now.

Almost a year ago, I met Cooper's mate, a human blessed with beauty, elegance, and poise, before he had officially claimed her. I'm not proud to admit that it had occurred to me to steal her out from under his nose when he was making a spectacular mess of their relationship. Not that it would have been as simple as that. They are fated mates after all, but my wolf adored her instantly. There was a connection I'd never experienced before, and it made me think that if she wasn't destined for Cooper, she would have made the perfect chosen mate for me. Not once have I thought the same about another woman, before or since.

However, I couldn't be happier that they worked things out. My wolf knew she wasn't ours, despite whatever was between us. I wouldn't recognise my own fated mate's scent if I took a chosen mate instead. The thought of that is unbearable. It seems like the ultimate betrayal.

I slow down as I reach the long driveway that runs down to her clinic. Pausing on the empty road, I sit in my idling car with the hazard lights on while I consider my options. Without knowing the layout of her property, I should stop here. If I drive down and she sees my headlights, I might frighten her. That's the last thing I want, but my wolf is eager to hear her heartbeat. To know she's here and is okay.

Maybe I should walk closer just to appease him, like the stalker that I am clearly becoming.

Parking at the side of the road, I open the door and hop out, planning to go the rest of the way on foot. Instantly, my enhanced senses pick up a loud thumping noise and I frown, trying to work out what it could be at this time of night. Suddenly, with one loud crack, it becomes clear what I'm hearing. Splintering wood.

When the indistinct murmur of two male voices carries to my ears on the breeze, my blood turns to ice. Someone is breaking into my mate's property. With no idea whether she is there or if she's hurt, panic grips me, along with a blinding fury that someone would dare threaten my mate.

I jump back into my car and force myself to drive quickly but carefully toward the clinic. Keeping my lights off, I want the element of surprise. I roll quietly to a stop and park behind the two abandoned vehicles outside. One sniff tells me that the large black SUV belongs to my mate. The smell of fear lingers inside the vehicle, despite the driver's door being left wide open. She was in a rush to get inside the building. A dark sedan has blocked her in, and the simmering rage building in my chest threatens to boil over.

They scared her, chased her, and then made sure she couldn't escape. These pathetic excuses for men are going to regret coming here.

They don't seem to be too concerned about being heard as they shout and crash around inside, searching for something near the front of the building. I circle around the back to get a sense of where Zoe might be. Much as I'd love to just barge in and end their miserable lives right now, it's probably not the first impression I want to make on her. She must be terrified. I'll do everything I can not to make that any worse.

Creeping up to the back entrance, I sense the animals waiting inside. They can sense my presence and have fallen silent, as most animals do in the presence of a dominant predator. With the frustrating mixture of hundreds of stale human scents and animals of all kinds, I can't lock on to where Zoe is, but she's definitely still in the building.

Using my supernatural strength, I break open the door easily, the lock dangling uselessly on the inside of the door as I shove it open quietly. Blinking eyes track me in the darkness, afraid to move in case they become the focus of the anger rolling off me in waves.

I'm halfway across the room when one door on the end wall cracks open slightly. My mate's scent drifts through, and my head swims with the desire to rush to her, pushing all rational thoughts of where I am and what's going on out of my mind for just a second. Opening it just wide enough for her to slip through, she steps inside and I see her profile briefly before she presses the door shut again, careful not to make a sound.

Hayley? It can't be.

My legs go weak as devastation unlike anything else I've ever experienced washes over me and crushes my soul. My sick mind is playing cruel tricks on me. Did I ever scent my mate? Or was that a figment of my imagination, conjured up by a wolf who was desperate to find her? I'm not sure, but I know one thing… this woman is not mine. Despite what my wolf wants to believe.

My body is convinced that we've finally found our mate, yet my eyes are telling me it's all a lie. It's Hayley standing in front of me. I don't know what's going on, but perhaps my wolf's connection to her has brought us here to help our friend. And she's clearly in trouble.

The moment she senses another presence in the near darkness, I watch the muscles in her slim shoulders tense. While waiting for her to turn and realise it's only me, I mourn the loss of something I never even had. My soul is destroyed, torn into tiny pieces. It felt so real. I could almost touch it. Taste it. I was already picturing what life would be like, living together within the pack. Building a new home. Starting a family… but it vanished in a heartbeat.

I'm still lost in my own thoughts when I notice she is staring at me without a flicker of recognition on her beautiful face. Moving slowly into the light so she can see me better, my wolf growls a low rumble of longing, which I'm not quick enough to smother. As the sorrowful sound fills the small space around us, her eyes widen in shock. She doesn't know what that noise is.

As she gasps and the light touches her face, I see it.

Silver eyes, not gold. It's not Hayley.

Twins.

Elation fills me, and without thinking, I rush toward her. I see the flash of fear in her eyes, and I regret it immediately. I regret it more when the gun she's holding goes off, and a sharp pain punches my side.

She throws the gun to the floor in horror and steps back, hands over her mouth. I stride forward and close the distance between us. My head is all over the place. I lost her and got her back again in the space of a few seconds. My wolf is demanding to get near. Entering her personal space, I lean in to get a big lungful of her intoxicating scent. She doesn't push me away and I rejoice when I hear her breath catch as my lips brush against her silky golden hair.

"You shot me?" I whisper, my gaze fixed on her neck where her pulse flutters under her creamy skin. She blinks up at me, like a deer caught in headlights, and it takes every ounce of self-control I possess not to reach up and stroke her cheek to comfort her. I want to, more than anything, but I'm a stranger to her. At least, for now. Resisting the urge, I focus on getting her safe. We'll have plenty of time to get to know each other once I get her away from here and far away from these men.

Straightening, I pluck the dart out of my stomach and place it on top of the cabinet behind her, and the clink as it hits metal seems unnaturally loud in the complete silence. Zoe winces and I see the guilt in her eyes. Shamelessly, I use the opportunity to move into her space again and feel the warmth of her body close to me. My chest is inches from hers as I dip my head until we're eye to eye.

"How long do I have?" I ask slowly, and her lips part slightly, about to speak, but then she frowns.

"What do you mean?" she whispers, staring up at me, confused.

"Well, I came here to help, but you just shot me with a tranquilizer dart. So how long do I have?" I repeat. This is a problem. A big problem. I'm not much good to her if I'm asleep on the floor.

"Maybe two or three minutes. It's not an exact science," she answers, looking me up and down, trying to guess my weight.

"Damn it." That's not long enough for me to get her away from here. "Angel, we're going to discuss what you just did some other time, but right now, I need you to listen to me and do exactly what I say."

I hustle her back through the door into an office and sit her in the chair. Fire flashes in her eyes at being told what to do, but she complies, still a little off-balance and probably in shock. She still doesn't know what I'm doing here. Me saying I'm here to help won't be enough to convince her.

"Once I go outside, you will lock these doors and stay right here. Call Cooper. Tell him Blake is here and what's going on. Don't open these doors for anyone, including *me*. Only Cooper or the police. Do you hear me?"

"How do you-"

She's about to ask how I know Cooper, but I hold up a hand to silence her. We don't have time for this. Zoe narrows her eyes at me. She has no intention of doing what I say. I can see it in her eyes and I ordinarily, I'd love it. Just not right now.

"Do you hear me?" I demand again, gripping her chin between my thumb and forefinger, tipping her head back so I can look her in the eye and show her how serious I am. I can't resist stroking her skin to soften my actions and enjoying the tingles that shoot through my fingertip as we touch skin to skin.

"I'm going to fix this, Zoe, but since I might be about to go for a little nap any second now, I need you to promise you'll do what I'm asking so that I can stop wasting time."

Her pale gaze softens and flicks to the spot of bright red blood on my pristine white shirt. Guilt washes over her features once again, and she nods reluctantly. Before I even realise what I'm doing, I press a soft kiss to her lips and run from the room, gesturing for her to come and lock it behind me. She stands on wobbly legs and follows behind. Slamming the door shut, I hold it closed until I hear the lock turn and her footsteps retreating to the far side of the room.

Turning back to the corridor, two heavy-set men stare back at me, pissed off at my unexpected arrival. One carries a crowbar hanging loosely by his side, waiting for me to make my move. He's mistaken if he thinks that flimsy weapon will protect him tonight. Normally this would be laughably easy, but I can already feel the effects of the tranquilizer on my thoughts and my movements. Everything is sluggish, and if Zoe is right, I only have about a minute left before I'm out cold.

Except I have a mate to protect, and there's no way I'm going to let them get anywhere near her while there's still a breath left in my body.

CHAPTER 7

ZOE

I touch my fingertips to my lips gently as I sit back down, dazed, and fire up the feed to my cameras again. They still tingle and burn where he kissed me. I don't think I've ever reacted like that to a man, particularly one that bossy. Whom I don't know. In the middle of a robbery. After I shot him with a tranquilizer dart. Before he went out to protect me, drugged up to his eyeballs.

I don't need the butterflies in my stomach or the goosebumps on my skin to know that this man is different.

Glued to the monitor, I watch him stand tall and bravely face the two men. His stance is relaxed and confident, but in his expensive suit and immaculate white shirt, he looks more like a high-priced lawyer than a brawler. I'm barely able to watch as the first of the thugs takes a threatening step toward him, crowbar bouncing against the palm of his other hand menacingly. Tattoos snake down his wrists and out from the edge of his sleeves. A distinctive jagged scar runs down the side of his neck.

These aren't kids looking to score some drugs, these are dangerous professionals. And they're not worried about one man standing in their way. Shit. I have a feeling I'm about to watch Blake get his ass kicked.

Dialling Cooper's number, I stand again and pace behind my

desk, eyes fixed on the screen. Moving lips tell me there are some quiet words being spoken. Good, talking is better than fighting. Blake can buy us some time until the police get here. I would offer them the code for the drugs, but I think we're well beyond that point now. We've seen their faces. If they were going to just leave, they would have run away by now.

"Zoe?"

Cooper's sleepy voice answers on the second ring, and I hear the rustle of sheets in the background as he sits up in bed to take the call. His voice is hushed and thick with concern. I don't think I've ever called my brother-in-law before, other than about their wedding plans. He immediately knows something is wrong.

"Cooper, I'm at the clinic. Two guys have broken in and I don't know what to do. Some guy named Blake just showed up and said to call you," I blurt out, speaking as quickly as I can because I want to eavesdrop on what's being said in the hallway.

"Blake? As in *Blake Steel?*" he asks. I hear more rustling, and I know he's already out of the bed, pulling on clothes.

"I don't know. Tall guy, with a suit and dark hair. Hot," I add for good measure, and then roll my eyes. I doubt Cooper really cares about that.

"He's gone out to tackle them, and told me to stay here, but he's going to get himself killed. I can't just hide and let him get hurt."

Cooper's footsteps on wooden stairs and the low rumble of another deep voice drift down the line. He's already on the move.

"That's exactly what you're going to do," Cooper says forcefully. "Believe me, Zoe, Blake can take care of himself… and you. Just stay put, and I'll be there as soon as I can."

"But-" I don't get the chance to tell him that Blake is about to go night-night before he cuts the call. Cooper can't do anything about that, anyway. I lower the phone and creep over to the door, pressing my ear against it to hear what Blake is saying to the two guys.

Maybe he's a lawyer? Maybe he'll be able to convince them to leave before the police get here and not do anything that will make this situation worse for themselves.

"Leave or I'll fucking kill you," Blake growls out, low and scarily confident. Okay, so he's not trying to de-escalate the situation.

"If you don't get out of the way right now, we'll have some fun with your girl while we get that code out of her. That's after we cut off your balls and tie you to a fucking chair so you can watch."

The tattoo guy speaks cheerfully, like he's talking about the weather forecast, not doing unspeakable things to the two of us. These men are pure evil. Blake must be terrified, even though he's doing a good job of hiding it. There's a brief pause, and then a chuckle from just the other side of the door. Blake's laughing. *What the hell?* Is that the drugs kicking in?

"Do your worst," he replies calmly, and my heart skips a beat. Is he crazy? They'll kill him.

There's a loud thud and the door rattles in the frame. The noises of a fight carry to my ears, huffs and moans, and the sound of hard knuckles hitting soft flesh. I run back to my computer to see what's going on. The sight of Blake holding one man off the ground, one hand twisted in the front of his hoodie, is the last thing I expected to see. His companion is slumped against the wall to the side, just below a large head-shaped dent in the plaster.

Blake lowers the man down a few inches, bringing him close to his face. Their noses are only inches apart. I don't know what he says, but the other man's eyes widen in shock, and he kicks his legs wildly, clawing at Blake's iron grip on him, desperate to get away.

Blake tosses him effortlessly down the hall and he lands in a heap with a sickening thud. The thief's arm bends awkwardly underneath him, and he cries out, but still continues shuffling backward. He's still trying to put distance between himself and Blake, who just stands there staring at him. With fists clenched by his sides, chest rising and falling with each heavy breath, my unexpected defender doesn't look like a lawyer anymore. He looks dangerous now, with his shirt torn open and his neat hair a mess. And sexy as hell.

Blake's gaze flickers back to my door for a second. He seems torn for a moment, but then his expression hardens as he takes a step away, zeroing in on the man scrambling on the floor, cradling his useless arm, and wailing like a banshee. Blake stalks forward like a predator hunting his prey with lethal intent. Without any warning, the other man suddenly lunges away from the wall and clutches Blake by the thigh, plunging something shiny deep into his leg. Blake grabs the back of his head and slams it into the wall again, rendering him unconscious once more. It's brutal but effective.

Blood pours from the wound on his thigh immediately. It's a nasty injury. I'm about to run to the door when Blake's voice booms out.

"Stay put!" he yells, and the other man freezes where he is, watching with horror as Blake yanks the scalpel free without so much as flinching and tosses it to the side. I know that command was really meant for me. He wants me to stay locked in my office as I promised. I grit my teeth and take a deep breath. It goes against every instinct I have not to help him immediately, but clearly, Cooper was right. Blake can handle himself.

On slightly unsteady legs, Blake drags the unconscious man close to his friend, grabbing a roll of bandages from the spilled contents of the supply closet as he passes. He binds their ankles and wrists quickly, leaving no doubt in my mind that he's done it before. More than once.

Gripping them by the scruffs of their necks, he drags them, one in each hand, into one of my examination rooms as I follow his every move on the video feed. Removing the key from the back of the door, he points right in their faces and says something that makes the conscious one pale even further. Turning on his heel to walk back out of the room, Blake locks the door from the outside and looks around, taking in the mess and carnage before shaking his head slightly. The mess is the least of my worries.

Blake's steps falter as he turns back toward my office and, for the first time, he walks with a limp, using one hand against the wall to keep himself upright. His navy trousers are shiny from the blood that has soaked through them. He's losing way too much. I need to look at that wound. I'm halfway across the room before I even realise it.

"Zoe, I can hear you thinking from here. So help me, goddess, if you leave that room, when I wake up, I'm going to put you over my knee," he warns. I hear him slump against the door and lower himself to the ground with a pained groan. Freezing on the spot, I loosen my grip on the door handle. How did he know?

"Did you call Cooper?" he asks, his voice sounding slightly slurred. The tranquilizer is kicking in. He won't be able to fight it much longer.

"Yes," I answer, kneeling down and pressing my forehead where I know his back rests just on the other side of the wooden panel. I can't believe what this stranger just did for me. He was magnificent. An overwhelming need to touch him, to hold him, washes over me.

"Good girl," he murmurs with satisfaction, and something stirs within me at his praise. "If he hasn't already, tell him to call Max."

"Okay. Blake?" I ask softly, needing to hear his voice once more before the drugs take him under. How am I having this reaction to him? It seems completely inappropriate to want to climb into this man's lap and kiss him senseless right now. Is this a reaction to trauma? Or is this why I'm single? I have to wonder, because I'm only attracted to men during life and death situations.

"Yes, angel?" His voice is weak now and I hear shuffling. The sound of his voice seems as if it's lower against the other side of the door now, as if he's lying down, unable to hold himself upright any longer.

"Thank you," I choke out. I want to say more, but what? The thud of his head hitting the floor and the lack of response lets me know he's out.

Jumping to my feet, I pull open the door carefully. Blake flops over onto his back as I open it wide. One hand limply holds the scalpel, as though he still thinks he can protect me in his sleep. My heart melts at the sight.

Glancing around me to figure out a plan, I make a mental list of what I need. Blake is slightly bigger than my normal patients. I'm not sure how this is going to work.

This isn't what he wanted, but tough. Those two guys are locked up tight, and I'm not letting him bleed out in my clinic. Leaning down to check his breathing, I can't resist stroking his cheek as he lies there, perfectly still. He really is stunningly beautiful. Slicing open his trousers reveals an expanse of suntanned, well-muscled thigh. One quick look assures me his femoral artery wasn't severed, which is good, but he's still bleeding heavily from the wound.

Leaping into action, I grab a tarp from one of my shelves and bring it out to the hallway, grunting and groaning as I try to manoeuvre his massive body onto it. I only get him half on, but it's enough. Dragging him into the next examination room takes every ounce of strength that I have. Blake is clearly more built than the well-tailored suit allows me to see.

I pull what I need down onto the floor with me. He might not be happy about this when he wakes up, but I'll gladly let him follow through on his threat if he's that annoyed about it. I have a feeling that being taken over the knee by Blake Steel wouldn't be a punishment at all.

Remembering my phone and that Cooper might call me, I run back to my office to get it. Even being away from Blake for a few seconds makes me uncomfortable. Rationally, I know there isn't anyone else here to attack me, but I still feel jumpy being on my own. I walk back into the exam room, checking my phone and see multiple messages from Hayley. Planning to call her on speakerphone as I stitch up Blake, I move toward the sink to wash my hands and freeze. My phone smashes to the ground as I slam my hands over my mouth to muffle my scream.

Blake's gone. Instead of the six-foot-something man I left lying sprawled out on the floor, there's a grey wolf.

An enormous one.

CHAPTER 8

ZOE

A gigantic, dark grey wolf is lying passed out on my clinic floor, injured. Just when I thought we were over the crazy part of this night.

I've never seen a wolf up close before. The vet part of my brain is in awe. The rest of me is looking out the window at the full moon, putting two and two together, and making ten. I'd like to think there is a reasonable explanation, but for the life of me, I cannot think of anything that is going to explain this. Other than the obvious. Which is that the man I just kissed is a werewolf.

An image of Blake lying in the same spot just seconds ago flashes into my mind, but it seems so absurd I push it away. I need to focus. I can freak out and worry about my sanity later.

The drugs pumping through his system mean he's not dangerous, for now anyway. As I edge closer, trying to get a look at his hind leg, I can admire what a magnificent animal he is. Thick grey fur covers his body. He's in perfect condition, except for the deep cut still oozing bright red blood out onto his glorious coat. In exactly the same spot as Blake was stabbed.

I bounce up and down, shaking my arms out and twisting my neck back and forth, like a fighter would before stepping into the ring. I can do this. It's just an animal who needs my help like any other. I push away all the other thoughts crowding my mind.

No one has arrived to help me yet — which is a relief because I have no idea how I would explain this. When I shave his leg and get ready to stitch him up, I'm stunned to see the torn flesh already appears to be knitting back together. It's inconceivable. Despite my shock as I run a hand through the luxuriously soft pelt of the animal in front of me, I shouldn't be surprised. If this wolf was a man just a minute ago, why wouldn't he be able to heal unnaturally fast? Anything seems possible now.

As a scientist, I'm unbelievably tempted to draw blood for testing while I have the chance, but this man just saved me. Not only would it be unethical, but it also seems like a massive breach of trust. He's risked his life, and he's only in this vulnerable position because of me. No wonder Blake didn't want me to come out of the room. He knew what I'd find.

It doesn't take long to close and dress the wound and then I stand back, not sure what to do next. I can't leave him here. The police are on their way.

"Hello? Zoe?" a deep voice calls from outside. "My name is Max. I'm a friend of Blake's. Cooper sent me. I won't come inside if you don't want me to, just let me know you're okay."

The silence stretches on as I hurry back into my office and bring up the CCTV feed again. A tall guy dressed head to toe in black is standing just outside my broken front door, looking inside but waiting patiently for permission before he enters.

"I'm okay," I call out. Max runs a hand down his jaw and rubs his chin, nodding.

"Good. Is Blake there too?" He looks around anxiously, a deep frown between his eyes as he asks after his friend. How do I explain this one? Max is his friend, but just how well does he know him?

"Em… he's fine. He's just…"

Jesus, I have no idea what to say. My vague response seems to have made Max concerned, and he fidgets on the spot. I swear he leans forwards and takes a sniff. Then I realize that's exactly what Blake did when we met. Blake mustn't be the only one of his kind.

"Zoe, what's going on? Can I speak to him?"

Oh god. Should I be afraid? Blake came here and protected me. He didn't hurt me. And if he and Max are friends of Cooper, it has to mean something. Cooper wouldn't put me in any danger. My sister would kill him.

"Not exactly. You should come in, I'll show you," I decide, shoving down the almost nauseating panic rising inside me at facing one of whatever these are. Judging by the worried expression on his face, I doubt he would have stayed outside for much longer anyway, not without knowing where his friend was. I don't blame him. I'd be the same.

Max is inside in a flash, long legs striding down the hallway to meet me. He gives me a quick once over as he approaches, checking to make sure I really am physically okay. Taking in the trashed reception, the supplies strewn across the hallway, and the blood-stained wall, he shakes his head.

"This is a mess. I'm so sorry this happened. Are you honestly alright?"

His tone of voice is full of genuine concern before he comes to a halt outside the closed door to the exam room where the grey wolf is still sleeping. Max knows exactly which room he is in. He can smell him. Holy shit. He is one.

I watch as his sharp eyes glaze over briefly before they dart to the closed door and then back to me.

"I'm getting worried here, Zoe. What's wrong with Blake? What happened?" Though he continues to speak in a friendly tone, it seems as if he's struggling to stay calm. I know the feeling. Deciding to trust my gut, I move to stand beside him and pull my keys out of my pocket. I don't miss the subtle inhale he does when I edge past him to the door.

"Blake tied the two intruders up next door, but he's... it's probably easier if I just show you. I'm going to need your help to move him anyway," I inform him. He stands behind me as I unlock the door and push it open to reveal the bandaged wolf still lying fast asleep on the tarp. I glance over my shoulder at Max, worried he might not understand, or might think I've hurt him. He could be upset his friend is unconscious, but he's none of those things.

"I shot him with a tranquilizer dart before I knew he was here to help," I admit sheepishly as Max continues to stare.

He stands there open-mouthed, looking from me to the wolf and back over again with wonder. A smile slowly spreads across his face as he takes in the sight before him.

"No fucking way…. This is brilliant!" he declares and bursts out laughing. He has to brace himself against the doorframe to keep from falling over. "This is the best thing I've ever seen."

He looks inside once more and bursts out laughing again, barely able to catch his breath. Wiping tears from under his eyes, he whips out his camera and snaps a picture despite my best attempts to get in his way. He's just too damn tall. Shaking his head, he seems to remember himself and tries to put on a somber face.

"Goddess, I'm sorry, Zoe. I know you've had a tough night, and this is an enormous shock… but you have nothing to worry about here. You're safe now, and you have nothing to fear from us," he tries to reassure me. I'd love to believe him, but my head is still spinning. It doesn't seem real. It just can't be.

Wrapping my arms around my middle, I move back out to the hallway, not keen to be cornered inside the room by a wolf and another man who can apparently turn into one, too.

"Okay, you said you need my help. What can I do?" Max asks, clearly deciding not to press the trust issue. I appreciate it when he moves over to the far wall and gives me as much space as possible. He must be able to sense my unease.

"The police are on the way. You need to help me lift him."

"That I can do," he says. He ignores my flimsy grip on one end of the tarp which I was preparing to drag and bends to scoop the massive animal up on his own. He lifts the massive wolf up onto the examination table with relative ease and steps back. I move to the other side, checking Blake's eyes and breathing once more. I catch Max watching me intently, clearly trying to hold back a grin.

"What?" I ask, not exactly sure why he finds seeing his friend unconscious quite so funny.

"Zoe, you have no idea how good this is. There are going to be legends about you." He looks like he's going to laugh again but pulls himself together. "Any questions for me?"

He leans back against the wall, arms down by his side, body language relaxed and open.

"Only about a million," I scoff, flinging my arms out to the side in exasperation and gesturing to the chaos that was my lovely clean clinic just hours ago. "But not tonight. I'm too exhausted."

He nods sympathetically and glances toward the door.

"Well, I can't help you with the robbery, but for all this stuff," he points to Blake lying perfectly still between us. "I know just the person."

I frown at him in confusion right before I hear footsteps charging into the room. Instantly, I am pulled into the embrace of my very heavily pregnant twin sister, Hayley.

And then it all clicks into place. Hayley's husband knows Max. Cooper sent him here to protect me. Cooper meant it when he said Blake can take care of himself. Seeing my brother-in-law standing beside Max, with the same tall, muscular build, same firm jaw, and same ridiculously alpha-male energy, it all comes together.

Cooper knows because he is one. Which means Hayley knows, too.

I narrow my eyes at her and peel her arms from around me angrily as she rambles on about being so worried and getting here as fast as they could, despite Cooper trying to make her stay at home.

"Hayley, you and I need to have a word in private," I hiss. She gulps and looks at Max, who nods. The cat is out of the bag, and she knows she's in big trouble. We're identical twins. I thought we had no secrets.

"Look Zoe, I was going to tell you, eventually," she stutters, looking at me with her big brown eyes, trying to look all innocent and pleading for mercy. She even has the audacity to rub a hand over her belly, as if reminding me of her condition so that I won't actually kick her ass. The sound of sirens interrupts Hayley. Blue and red flashing lights cast moving shadows across the walls and ransacked mess of the clinic, just as tyres screech to a halt outside.

"Saved by the bell," Max announces dryly, raising his arms in surrender and marching toward the front door, as two officers get out of their car, guns raised.

CHAPTER 9

BLAKE

As I uncurl my stiff body, I bury my nose deeper into the soft blanket that smells like heaven. The fog clears from my brain, and the cold air and hushed voices drifting underneath the door bring me back to my senses. I sit up slowly and fight back the wave of nausea that washes over me. Squinting against the bright lights of what appears to be a domestic utility room, I rub a hand over my head and try to figure out how I got in here.

The last thing I remember was propping myself up against the door to Zoe's office, struggling to keep my eyes open, and praying that I wouldn't shift to heal once the drugs kicked in. Given I'm stark naked now, and not lying where I fell asleep, I think can safely assume that's exactly what happened.

Feeling groggy, I haul myself to my feet, but one of my legs gives way and I land hard on my knee on the tiled floor. Biting back a curse, I try again, this time gripping the countertop beside me to pull myself up to standing. A dull ache in my leg draws my attention to the neat row of stitches beneath the loosened white bandage strapped around my thigh. I touch it carefully, reverently, because it smells like her. My mate. I can't help but smile.

Zoe took care of me. Which means she knows what I am and didn't run screaming. It's a start.

The sound of Max's laughter reaches me, and I raise my fist to pound on the door. A hushed silence falls on the other side. My temper flares when the door doesn't open immediately. Max isn't moving fast enough. I need to see her and make sure she's okay. It nearly killed me to know I was going to leave her helpless with those two creeps in the same building. Well, maybe not exactly helpless considering my predicament.

Max flings open the door and stands there smirking at me like an idiot when I growl at him.

He knows.

"Well, well, well. Look who decided to get up from his nap?" he drawls, trying his hardest not to laugh. I ignore him. He can slag me all he wants later. My focus is on one person and one person alone.

Zoe is leaning against the far wall, as far away from me as she can possibly get. She's wide-eyed and freaked out, and I can't blame her. My heart aches at the distance between us. I long to take her in my arms and reassure her, to make sure she never feels fear like that ever again.

Her blonde hair falls in waves around her shoulders and she's casually dressed in soft-looking leggings and a fitted t-shirt. She's stunning. Wanting to get closer, I take a step toward her, but Max places a hand in the middle of my chest to stop me. Another growl is past my lips before I even realise it, and Zoe shrinks back even further. Max narrows his eyes at me and shakes his head.

"Put some clothes on, big guy, if you want to speak to your lady," Max suggests, tilting his head toward my naked body. Shifters think nothing of nudity, but he's right. I don't want to alarm Zoe even more.

Max hands me a change of clothes. He must have taken them from the back of my SUV, and I nod at him in gratitude. As I step into my boxers, I glance at Zoe again. Her gaze is fixed firmly on my crotch, where I am already sporting a semi just from breathing in her tantalising scent.

She swallows hard, then her eyes flick back to mine as she realises I've caught her staring. Arching her back subtly, her fingers curl as her body reacts to me, and her nails scratch gently against the paint on the wall behind her. It should be my back she's digging her nails into, or my sheets her fingers are curling into. And it will be soon. Hopefully. I need to be patient. Easier said than done, though. Alphas aren't known for waiting for what they want.

"Are you okay? Did they stay locked in that room?" I ask in a serious tone and she nods, still watching as I pull on my trousers and button up my shirt, wishing that I had something less formal to put on. The relief allows me to breathe properly. I wouldn't have been able to forgive myself if something had happened to her while I was asleep on the floor.

"Is she okay?! Blake, when I got here, she was about to sew up your furry butt. She was incredible, so calm," Max declares with pride. Zoe's expression tightens at his words, and I grit my teeth, taking a few steps toward her. She broke her promise.

"Max, were the police here when you arrived?" I ask, and Zoe takes a deep gulp of air. Busted.

"No. They came later, after Hayley and Cooper arrived. You'll need to give a statement tomorrow, by the way. We told the cops you headed off on foot to get help."

I nod along to what Max is saying, but my eyes never leave Zoe's. She fidgets uncomfortably.

"Where's Cooper now?" I inquire. Max is oblivious to the growing tension in the room and keeps talking.

"Hayley came with him. He took her upstairs to get some sleep. He'll be back down in a minute," Zoe offers before Max can reply, her voice like honey. It soothes my nerves to hear her speak. Tonight was tough. If she's not in shock, she must at the very least be exhausted.

"And why aren't you resting, Zoe?" I ask, my tone sharper

than I meant it to be, but the dark circles under her eyes worry me. She has to be running on fumes. I continue to edge closer, pausing again to gauge her reaction. She narrows her eyes at me, perhaps not enjoying being questioned or my bossy tone.

"Because I'm a big girl who can decide for herself when she goes to bed," she fires back at me. "And—"

She's about to say something else but stops herself and presses her lips firmly together instead. I want to know every thought that goes through that pretty little head of hers. I know it's important, otherwise, she wouldn't have started to say it.

"And what, angel?" I whisper, finally getting to within a few feet of her. If I reached out, I could touch her, but she's still skittish.

"Nothing," she says in a stubborn tone, folding her arms across her chest and holding my gaze, challenging me. Oh yes. My girl has some backbone, even when she's unsure, or maybe especially when she is.

"She wouldn't leave until you woke up. She was worried about the side effects of the anaesthetic," Max offers in her defense. "Or that was her excuse anyway."

Zoe scowls at him and refuses to look at me, her cheeks pinking slightly in embarrassment.

"Leave." It's an order, albeit calmly given. Max sighs before turning on his heel to head for the door without a backward glance. As the door clicks shut behind him, Zoe turns back to face me.

"Do you always just boss him around like that?" she asks, but I couldn't care less about Max right now.

"Is it true? Did you stay awake just to make sure I was alright?" I need to know, because it's one thing for her to be affected by the bond when I push my way into her personal space, but it's another thing entirely for her to care for my wellbeing when she must be tired, scared, and confused.

"I'm a veterinarian. Caring for animals is in the job

description," she quips, narrowing her eyes at me, as if she doesn't want to confess that she went above and beyond for me.

"Is that all it was? Just your duty?" I press, again stealing a few more inches of the distance between us. This is torture, being so close and yet so far.

"You rescued me. It would be selfish not to make sure you stayed alive after I was partly responsible for what happened," she concedes. I notice when she registers exactly how close I am now. Closer than a stranger should be, yet she doesn't move away or tell me to stop.

"Zoe, you shot me. You're one hundred percent responsible," I say, purely to provoke her. I love the way her eyes shine when she's irritated.

"You scared the life out of me. What was I supposed to do?" she counters, raising her voice in annoyance. Nobody speaks to me like this. I love it.

"Are you scared now that you know what I am?" I ask, leaning closer and allowing myself to take in as much of her delicious scent as I can. She hesitates, pulling her pillowy lips into a sexy pout.

"Should I be scared of you, Blake?" There's a hint of teasing in her breathy voice. She's enjoying this back and forth as much as I am. Goddess, she's so sexy. I think I'll enjoy fighting with her for the rest of our days.

"I love the way you say my name," I whisper, and she blinks at me, disorientated by the change in subject.

"You didn't answer my question." She presses her palms flat against the wall behind her as I ease in, our chests almost touching. Her eyes dance, giving away the fire inside her.

"You never need to fear me, Zoe. I would protect you with my dying breath. But you left your office before help arrived. Even after you promised me you wouldn't," I remind her, brushing her hair back from her shoulder and allowing my breath to tickle her sensitive skin. "I told you what I would do."

She sucks in a breath and her dusky pink lips part. Goddess, those lips. I can't decide whether I want to suck them, bite them, or fuck them.

"That's presumptuous," she counters, squaring her shoulders and defying me once again. "You might have helped me, but I don't owe you anything."

"No, you certainly don't. If you never speak to me again, getting shot will still have been worth it just to meet you. But I would like to see you again."

Mustering my courage, I take her delicate hand in mine and bring it slowly to my mouth, kissing the back of her knuckles. A thrill runs through me as I feel the sparks erupt between us. The corners of my lips turn up in delight at this new sensation. It's absolutely incredible and I pray she can feel it the same way I do.

Zoe aims a stunned look at our joined hands, where my lips touched her skin. She shakes her head to break the trance, and my heart sinks. Suddenly, the spark is gone, and she looks like she might fall asleep on her feet.

"This is all too much," she says, looking up at me earnestly with those pale grey eyes. I nod. She's right, it is. I shouldn't be pushing her.

"You're right, and I've probably overstayed my welcome. Please, go get some sleep. You're safe here with Cooper tonight and you'll get a better sleep without strangers in your house," I suggest, and she nods. I take a few steps to leave, but she grabs my hand and gently pulls me back. Her other hand wraps around my wrist, and I'm not certain if she even knows why she's grasping me like this.

"How do I... I mean if I wanted to...?" she stutters, her cheeks turning rosy as she looks anywhere but directly at me. A cute little line appears at the top of her nose when she frowns. She's still reluctant to say what she wants.

"I'll come back after you've had a rest. Then you can ask me anything you want, including where I'm taking you on our first date," I say with a wink, smiling softly at her uncertain expression. "You were incredibly brave this evening, angel. Thank you for taking such good care of me, it means a lot to me," I add, before pressing a kiss to the top of her head and forcing myself to walk out the door.

She stands in the doorway watching me leave, and even though it's difficult to walk away from her, I'm on cloud nine.

CHAPTER 10

ZOE

The bed dips as someone pulls back the covers and climbs in beside me. I crack open one eye but slam it shut again when I'm blinded by the sun streaming in through the window. The curtains are wide open. I was too tired to bother closing them when I fell into bed last night. It can't be morning already. I'm still exhausted.

"Please tell me last night was all a horrible dream," I groan as I roll over on my side to face my sister. Her hands are tucked under her cheek and her pose mirrors mine exactly. It reminds me of when we were teenagers, and we'd climb into each other's beds late at night to gossip about school and boys.

"I wish I could, sweetie," she says sadly, stretching out a hand to brush the hair back from my face. "But it's going to be okay."

I blow out a breath and screw my eyes shut, wanting to pretend for another minute that my clinic wasn't destroyed last night and that I don't have a whole mess to deal with today. The police arrested the two intruders last night, but the clinic is still a crime scene. They said it'll need to stay closed today while they go back over it in daylight for evidence and dust for prints. I'm getting a headache just thinking about it.

Sitting bolt upright, I bury my face in my hands and force myself to calm down. There's no point freaking out. I will get it all done. I just need to keep going, doing the next thing, until I'm back on track. Hayley hooks an arm around my waist as I move to get up, and pulls me back down onto the bed.

"Now don't freak out, but I may have done a thing," she confesses. I grimace and shake my head at her slowly. Dread fills me. Knowing her, it could be anything.

"No, Hayley, no. What did you do?"

"Lie back here for a minute and I'll tell you."

She pats the space beside her on the mattress. I sigh, but do as I'm told, even though I'm aware of what she's doing. I know all her little tricks. It's hard to stay mad at someone when you're comfy in bed. I have a feeling I'll manage it, though.

"I don't have time for this, Hayley," I complain, and she bites her lip nervously before reaching behind her and producing a phone. My phone, to be exact.

"Actually, you do," she admits and then winces when I snatch it out of her hand.

"Oh my god, Hayley. Did you break into my phone?" I moan, pulling up my messages and call history. Face ID is great unless there's someone wandering around who looks exactly like you, then it's completely useless.

There are messages from Doc, the previous owner of the clinic who retired locally, agreeing to handle any emergency call-outs. Jenny, my part-time secretary, has happily agreed to cancel all non-urgent appointments for the next couple of days. I stare at Hayley, completely stunned, as she pulls the phone back out of my hand and places it gently on the bedside table.

"Cooper and Max took care of the animals in the clinic. Blake has someone lined up to replace the doors as soon as the police have left. Doc is thrilled at the idea of getting to go out on a few calls. He sounds like he's bored at home, to be honest. You should hire him back."

"Jesus, Hayley, that's great, but you can't just…" I try to explain, but my protests fall on deaf ears. Hayley is purely results-focused.

"I'm your twin sister, and I can feel how stressed out you are. You've barely taken a day off since you bought the place. I know that's part of having a new business, but you don't have to deal with all of this on your own. Please, it'll make me feel better if you have help."

God, she's bossy. We need to have a serious chat about boundaries, but I do appreciate what she did. I can breathe again knowing the appointments and the animals are taken care of.

"You're impossible," I mutter, but she smiles as if it's a compliment.

"You sound like Cooper," she says with a grin, knowing she's gotten away with it. As usual, my sister is a pain in the ass, but she's usually right. Her heart is in the right place, but her methods leave a lot to be desired, though.

We lie there in silence, our breathing synchronising slowly. Just like when we were younger, the tension ramps up until one of us breaks and blurts out what we really want to say.

"I wouldn't have told anyone," I blurt out, wounded that she never confided in me about something that's such a big part of her life. Hayley reaches out and hugs me tight, or as tight as she's able to with her giant bump squished between us.

"Zoe, I know, but it wasn't my secret to tell. Plus, it wouldn't have been fair to burden you with it," Hayley says with certainty. My sister does nothing lightly. She's thought long and hard about this. Much as I hate to admit it, she's right again. It's Cooper's secret to share with whomever he wants. I can understand why that circle would be small.

"I told the officers that the cameras are just for show, that they don't actually record anything. I'll destroy any footage that's there," I confide and Hayley nods gratefully, eyes shining with relief.

"Thank you." She holds my hand and gives it a squeeze.

"So, is Blake still here?" I ask, trying not to seem too interested. She snorts out a laugh, rolling her eyes.

"Why, Zoe? Did you take a shine to Blake Steel?" she teases, and my cheeks burn hot as I blush. Guilty as charged.

"*Maybe*. He's intense, isn't he?" I comment casually, watching closely for her reaction. "Is that normal?"

For werewolves, I want to add, but I don't need to. She knows exactly what I mean.

"Yes. Especially among alphas, it is," she answers carefully. "Their wolves are extremely protective."

"And Blake's an alpha?" I guess, and Hayley nods. Of course he is. Bossy and used to getting his way. A prime physical specimen. I think back to how the animals in the clinic became submissive in his presence. They knew who the top dog was as soon as they sensed him arrive.

"It's not just because he's an alpha. Blake is so intense around you because his wolf has decided he likes you. He wants you to be his."

"I'm sorry. Did you just say *his wolf* likes me?" I repeat, and Hayley laughs.

"I won't speak for Blake, but the first time Cooper and I met, as soon as he picked up my scent, for him, that was it. He hadn't even seen me, but his wolf decided there would be no one else."

My eyes nearly bug out of my head at that. I know all about wolves' mating habits in the wild, but it never dawned on me that would transfer to these men.

"Sorry, Hayley, but that sounds like a line. A good one, I'll give him that, but…" I say incredulously. There's no way. Falling for someone by their scent. It's crazy.

"If it's so ridiculous, tell me what happened with you and Blake last night, Zoe? No sizzling chemistry? No overwhelming urge to rip his clothes off? Even now, you're not secretly thrilled that he's still close by?" she taunts, and seems rather displeased with my dismissal of her relationship with Cooper. I feel called out. She's describing my reaction to Blake to a tee. Lifting a hand, I touch my lips as I remember our brief kiss. It felt magical when it happened. Could it really become something?

"I didn't mean to suggest that you guys don't have something special. But it's a lot to take in. And come on, Blake seems fancy. I doubt I'm his type."

I look away as she frowns at me. She's brimming with self-confidence, and everyone loves her. I doubt she could even imagine feeling less than.

"Full disclosure. I know you're his type because he told me before that he would have pursued me if I wasn't with Cooper," Hayley admits, rushing her words to get that bombshell out.

"*What?!*" I shout. "Oh wonderful, I get it now. So he only likes me because I remind him of *you?*" I thump my head back against the pillow. I knew it was too good to be true.

"No, Zoe, you're not paying attention. He only liked me because I reminded him of *you*. He just didn't know it yet."

"Seriously, Hayley. That doesn't even make sense. What am I supposed to do with that?"

I stare at her, exasperated. It was already bizarre that a wealthy, stylish man as good-looking as Blake comes to my rescue and wants to take me out. Now I find out he's got the hots for my sister. I wrinkle my nose, thinking about his gleaming black SUV, his immaculate shirt, and trousers. I don't even own my car, and I'm constantly dirty. He's the exact opposite of me.

"Get to know Blake. He's a good guy, Zoe. You can take him at his word," she assures me. "If you give him a chance, you won't have doubts for long about how genuine he is."

She's grinning at me as if I've just won the lottery, but doubt lingers at the back of my mind. Sure, he's coming on strong now, but that's because I'm the damsel in distress and he had this connection with Hayley in the past. In the cold light of day, it'll be a different story. Like most men, the first time I have to run out in the middle of the night or cancel plans at the last minute because of an emergency, he'll decide I'm not for him. It would be nice to have some company other than my sister in my bed, though.

"I've forgotten how to even date, Hayley," I moan, hiding my face with my hands. She clasps her hands together with glee.

"Ha. Believe me, you won't have to do a thing. Just be yourself and enjoy the ride."

CHAPTER 11

BLAKE

The noise of the shower turning off upstairs distracts me from what Max is saying. My wolf is itching to see his mate again. It nearly killed him to stay away last night, even though we didn't go far.

"I'm wasting my time," Max mutters as I continue to ignore him, and Cooper laughs. They're perched on stools at the small kitchen island, watching as I open and close every cupboard in the kitchen. As I bang the last one shut, probably louder than necessary, I whirl around to face Cooper.

"What on Earth does she eat? *There's no food here,*" I complain as I yank open the practically empty fridge again and pray for inspiration.

"That's probably a good thing. You can't cook, remember?" Max comments, watching with disbelief as I pull out a frying pan and a few basic rations and set to work.

"I can feed my mate," I mutter, cracking eggs into a bowl and adding some milk, flour, and oil. Max's eyebrows shoot up as he glances at Cooper to gauge his reaction to my admission. Max has already guessed and even if Cooper hasn't yet, there's not much point in denying it. He's the only other alpha I've heard of with a human mate. Plus they're sisters. I have a feeling I'm going to need his advice.

"Thought as much. The cooking is a dead giveaway. I did the same for Hayley before she knew. Dinners, picnics... taking her for lunch," he admits, a soft smile crossing his face at the memories. He knocks back the rest of his coffee and stands as Hayley enters the room. Bending down, he presses a kiss to her lips and whispers hello, his hand resting on her swollen belly. They gaze at each other adoringly for a moment before he wraps an arm around her shoulder and steers her to the door.

"I think you've got everything under control here. We'll get out of your way," Cooper says, leading a reluctant Hayley away.

"But—," she objects before he interrupts her, dipping his head to meet her eye.

"No buts. Zoe's fine. She has a couple of days off and Alpha Steel will make sure she rests, won't you?"

He directs the last part at me, and I nod emphatically.

"I'll take care of her, Hayley. I promise."

She finally relents and allows herself to be pulled further along. Even though objectively they look almost completely identical, I'm able to see subtle differences between them, other than their eye colour. Hayley's hair is a paler shade of blonde, and her frame is leaner. Zoe's slim, but she has curves in all the right places.

"Be patient with her. She's the best, but she's stubborn; she's going to struggle with this," Hayley warns me, before shouting up the stairs, "Bye, sis, I'll call you later!"

"Wait, what? *You're leaving?*" Zoe rushes down the stairs wrapped only in a white fluffy towel and stops short as soon as she spots Max and me standing in the kitchen. Tugging the towel tighter, she smooths it down so it covers as much as possible, which isn't much.

"Yeah, we need to get back. We have a scan today, and everything seems to be under control here. I'll call you later, ok?"

Hayley says, leaning in to give her sister a hug before Cooper practically drags her out the door.

Zoe spins around and our eyes lock. Her tanned shoulders are exposed and rivulets of water run from the ends of her wet hair down between her full breasts. The towel is not quite big enough and barely covers her ass, leaving her long legs on display. I'm delighted with the view, but not thrilled that Max is enjoying it, too.

A rumble starts deep in my chest and Max slaps a hand over his eyes before I even say a word. Zoe's hand moves to her chest and she rubs it, like she can feel the vibrations there.

"On that note, I'm out of here. I'll hold the fort for as long as you need," Max promises before averting his eyes and practically running for the door. "Zoe, it was a pleasure. I hope the next time we meet will be under more pleasant circumstances."

The door clicks shut, and now it's just the two of us.

"Sorry," Zoe says, adjusting the towel around her body. She doesn't move to leave, just stands rooted to the spot, her fascinated gaze taking in the utensils and ingredients I've pulled out as I make myself at home in her kitchen. My feet move of their own accord until I'm standing right in front of her.

"What do you have to be sorry for?" I ask, reaching up to trace the path of a water droplet sliding down her neck to her collarbone.

"I don't remember, maybe being practically naked?" she whispers. I'm glad I'm not the only one whose brain has turned to mush.

"You don't ever have to be sorry about being naked around me. You look amazing in that towel," I mutter, staring at the offending article, wishing it would magically disappear. It's blocking my view of the rest of her, and I long to see every curve and dip of her body. Knowing her pussy is exposed, just inches above the hem of that flimsy bit of material, tests every ounce of my self-control.

I tip her chin up with my index finger and pause. When our

lips are millimetres apart, I hold my breath and wait, needing to check if I'm overstepping here. Her luscious pink lips call to me, begging for me to kiss them, but I need to be sure. I'm afraid to startle her by moving too fast.

"Zoe?" My mouth brushes hers as I speak. "May I?"

She knows what I mean. Her racing heart is beating just as hard as mine. She gives me an almost imperceptible nod, but I'll take it. Sliding my fingers into her hair, I cup the back of her head in one hand as I take her lips with mine in a brief but sensual kiss. Her taste explodes in my mouth and I groan, desire surging through me.

Even though I'm tempted, I don't push my luck and try to deepen it further. Releasing her reluctantly, I remain exactly where I am but keep her pressed to me, enjoying the feel of her against my body.

Her expression is stunned as she gazes up at me. I know the feeling. Every cell in my body sings from that fleeting kiss. It's like coming home. Everything about being here with her feels right. I can't even imagine what it would be like when we finally come together.

"Why do you have that?" Zoe asks, gesturing to the frying pan I'm still holding in my left hand. I didn't even realise I still had it until now.

"I'm making pancakes. Get dressed while I put some more coffee on," I order, and she nods. As she turns to go, I can't resist the urge to give her a gentle slap on the backside. She gasps and spins around, mouth hanging open, to stare at me wide-eyed. Maybe that was a bit cheeky, but I couldn't resist.

"You promised me you'd stay locked in that office. Consider yourself lucky you're not getting a proper spanking," I admonish with a grin, and she stiffens, shocked at the brazenness of my words. I worry for a second that I've judged the moment wrong because she shoots me an angry look and stomps off.

If it weren't for the fact that I can smell how much the thought of that punishment appeals to her, I'd swear she was genuinely angry at me. The passion inside her turns me on so much. She's going to challenge me at every turn, and I'm never going to get enough.

Five minutes later, she returns in a loose sweatshirt and leggings, fresh-faced without a scrap of makeup on. She's beautiful. Zoe has her toffee-coloured hair pulled back in a long plait and all I can picture is wrapping it around my hand as I take her from behind. I only found her less than twelve hours ago and I'm already worried I might die just from not being inside her. Shifters normally mate immediately and mark each other within days of meeting. However, Zoe's human, so the rules are slightly different. I can't push her too fast or she'll run.

Cooper couldn't even speak to Hayley for weeks after he found her. How the hell did he manage?

"Something smells good," she comments as she sits shyly down at her own dining table. She watches me add some pancakes and maple syrup to a plate, along with some fruit. I plonk the giant pile, along with a steamy mug of coffee, in front of her. She moans in a way that should not be heard outside of the bedroom as she takes her first bite and licks some syrup off her lips. It's not helping my situation.

"Don't take this the wrong way, but you're not exactly well stocked. I need to go into town to give my statement at the police station. I can pick you up some groceries if you'd like?"

Joining her at the table, I watch with delight as she tucks into her pancakes with gusto. I'm proud as punch that she seems to like them. It's not lost on me that I am already whipped.

"Why would you do that? That doesn't make any sense."

Her brow creases in genuine confusion as she drains half the mug of coffee in one go and sits back, eyes closed.

"It'll save you the trip if I bring it back with me," I explain, just as perplexed.

"But it's out of your way." Her frown deepens.

"Out of my way? To where?"

She thinks that I'm going to leave and go on my merry way.

That we'll just swap phone numbers and maybe I'll call her in a week to arrange some crappy first date. Hayley clearly hasn't explained much to her at all.

"Your way away! From here! I don't know where you live." She sounds exasperated, and she's looking at me like I have two heads.

"Angel, I'm not leaving you here on your own tonight after what you went through. So, what's going to happen is this, I'm going to go give my statement, then I'll pick up some food from the shops. You're going to take it easy. When I get back, we'll eat and then go to the clinic and start tidying up."

"That's ridiculous. You don't have to do that," she argues, still not seeing it. "I don't need a babysitter."

"You're right, I don't have to do it. I *want* to do it, and I'm *going* to do it even if you say no."

She's not the only bossy one here.

"Fine. Do what you like. You'll be sleeping outside, though."

Her eyes flash as her feisty side shows itself again, but she can't out stubborn an alpha wolf. She's a witness to a crime. Someone could show up out here to intimidate her. She might get scared once the dark creeps in again. No way am I leaving her alone.

"I'm a wolf. It won't be the first time," I reply with a cocky smile, and that finally breaks through. She laughs and shakes her head, resigned to accepting some help as though it's the worst thing that's ever happened to her.

"Fine, but I'm coming with you. I'll get groceries while you're in with the police."

She rolls her eyes, pretending it's the biggest imposition in the world to accompany me on a trip into town. I knew she would never stay at home. Now I get her trapped in a car and all to myself for a few hours at least.

"I told them the cameras were just for show, that they don't record anything," she admits, staring into her mug to avoid meeting my eyes as she always does when I pay her a compliment or she does anything nice. I reach across the table and place my hand over hers. It looks so tiny and delicate hidden under mine.

"Are you sure, Zoe? I don't want you to get into any trouble."

My heart swells with gratitude. She lied to the police to protect me. Us. She smiles with a quick nod before pushing to her feet and snatching the empty dishes off the table.

"Yeah, well… you got lucky. I don't think Hayley would appreciate me opening that can of worms."

She's quick to pretend it's only Cooper she's protecting, but I know she did it for me as well.

I'll let her keep her act up, but she's not fooling me.

CHAPTER 12

ZOE

There are so many questions swirling around in my brain that I barely register Blake taking my hand as he helps me climb into his SUV. As he strides confidently around to the driver's side, wearing his tailored suit and looking every inch the suave business executive, I squirm uncomfortably in the high-class vehicle. The leather seats are buttery soft, and one look around at the spotless interior tells me he's not used to having people with mucky boots like mine climbing in and out of this thing. It's immaculate.

"So, you like things neat?" I ask, as I make sure I don't knock any more dirt off my shoes onto his spotless floor.

"I suppose so, but you don't need to worry about that." He glances over and notices the way I'm sitting rigidly in my seat. Damn right I'll worry about it, but not the way he's thinking. I don't care about his floor, but my job and my life are definitely not neat.

"Hmm," I continue. "You live in Black Hill?"

"I do." Blake keeps his eyes on the road, but I can tell he's paying close attention to my every word. It's both refreshing and unnerving to have someone's full attention.

"Alone?"

It's a reasonable question, but I cringe internally as soon as the word is out.

"No, not alone," he says hesitantly. When he sees my hands twisting in my lap, he reaches out a hand and covers them. "With about fifty other wolves. I live in the packhouse in my own apartment. On my own."

"Like Hayley and Cooper in the lodge," I reason out loud and he nods. My sister really could have hung around and given me some more detail about this whole wolf shifter thing. I'm flying blind here.

"And you run your own business?" I ask, but he shakes his head this time, unsure of how to answer.

"Not my business, the pack businesses; I manage them and all of the assets for the benefit of the pack. But yes, that's what I do all day."

That explains the suits, kind of. Cooper does the same and is always far more casually dressed.

"And all night?"

Blake looks at me, eyes shining with something like delight. He wasn't expecting me to ask him that.

"My other job," he admits with a shrug. "But I'm normally a homebird. I tend not to get up to anything too exciting."

Holding eye contact for a second longer than necessary, his gaze seems to burn into me as he hints at his underlying meaning. He's not out dating or sleeping around, but he would say that, wouldn't he? It shouldn't matter, but somehow it does.

"You don't seem too sure," I observe, and he frowns again.

"I'm sure, angel."

"Hmm."

I go back to looking out the window as I consider the last twenty-four hours. Not even twenty-four. I was happily living my quiet, insignificant life in the country, taking care of other people's pets and livestock. Not a man or a date in sight. Chats with Earl were the closest to flirting I've come in months.

Now I'm sitting beside a gorgeous, charming man who genuinely seems to be interested in me, but there's a catch. Of course, there's a catch. He's a wolf in sheep's clothing, and we couldn't be more different. Hayley seems to think this is some mystical, predestined pairing, but it seems unlikely that anyone would put the two of us together. The chemistry is off the charts so maybe they got one thing right, but the rest?

"Penny for your thoughts?"

Blake twists my hands apart and takes one of mine in his to stop me from wringing them. I'm a nervous wreck, which makes me even more amazed at how confident he is. We've only just met, yet he seems to be so sure that we are inevitable. He's so comfortable showing affection, like we've been together for years rather than meeting only hours ago.

"You're a busy man. I'm a busy woman. You don't exactly live nearby."

I'm pointing out the obvious pitfalls to whatever's going on here, because I don't think he's thinking with his head.

"Are you too busy to go on a date?"

His smile is boyish, and I can't help but smile back at him as he gives my hand a gentle squeeze.

"You know what I mean."

"I do. But angel, we only just met. I think you might be getting ahead of yourself," he says with a smirk, and I laugh. He knows Hayley must have told me what's going on here. Instead of trying to convince me we're meant to be, he's still just harping on about this date.

"This is it."

Glad to have an excuse to end that conversation, I point out the police station, but Blake is already pulling in. He's out of the car and opening my door before I get the chance to do it myself. Awkwardly, I nod at him and slip past, but somehow, he makes it to the door ahead of me and holds it open. I'm not used to this, and I don't know how to behave when someone is so focused on me.

Immediately, all eyes in the small reception area turn toward us. As I skirt by Blake, moving away to put some distance between us, I can feel everyone watching. The way he stands close and places one possessive hand lightly on my lower back as I pass, makes it clear we arrived together. Even through my clothes, I swear my skin is on fire where he touches me. Every one of my senses are heightened, completely tuned in to where he is and what he's doing.

"Hi, Zoe," Mel singsongs.

Mel is Doc's daughter and works as a clerk at the station. She has a massive grin on her face as she takes in Blake's charming smile, casual attitude, and my obvious discomfort.

"I was so sorry to hear about your break-in. Is this the hero of the hour?"

She bats her eyelashes at him and I roll my eyes. No doubt he gets this wherever he goes.

"Something like that. Is John here? Blake has to give his statement." I'm eager to hurry this along. There are enough ears listening to this conversation that I can be sure the entire town will know every detail before I walk back out the door.

"He is. Come right this way," Mel stands, fixing her clothes as she takes Blake in from head to toe. It's rare we see a man dressed as well as him around here. He stands out like a sore thumb, but he seems to get the vote of confidence from her. As Blake goes to follow Mel through to the back, I turn to leave, but he catches me by the fingertips and pulls me back. He drops his keys into my hand and wraps my fingers around them.

"Just get some essentials. I'm taking you out for dinner tonight, remember?"

He gives me a wink before walking back in the direction Mel is pointing. My heart races from the small bit of skin-to-skin contact and I'm about to melt into a puddle right here.

"Damn," Mel whispers, swooning as he leaves. "Where did you find him?"

"He found me," I answer before I even think about it.

"Well, aren't you the lucky one?"

She sighs as we both watch his tall frame move with grace through the haphazardly arranged desks, finding John on the first try. There is no hint of a limp or any other indication someone stabbed him in the leg last night. It's remarkable.

Blake reaches out a hand and John takes it immediately. They chat away like old friends, smiling and friendly, and I shake my head. I can't imagine what it would be like to be so self-assured all the time. Blowing Mel a kiss goodbye, I push back outside and march down the street to the grocery store.

Everyone stops to give their well-wishes and offers of help. This really is just the nicest town with the kindest people. I'm glad I left the clinic and came with Blake. I was feeling so bad about cancelling appointments and letting people down, but it's clear now that people understand. They just want to make sure I'm okay.

As I juggle three overstuffed bags and a loaf of bread under one arm, I spot Blake leaning against the car, waiting for me. With all the interruptions, that took longer than I thought.

"Shit, sorry!" I mutter as I catch the unhappy look on his face.

As I jostle the bags, trying unsuccessfully to get the keys out of my pocket without dropping something, Blake jogs to meet me. Without saying a word, he leans in close, slips his hand into my back pocket, and fishes out his keys. Unlocking the car, he carefully scoops the bags out of my grasp. My core clenches and a jolt of pleasure shoots through me at that slightest touch. This man has such an effect on me it's terrifying.

"I gave you the keys so you could drive to the shops. Then you wouldn't have to carry everything so far," he comments as he opens the boot and places the bags inside. I shrug, and I can see his shoulders tense. As much as I'm enjoying spending time together, I'm having much more fun winding him up. He makes it far too easy.

"I enjoy walking," I reply, and he glances at me, eyes narrowed.

"That's not the point," he replies sulkily. It really was a sweet gesture. There are plenty of men I know who barely let their wives near their cars, let alone someone they met yesterday. I decide to throw him a bone.

"Thank you, though," I whisper. As he reaches past me to open my door, his gaze lifts to mine. Without thinking, I give him a quick peck on the cheek and hop inside. He grins at me and shakes his head as he makes his way around. Blake settles into his seat and gives me a self-satisfied smile. I'm happy with how thrilled he looks with just that small display of affection.

"John asked about the cameras. He wanted to know if it's true they don't work," he says, pulling back onto the road and heading for the clinic once more. "Thank you again, Zoe."

He reaches over and takes my hand in his without even looking, like this is just the norm for us.

"It's the least I can do," I say dismissively, but he stares at my profile until I look at him. "It's not a big deal."

"No really, thank you." I nod this time, accepting his gratitude, and he seems happy with this.

"Also, he wanted to know what I was doing out there at that time of night."

I've been wondering the same thing. I wait with bated breath for him to explain to me how he knew I was in trouble and where to find me. Or, what excuse he's given John. Maybe he was bringing me an animal to look at.

"I told him we're dating. He looked gutted," he says with a sly grin. I can tell he feels terrible about it.

"*You what?!*" The words come out in a high-pitched, manic squeak, but I'm too shocked to care.

"Yep. Told him it's serious too," he continues unashamedly.

"Oh, Jesus. Now everyone is going to hear that."

I put a hand to my head as I think about how quickly that bit of gossip will have travelled around the town. It's the only part about small-town living that I hate. Everyone knows everyone else's business. If I thought being asked why I'm single every day was bad, I know this will be way worse.

"They already knew, angel." His expression is deadly serious as I stare at him, confused. "Last night, I told Earl that I'm going to marry you."

CHAPTER 13

BLAKE

"Now who's getting ahead of themselves?" she shoots back. Her eyes are wild, and she takes a deep breath to steady herself. I brace myself for the onslaught, but it never comes. I wanted her to give out to me, to berate me for talking to other people about her, because when she's all riled up, she's honest. Right now, I'd give anything to know what she's thinking, but instead of fighting with me, she falls silent for the rest of the drive back.

I force my hands to relax on the wheel, giving the impression that I'm calm and confident. I'm anything but. If I push her too hard, though, she might shut down completely.

We get back to the house and, despite her protests, I carry in the bags. We unpack them in silence. She huffs as she closes the fridge with a bang. The jars within rattle as she turns around and leans back heavily against it, her eyebrows drawn together in a frown. Here we go.

"So, I could just be anyone?" she demands. "You get one whiff of my scent, without meeting me, without talking to me, and bam, that's it. Just like that?" She snaps her fingers for emphasis and I see a flash of guarded emotion in her eyes. Hurt maybe?

"No, not just like that," I argue, but she looks away, tuning me out as she stares out the window.

"It's chemistry. Pheromones. Not fate or destiny. I could be anyone. I believe that you're attracted to me, but it's not real, Blake. If you told Earl that you're going to marry me before we even laid eyes on each other, that's all I need to know." She locks eyes with me, defiance shining bright in her silvery grey eyes, chin lifted, and her full lips set in a determined line.

"That's all you need to know?" I repeat, resting my hip against the kitchen island directly opposite her and casually stuffing my hands in my pockets so she doesn't see that they're balled tightly into fists. The mate bond means everything to wolves. It's sacred. To hear her deny it is hard, but it's what I expected.

"To know it's not real. Whatever this is, it's not *real*."

"You think what Hayley and Cooper have isn't real?" I challenge, pushing off the counter and saunter across the space toward her.

"Well, no. I know they're mad about each other—"

"Tell me, do you really think that how Leah and Rex feel about each other isn't real?" I demand a little more forcefully, my voice slightly raised. Her mouth drops open, and she curses, before raising her eyes to heaven. Leah is Zoe's younger sister. She recently moved in with Cooper's brother and they're deliriously happy.

"Oh my god. Duh Zoe, he's Cooper's brother. Of course, he's a wolf," she mutters to herself, lifting a palm to smack herself gently on the forehead. I catch her hand and force her to look at me.

"Are you telling me that your sisters are committed to men who they're not suited to?" I press, and she glares at me angrily.

"Of course not. After what Hayley went through, she'd never let that happen again."

Hayley was in an abusive relationship before she met Cooper. She managed to get herself out of that situation and move on. She's no pushover.

"So, what's your point, Zoe? If both of your sisters are madly in love with their mates, is it so hard to believe that fate can get it right?"

Zoe grits her teeth and keeps her mouth firmly shut as she mulls over what I've said. There's something else, but she's too stubborn to say it. Placing a hand on either side of her head, caging her in against the fridge, I move closer to remind her exactly how strong those pheromones are.

Her palms stay pressed against the fridge and she barely breathes. I know what she's doing. She's trying to avoid breathing in my scent, but it's not quite that simple. She's trying to be rational, that scientific brain of hers struggling to accept something that she can't explain. I can empathize, but I'm not thrilled about it.

"My point is, that for all I know, you could have hundreds of scent matches out there. I mean, you thought it could be Hayley when you met her. Maybe there's someone else you'll feel even stronger about."

I stare at her in disbelief and struggle to contain the anger boiling up inside me.

"And what if some other guy turns up and claims I'm his fated mate? How am I supposed to know what to believe?"

Before I can rein in my temper, I slam a hand against the fridge door. Hanging my head while I fight to calm myself, I'm aware her heart is racing madly and I hate that I've frightened her. I try my best to push my wolf back down, so he doesn't shine through in my eyes.

"*You are mine*," I grit out. "If anyone else tells you otherwise, they're a fucking liar."

Just the thought of her with another man makes my lungs burn and my skin itch with the desire to shift and tear something apart. Nobody else will ever touch her again. She belongs to me.

"Convenient," she whispers, quiet but still unmistakably feisty. I lean in and bury my face in her neck, pressing a kiss to her pulse. She's perfect. Soft but fiery. Honest and quietly confident.

"There is *no one* else for me. I've been waiting so long to find you, Zoe. You might not believe me yet, but I will never want anyone else the way I want you." Gripping her neck, I feather gentle kisses up from her shoulder all the way to behind her ear. Her skin is so soft against my lips as I scoop her hair out of the way and kiss gently along her jaw, from her ear to her chin. Angling her head back to give myself better access, I nuzzle her neck. She tastes delicious.

"Blake, you can't know that. We don't know each other," she mumbles, gasping as I grip her waist with my other hand and pull her body close to mine. There are millimeters between our mouths and we're both breathing heavily now.

"Then let me get to know you, and you'll see what I already know." My lips brush hers as I whisper. She moans and I don't give her the chance to answer. Her body's reaction to me is enough. The scent of her arousal hangs thick and heavy in the air, as the evidence of my desire is pressed hard against her stomach. I lean in and take her mouth with mine, pouring every ounce of my attraction, of my feelings for her, into that kiss.

Despite her disbelief, I do have feelings for her. We've only spent a day together, but I can see how intelligent, brave, and kind she is. She's stunningly beautiful, even if she's not comfortable with it and tries to hide it. Still, it's more than her beauty or her brains. I can feel in my soul that we could have an amazing life together.

"Blake..." She sighs as we part for air and I rest my forehead against hers. As she clings to my shoulders, she trembles in my arms. I want nothing more than to carry her upstairs and bury myself deep within her tight pussy, to claim her right now as my own. It would be glorious between us, but I know that afterward, we'd be right back to where we are now. It will fuel her argument that my desire for her is purely superficial. I need to show her it's more than that.

"Zoe, you are the sexiest woman I've ever met." I roll my hips into hers to prove my point and she moans again, eyes screwed shut against the all-consuming need that I know all too well. "But I'm going to prove to you it's more than that before I take you to bed and show you how amazing our chemistry really is."

She opens her eyes and blinks up at me, her expression languid and drunk with lust. Her face is flushed, and I imagine this is what she'd look like underneath me. Sated and satisfied.

"Sorry?" Dazed, she grips my shirt in her fists and tries to wrap her head around what I'm saying.

"I'm saying get your sexy ass dressed and ready for our first date before I lose control and fuck you all night long."

"Date? Where are you taking me?" she asks breathlessly, making a valiant attempt to regain her composure.

"I have no idea what's around here, so lady's choice."

She places her hands on my chest and pushes. I step back to give her space as she lazily takes me in from head to toe.

"Sounds good. But if we're going into town, you're going to have to get changed. I can't be seen with a man dressed like that."

I frown and glance down at my crisp white shirt. I pride myself on looking good. Whenever I pictured meeting my mate, I wanted her to be proud that I'm her mate. Zoe clearly isn't into it.

"Your wish is my command," I agree reluctantly, willing to go along with it if it means another few hours in her company, and another chance to win her heart. But when she laughs and takes my hand, leading me toward the stairs excitedly, I start to get nervous.

"They're my brother's clothes. He's about your size and I know he won't mind," she says sweetly, opening the closet in the guest bedroom and pulls out a red and black flannel shirt. I immediately regret my decision. Zoe smiles innocently at me, and I know it's a test. I've seen the way she looks at my car and my watch. She's already formed an impression of me and my life. If I refuse, it'll prove her suspicions that I can't fit into her world and that we're not really compatible.

Never one to back down from a challenge, I take my time

unbuttoning my shirt, delighting in the way her eyes trail over my bare chest and abs as I do. She blushes as I take the shirt from her hand, letting our fingers brush and enjoying the sparks as we make contact.

"Perfect. Does he have some jeans I can borrow, too?"

CHAPTER 14

ZOE

I realise I've made a terrible mistake the instant Blake drops his trousers. Gobsmacked, I stare mutely at his long muscular legs and the substantial bulge in his tight black boxer briefs. He snatches the pair of black jeans I'm holding from my grasp and steps into them.

As he pulls them up to his hips, his fly cups his package, thrusting it up and out, and like boobs in a push-up bra, it looks even more impressive. *Oh God*. I know I've seen him naked briefly, but he's so close now I could reach out and touch him. I continue to admire his impressive physique as he tucks himself away and closes his fly before buttoning up the shirt and hiding his chiselled abs from view.

I thought I was so clever, thinking I could throw him off balance and level the playing field a bit. He looks far too good in a suit. I thought he might be less intimidating in normal clothes, but he looks just as handsome, only in a different, more rugged way. Both versions have the ability to flood my panties on sight.

"Is this what you had in mind?" Blake asks, arms out the side as he shows off his new look. His expression is smug. He knows he could wear a paper bag and look sexy, damn him.

"You might blend in a bit more now." Not that Blake would

blend in anywhere. His aura pulls your attention to him, and those model good looks keep it there.

"Your turn." He gestures to me, and I'm mesmerised, watching his lips as they move. They look so soft and luscious, full and inviting. They're a sharp contrast to the rest of his features, which are strong and masculine.

"Hmm?" I catch myself ogling him and force my gaze from his mouth back to his slate-grey eyes, which are studying me as always from behind thick black lashes. Amusement dances there. He's enjoying this, and I must admit I am, too.

"Right, right." With a shake of my head, I snap out of my trance. "Go grab a beer or something. I won't be long."

"Take your time. I'm not going anywhere."

Those words are loaded with meaning. He cups my chin gently and presses a soft kiss to my lips before disappearing back downstairs.

I hate getting dressed up. Hayley loves it, but I don't. She's much more at ease being the centre of attention. Me, not so much. Logically, I know I look almost exactly the same as my stunningly, beautiful twin sister, but I don't feel like I look the same.

It could be the profession I've chosen or being hit on way too many times by guys who only want one thing, but I've always felt uncomfortable when people focused on my looks. Working as a vet, I'm either dressed in scrubs or covered in muck. With so little downtime, I don't have much chance to get dressed up, which suits me fine. Normally.

Now, though, I wish I had Hayley's wardrobe, because I have a gorgeous man downstairs who wants to take me out, and I don't have a clue what to put on. I dig out my tightest pair of jeans and a white silky top Hayley left behind. A swipe of mascara and lip gloss later and I'm done. Hopefully, Blake appreciates low maintenance.

I skip down the stairs and stop at the entrance to the kitchen. Blake is leaning back against the island with his legs crossed and a beer lifted to his lips, looking effortlessly sexy. The moment he sees me, he stops drinking and places the bottle down on the counter slowly. He nonchalantly pushes to his feet and prowls forward. I take a small step back as he closes in, looming large in front of me. Catching me around the waist, he drags me toward him gently.

"You're beautiful."

He looks me straight in the eye as he speaks, and it's as if he's staring into my soul. It's only when he takes my breath away with a devastating kiss that I realise why his words had such an effect on me. He didn't say that I *look* beautiful. I melt into his embrace and run my hands up his sides, roaming along his waist to his chest and across his muscular back. He's rock solid, built like a Greek god. Taking a deep breath, I allow myself to finally relax and enjoy it.

"Angel, we need to leave now, or I won't let you outside this door." He nips my bottom lip and pulls away, eyes dark and heavy-lidded. "We'll pick this up again later," he promises, stepping back and gesturing for me to lead the way. I try to look unfazed as I walk past, but he has me rattled. He keeps doing and saying the perfect things.

Could the mate bond really get it this right?

He makes no comment when I say I'm driving or when I pull up outside a rustic bar, that I know has some good food, on the outskirts of town. He merely hops out and escorts me inside, one hand resting gently on my lower back as he holds the door to the bar open for me.

You could hear a pin drop when it shuts behind us, every head turning to look in our direction. Blake smiles confidently at anyone who meets his eye, one arm wrapped around my waist, unashamedly acting like we're a proper couple.

"Zoe, oh my gosh! I'm so glad you're alright, I heard what happened," Mandy slips out from behind the bar and shows us to a table at the back. She nods at Blake and smiles. "And I'm glad you didn't listen to Earl."

"Thank you, Mandy. If you hadn't helped me..." He frowns and swallows as if he can't even bear to finish his sentence. "You work here, too?"

"I pick up the odd shift here and there," she answers warily, handing us our menus. He watches her intently.

"What about your son?"

"Not that it's any of your business, but he's old enough to put himself to bed. I work while he sleeps, and I sleep while he's in school. It's not ideal, but..." She shrugs and lifts her chin, daring him to comment further. Blake merely nods, but he continues to watch her as she walks away.

"How did you know she has a son?" My curiosity is piqued as I look back and forth between them. Do they know each other already?

"She's a wolf. I can smell an adolescent male on her. She doesn't have a pack to help her." He looks troubled when he turns back to me. "It's hard enough raising a shifter and keeping it secret, even with the protection and support of the pack. Doing it on your own must be tough."

"Why isn't she part of a pack?"

"I don't know. Could be lots of reasons. She might not have been raised in one. Maybe she decided she wanted to be on her own." Blake shrugs but I get the impression it's a bigger deal than he's letting on. "Anyway, Miss Walker, back to our date. What do you recommend?"

He flashes me a warm smile as he scans down the menu, resting his hand on top of mine and lacing our fingers together. Even though the nosy locals are staring at him like he's some kind of alien species, he remains completely focused on me and seems genuinely happy just to be here with me.

"Steak," I reply, as Mandy reappears beside us. He gives me his best wolfish grin before slamming the menu down on the table.

"Sold."

Mandy jots down our orders and disappears again, seeming

nervous after Blake's questions. He rubs his thumb absentmindedly across the back of my hand, and we gaze into each other's eyes, grinning like a pair of smitten teenagers. We fall into easy conversation and laughter, enjoying our meal and a few beers. Blake looks more relaxed than I've seen him. He beams as he tells me story after story of the mischief he and Max used to get up to as bored teenagers. I'm really enjoying his company, and every time our legs touch under the table, or he traces his thumb across my knuckles, I'm reminded of how strong our connection is.

Maybe it's time for me to stop over-thinking everything and just go with it. It doesn't seem to have worked out too badly for my sisters.

"Zoe!" Our moment is broken by the arrival of Matt, who pulls me up out of my chair and into a firm hug. Matt and I had a couple of dates back when I first arrived and mistakenly thought I had time to set up a clinic and date. He's a local farmer, an all-round good guy, and even though it never went further, we've stayed friends.

"Hi." I awkwardly step back out of his arms. "Um, Matt, this is Blake. Blake, this is Matt."

Blake stands and extends a hand to my friend. Matt's a big guy, but Blake is bigger.

"Nice to meet you, Matt," Blake says coolly. "Join us." He's polite and welcoming, but his shoulders are tense. In the dim light of the bar, his silver eyes almost look like they're shining.

"No, I don't want to intrude. I'm just glad to see you're okay," Matt squeezes my shoulder before moving off with a tip of the head to Blake. As I sit backdown, he doesn't immediately take my hand. He's been holding it all night, barely letting go to let me eat, and I miss it. I tuck my hands together in my lap and watch Blake as he gestures to Mandy for the bill.

"So, you and Matt…" He keeps his gaze fixed on the table and I notice the muscles along his jaw are clenched tight.

"Dated. Yes," I say, curious to see how this will play out. "Briefly."

Somehow, I can feel his jealousy, but also his unease. He doesn't want to make me feel uncomfortable. He nods and pulls his own hands under the table, rubbing them on his thighs as they bounce rapidly up and down with nervous energy.

"And you've… ?" His brow furrows, and I can clearly see he's uncomfortable even asking.

"Kissed," I finish for him. Nodding again, he keeps his gaze down. He shakes his head, and I notice the tendons in his neck constrict beneath his skin, wound tight as strings on a guitar. It's like watching a storm cloud build and churn as he struggles to contain himself.

"I know it's none of my business, but I have to know," he grits out, with what can only be a low growl starting deep in his chest. Primal and possessive. He finally lifts his eyes to mine, and I see exactly what he's trying to control. His eyes are glowing, and his expression is thunderous and dark.

"Know what?" I whisper, fidgeting in my seat. His wolf is staring straight back at me, and the shift in his energy is palpable. He's as much an animal now as a man, and for some fucked up reason, it's turning me on. Pressing my thighs together, I attempt to ease the ache building inside of me. This can't be normal.

"Has he touched you? Has he tasted you?" His voice is low and gravelly. Using his knee, he forces my legs apart under the table and I gasp as he reaches out to trail his fingers along the seam at the crotch of my jeans.

"*Blake…*" His name comes out as a moan, and I whip my head around to check whether anyone overheard and is watching us.

"Has he Zoe? Has he felt what's mine around him?" He grips my thighs and drags his hands from my knees all the way to my pussy before rubbing my clit roughly through my jeans. A jolt of pleasure shoots through me and I struggle to stop a loud moan from escaping me.

"Jesus, Blake. No, nothing like that!" I hiss. My head is spinning with the sudden turn this evening has taken. I'd slap any other man for asking me anything like that, but it seems to pain him to ask so I relent. Plus, something about his possessiveness stirs my desire.

What's mine. His claim is doing spectacular things to my insides.

"Good." He's up and out of the chair with lightning speed. He slaps some money down on the table and drags me up out of my chair, holding me close. Pressing a hand to his chest, I feel his heart racing. Mine must be the same.

"Are you okay?" I'm genuinely concerned. He takes my hand from his chest and kisses the palm, sending more delicious sparks skittering across my skin. Hunger shines from his eyes and I've never been so aroused in my life. He looks like he wants to eat me alive. As his gaze drops to my lips, I lick them and he growls again.

"I will be. As soon as I get you home and show you exactly how a wolf worships his mate. You won't even remember Matt's name by the time I'm done with you."

CHAPTER 15

BLAKE

I don't remember anything about the drive home except the feel of Zoe's hand resting on my thigh. The rest of it's a blur. A few times, out of the corner of my eye, I see her looking over at me, but I continue to stare straight ahead. This woman has me out of control. As we pull into her driveway, I lift her hand to my lips and kiss her knuckles, finally daring to look at her. My heart soars as she gives me a soft smile. She's still here with me, still in the moment, and she's breathtakingly beautiful.

Pulling to a stop in front of her house, I slip out from behind the wheel and around the vehicle to reach her door in record time. I open it wide and hold out my hand, waiting to see if she'll take it, and accept what I'm offering. As soon as she places her delicate hand in mine, I pull her into my arms and hold her tight to my body. Pushing the car door shut behind Zoe, I bury my fingers into her hair on either side of her face and stare into her beautiful eyes.

Crowding close until there's no space left between us, I loom over her. Our faces are mere inches apart, as I breathe her in and use the very last dredges of my control to force my next words out.

"Zoe, I want to taste you, to touch you. But if you tell me

you're not ready, I'll stay out here and run it off. I'll still be back in the morning to make you breakfast. It won't change a thing."

Leaning down, I press my forehead to hers and close my eyes. She slides her hands up my chest and drapes her arms over my shoulders. I hold my breath and wait for her answer. As much as I yearn for her with every fibre of my being, I don't want to put any pressure on her.

"Blake…" she murmurs, and I open my eyes. "Come inside."

"Thank fuck," I mutter, bending to grab her behind the thighs and hoist her up into my arms. Marching towards the house like a man possessed while she giggles in my ear, I snatch the keys out of her hand. Unlocking the door and kicking it closed behind me, I toss the keys to the floor and press her against the nearest wall. Smashing my lips against hers, I pin her in place with my hips, running my hands over her sexy curves.

"Zoe," I groan as I trail my hands up her sides, savouring the feel of her silky skin. As I feather touches across her ribs, she squirms and sighs against my lips. Every little movement and those noises she makes drive me crazy. Reaching around, I open the clasp on her bra, lifting it away so I can take the weight of her breasts in my hands. Stroking the undersides before circling around each nipple, I roll her stiff peaks between my thumbs and index fingers. Breaking our kiss, I pull up her top and bend to take one between my lips.

The moan that passes her lips as she arches against my mouth goes straight to my balls. Pushing my hips forward, I rub my aching cock against her, and from the gasp that escapes her, I know it's hitting the right spot.

"I want to hear you make that noise every day for the rest of my life," I grit out, moving my hands down to grip her waist, still sucking and biting her nipples. Continuing my exploration, I blaze a trail with my lips along her fragrant, soft skin. Kissing across her collarbone, her shoulder, and up the column of her neck is the ultimate temptation. Her marking spot is right there.

My teeth descend in an instant, punching through my gums,

ready to stake my claim. Burying my head in her neck, I force my wolf back down and distract myself by thrusting hard where we're lined up perfectly.

"Take it off," I order, pulling back to watch as she gathers the hem of her top and peels it over her head seductively, taking her open bra with it. Her breasts are firm, her waist trim, flaring out to soft, womanly hips. She's perfect.

Her face is flushed and her hair sticks up all over the place, disheveled from when I clutched the silky strands. Dazed, she blinks at me wide-eyed, her bottom lip pulled between her teeth. She complied. My defiant little mate did as she was told, and it pleases me to no end.

"Good girl," I murmur as run a finger along her chin, tugging her lip free with my thumb before diving back in for another sensual kiss. She hums and wraps her arms around my neck, melting into me.

Spinning away from the wall, I cross the short distance to the living room, dropping her to her feet and twirling her so she faces away from me, legs touching the edge of the sofa. Sweeping her hair over her shoulder, I kiss, nip, and lick my way down the back of her neck between her shoulder blades. Impatient, I reach around and pop the button on her jeans, dragging the zipper down ever so slowly.

She shivers as my breath skims the back of her ear, and goosebumps dance across her skin. Looking over her shoulder, I have a perfect view of her pebbled nipple and can't resist taking one in my fingers and tweaking it hard. A stifled cry escapes her, somewhere between pleasure and pain.

Sliding my fingers down her taut stomach, I slip my hands inside the stiff denim material and shove her jeans over her hips, tantalisingly slowly. She wiggles to help me as I drag them all the way down to her ankles. Kneeling, I lift her feet one at a time to free them.

"You're stunning, Zoe," I tell her as I admire her sexy body, caressing the back of her calves and knees, along her sleek thighs and shapely hips as I get back to my feet. She's utterly and absolutely perfect. Gritting my teeth, I smooth my hands over her firm ass and let one drift around to her front. Slipping into her panties, I dip into her delicious wetness and drag it back up over her clit, teasing her with small flicks of my finger and long slow strokes. She calls out as I plunge a finger inside her, my chest pressed hard against her naked back.

Without a word of warning, I step back and bring my hand down hard against her ass. The ringing of the loud slap fills the silence of the room. She gasps and rocks forward onto her toes, taken completely by surprise. Steadying herself, she tips her head back, her toffee-coloured hair brushing against her lower back as she groans low and husky.

"Blake!" I've caught her off-guard. Her tone is one of mock horror, but I hear the undercurrent of pleasure in her voice, and my cock twitches, coming to life at the possibilities. She loved it. This woman really was made for me. I wrap the ends of her hair around my fist and tug gently, tipping her head back even further as I rub her tender ass cheek to ease the sting. Bringing my lips to her ear, I whisper, low and commanding.

"That's for leaving that damn office when you promised me you wouldn't." She swallows hard and her breathing comes in shallow little pants now. That skimpy scrap of material she calls underwear does nothing to hide the scent of her arousal. They've soaked through anyway.

"You already spanked me," she whispers, cheeks pink as though she can barely say the words, and her gaze darts to meet mine. I can't help the smile that crosses my lips as I lean in close and take her earlobe in my teeth. My mate hasn't indulged her love of being dominated before. I'll gladly help her with that.

"Angel, if you think that gentle love tap was a spanking, you're in for a big surprise." I kiss her shoulder and turn her back around to face me, before lowering her onto the cushions. "Scoot forward," I instruct, and again, she complies instantly, shimmying closer until she's perched on the edge, eyes locked on mine. Goddess, I love that.

Dropping to my knees in front of her, I kiss from the inside of one knee up her thigh. She watches, fascinated, as I hook my thumbs inside her panties and drag them off. Lifting them as she watches, I press them to my face and inhale deeply. Her scent drives me wild. Unable to resist, I reach down to grip myself, needing some friction to ease the unbelievable urge to strip and bury myself deep inside her.

"Fuck, Zoe… you smell so good. I know you're going to taste even better."

She drops her head back against the cushions as I run my nose up her thigh and hip, grazing her skin with my lips. I'm enjoying the restless way she squirms and fidgets.

"You have a dirty mouth, Blake Steel," she teases, voice deeper and thicker with desire. I use my big body to shove her thighs wider abruptly, positioning my shoulders so she can't squeeze them shut again.

"I'll have to find something better to do with it, then."

CHAPTER 16

BLAKE

Holding eye contact, I finally close my mouth around her juicy cunt, and suck her clit into my mouth, flicking it with my tongue before licking along her slit.

"Blake!" she cries and reaches out to grasp my hair tightly in her hands. "Fuck!"

Lips pressed against her skin, I slide my hands down her body, barely touching her with my fingertips. With increasing pressure, I slip two fingers deep inside her, making her quiver beneath me. I continue to thrust and pulse my digits, simultaneously pleasuring her legs and clitoris. She moves with my motions as I hear my wolf howling inside me, filled with pride.

I push her hips down, holding one hand firmly against her lower abdomen as I increase my pace, pumping harder and faster now, stretching her wider while she clenches down around my fingers. Even her sweet little pussy wants me inside her, but not yet.

"Blake, oh God… I need…," she calls out, gasping as her head and shoulder lift from the couch as I press the heel of my hand hard against her. Her eyes find mine and she is adorably messy and flushed, her chest a pretty shade of pink.

"Please, Blake, I want you. I need you inside me," she pleads, and my cock nearly punches through these agonisingly tight jeans at her words. I want her more than anything, but not tonight. We only met last night. I can't give her any reason to doubt my intentions, but it's torture. I want to break and give her what she's begging for. The idea of pushing her down and pounding into her right here and now seems like heaven.

"You're doing so good, angel." Mumbling against her sensitive flesh, I concentrate on giving her what she needs. She moans, tensing her ass, and squeezes even tighter. My girl likes praise, and why wouldn't she? She'll be getting a lot of it from me. I hum appreciatively and the vibrations from my voice carry to her most sensitive area, sending her spiralling closer and closer to the edge. The silken inner walls of pussy clutch at my fingers, as if seeking to pull me in. Her body feels empty, demanding to be filled, and I want it to be my hard cock that does it.

Zoe drags her fingernails across my scalp and down my neck, sending electric sparks across my skin and to my groin. She presses them hard into my shoulders, hard enough that she will leave marks. My wolf preens, enjoying how caught up in the moment she is.

"Give it to me, Zoe. I need to feel you come for me," I growl out and she tosses her head, refusing to give in. Her eyes are glassy and unfocussed, lost to the whirlwind of sensations.

"Blake," she whispers, sounding overwhelmed.

I know the feeling.

Her stomach tenses and she goes rigid just before her climax hits. She convulses around my fingers, arching forward, her pert breasts pushed out and too tempting to resist. I bite down gently on her nipple as her tight little body milks my fingers. I can hardly wait to feel her sweet little pussy clench around my cock when I claim her as my mate. She continues to pulse and twitch underneath me as the aftershocks continue.

I watch, amazed, as she finally comes down from the last wave. She falls back against the cushions, arms hanging loose by her sides and eyes closing softly. Rocking back onto my heels, I admire her beautifully flushed body, stroking my hands over her thighs and down her legs, before pulling her panties on and carefully tugging them up to her hips. She doesn't even seem to notice.

In one smooth move, I lean down and scoop her up in my arms, pressing a soft kiss to her lips and then her forehead as I carry her upstairs to her room. Manoeuvring her gently under the covers, pulling them up to her chin to make sure she doesn't get cold. Running a hand through her hair, I take a moment to appreciate just how lucky I am. I had almost given up hope.

As I stand up, her hand shoots out to grab my wrist, and she gazes up at me with confused, drowsy eyes.

"Blake… please don't go," she mumbles, sounding half asleep. "I don't want to be alone." The subtle note of fear in her voice makes my chest ache.

"I'm not going anywhere, angel. Go to sleep. I'll be back in a minute," I promise. Her fingers loosen and she slowly releases me as she sinks back into the pillows, totally exhausted from the last few days. She's been through so much. The few hours of sleep she got couldn't have been enough. She needs to rest.

Stepping into the en suite, I strip off my clothes and free my aching cock. Tonight was all about Zoe but damned if I didn't want to get involved, to plunge my cock deep inside her and discover exactly what her dripping wet pussy feels like.

"Fuck," I mutter, shaking my head as I turn on the shower, turning the temperature down as low as it will go before stepping inside. My insides are on fire and I long for her. My rock-hard erection doesn't budge, refusing to go down as I let the cold water sluice over my tense body. There's no way I can go back out and climb into bed beside her like this and I certainly won't be able to sleep.

Resting my forearm against the cold tiles, I wrap my hand around my cock. With a groan, I drop my chin to my chest, closing my eyes as I stroke the hard shaft firmly up and down.

Goddess, it feels good. Giving into the fantasy building in my mind, I imagine it's Zoe wrapped around me. The slippery sensation of her juices all over me as I push my way inside her. Thrusting into my palm, my balls tighten as I recall her messy hair, rosy cheeks, and soft moans. The way she followed my instructions eagerly. I wonder if she would be as willing if I asked her to take me between her sensuously full lips.

"Let me watch you."

Zoe's whisper from the bedroom is barely audible above the cascading shower. If it weren't for my enhanced shifter hearing, I'm not sure I would have heard her at all. Briefly, I wonder if she was talking to me or to herself? Either way, her wish is my command. I turn in the shower so my arm now rests against the steamy glass, giving her a clear view of my fingers wrapped around my cock.

I lift my gaze and lock on to hers. Her pale grey eyes shine from under half-closed lids, and she looks sexy as hell with her hair fanned out around her on the pillow. The sheet has fallen to her waist and her perfect breasts are exposed, nipples stiff in the cool of the room. I don't need to remember how she looked earlier. Just looking at her now has me as turned on as ever.

"Zoe," I groan as I pump my fist up and down slowly but firmly, rocking my hips as I thrust into my hand to add to the sensation. She rolls onto her side but our eyes stay fixed on each other as I go higher and higher, picking up the pace as I chase my release.

She opens her mouth and flicks her tongue out to wet her lips, and that's all it takes for my thoughts to dive into the gutter. In an instant, my mind conjures up the image of her licking my cock, opening her soft mouth as I feed it between her lips with a hand buried in her hair. It's enough to send me over the edge, and I shove my hips forward one last time and still with a loud groan. My cum shoots out in thick spurts against the glass shower door as I shout her name and screw my eyes closed.

The force of it makes me see stars and my knees almost

buckle. I've never experienced any like it. When I force my eyes back open, panting hard, she's still watching me intently, chest heaving and eyes sparkling with excitement.

"You like to watch me, angel?" I say as I step out and wrap a fluffy white towel around my waist. She nods as she rolls onto her back and sighs happily, her breathing a little calmer, keeping her eyes glued to me as I dry off and slip back into my boxer briefs.

"That was so hot," she admits, nipping my shoulder as I slide under the covers beside her.

"You're so hot," I retort, wrapping an arm around her shoulder and tucking her against me so her cheek rests against my chest. When she throws a leg over mine, curling her languid body into mine, I grin.

This is perfect.

It might not be the first meeting I'd hoped for, but at the end of the first twenty-four hours, we've ended up exactly as I would have dreamed.

In each other's arms.

CHAPTER 17

ZOE

There's a furnace against my back when I wake from the deepest sleep I've had in years, and the delicious warmth is amazing. It seems like a dream, so I lie still to linger a few more moments and savour it. When I finally stir, edging towards the side of the bed, Blake's arm tightens around me and pulls me tight against him. He's spooning me from behind, his legs tangled with mine. His relaxed, even breathing tickles the back of my neck.

Lifting his heavy arm, I slip out from underneath him as quickly as I can. I roll off the side of the bed and scan the ground for something to throw on. Pulling on Blake's discarded shirt, I tiptoe down the stairs and fill the kettle, pulling two mugs from the cabinet and letting my mind wander to the events of last night.

A buzzing noise from the sitting room catches my attention and I spot Blake's flashing phone lying in the middle of the floor, not too far from where he carelessly threw my keys. My gaze drifts to where he pressed me against the wall, and I smile. It was so hot. I've never felt so wanted.

I pick his phone up and go to place it on the hall table when it immediately rings again in my hand. Max and five missed calls. I hesitate for a moment before answering.

"Max? It's Zoe here," I say, placing the phone on the counter on speaker as I go back to making coffee.

"Zoe, hey! I take it Blake's still with you?" I can hear the smile in Max's voice. It would seem he's thrilled his buddy didn't get sent packing last night.

"Yeah, he's still here. He's asleep though. Do you want me to wake him up, or have him call you back?" I ask, dropping some bread into the toaster and pulling out the butter and jam.

"I'm sorry, for a second there I thought you said he was still asleep," Max repeats in disbelief.

"I did."

"But it's after ten." Max seems completely stunned. Blake is obviously a morning person.

"Yeah, well… we didn't exactly have a good night's sleep the night before," I offer.

"You maybe, but he spent a good portion of that night unconscious, remember? He should be well rested."

"Hilarious," I grumble sarcastically. Max will never let him live it down.

"He's really in bed? Blake never sleeps. What did you do to him, woman?" he teases. "Actually, I don't want to know!"

"I sleep sometimes," Blake interrupts, sauntering in and wrapping his arms around me from behind, pressing a sensual kiss to my neck. He grips my chin and turns my face toward him, before kissing me again on the lips, deeper this time, and my legs turn to jelly. His black hair is all mussed up, and he's dressed just in tight boxers and a t-shirt, looking sinfully sexy. Seeing him sleepy and tousled makes him look almost boyish.

"Barely," Max shoots back. "I hate to interrupt, but I wasn't able to put off your council meeting this afternoon. Do you want me to go in your place?"

"No, I'll go, but would you meet everyone when they arrive and get them settled? I'll only get back just in time." Blake never takes his lips from my skin as he speaks, dragging the shirt down my shoulder so he can kiss his way from my ear to my shoulder blade.

"You look sexy in this thing."

His voice comes out in a low growl. His clever hands find their way under the hem of the shirt, skimming up along my thighs, stomach, and higher along the sides of my ribs. It's the one he wore out to dinner last night. I had an intense to desire to drape myself in his smell. It's intoxicating, just like the man himself. I bite my tongue to stop the moan threatening to tumble from my lips.

"Sure thing, boss. Bye, Zoe," Max calls out.

"Bye, Max." I try to sound casual, but my voice comes out high-pitched and squeaky as Blake continues to torture me with caresses. Max chuckles as he disconnects and finally, I can relax. The second he's gone, Blake spins me to face him before pinning me against the counter.

"Last night was amazing," he murmurs into my ear. His hot breath and the reminder of what we got up to send a jolt of desire straight to my core. Stubble covers the lower half of his face now, and it scratches my sensitive skin slightly as he kisses along my jaw, burying one hand into the hair at the nape of my neck.

I nod enthusiastically. Amazing doesn't even begin to cover it. It was mind-altering and life-changing. Any doubts I had about two people being matched together based on some magical, instant reaction, have been obliterated. He knows what I want and what I like better than anyone else, including me.

"But I... you know, and you didn't. And then you had to..." I'm a grown woman, but I can't make myself say the word masterbate.

"I had to rub one out so I didn't climb into bed and fuck you senseless all night?" he says shamelessly, and I blush. He presses a kiss to my lips and forces me to look at him.

"Angel, believe me, getting to see you come for the first time was all I wanted. For now. We have all the time in the world to enjoy the rest," he promises.

I blink up at him, marvelling at how certain he seems of all this. I keep trying to dismiss it as an act, but then I think of Hayley and Leah. This is a reality for them. I just need to be open to the idea that he's genuine and keep my skepticism at bay.

"Okay," I whisper, and he smiles before his face turns serious again.

"Then why did I wake up to an empty bed?" he asks, his voice low and husky with sleep. There's an unmistakable edge though, and God help me, I'm giddy at the thought that I might be in trouble.

"I wanted to make you some coffee," I squeak when he trails his hands up the back of my legs, tickling that spot where my thighs meet my ass.

"Well, in that case, thank you," he whispers, giving my backside a firm squeeze and placing a soft kiss on my lips before pulling back. He steals the mug of coffee from the counter behind me and brings it to his lips with a smug smile. Blake knows exactly where my mind went. He's enjoying this.

"You need to work?" I ask, and he growls in frustration.

"Unfortunately, but I can come straight back."

I'm shaking my head already, thinking of all the things I should do around here to get the clinic back up and running, and catch up on missed appointments. It doesn't make any sense for him to come back just to watch me work. He dips his head, so we're eye to eye.

"I'm not leaving you here on your own. Come with me and see the pack. I know Hayley cleared your diary today and tomorrow as well." He grins at me triumphantly, delighted that he has this nugget of information to lord over me.

I don't miss that he said to come and see the pack, not his house or where he works, because he knows the veterinarian in me will be too curious to pass up an opportunity like this.

"We have a clinic, too. It's new. I'd love it if you could have a look and tell me what you think," he adds, dangling another carrot in front of my nose.

A shiny new clinic? I bet they have all sorts of fancy equipment. Are they set up to treat humans or animals? Do the physicians there qualify in human medicine or veterinary practice? Blake's steely eyes crinkle at the corners as he grins, waiting, and sees the moment he has me. It's too tempting.

"I suppose I could come and see your clinic."

A smile spreads across my lips as he pretends to be offended that it's not him I'm interested in.

"Of course, to see the clinic," he smiles back. "Fifteen minutes, sweetheart, then we're on the road."

"Sure thing, boss," I reply, using Max's sign-off from earlier. Blake growls, and presses me harder against the countertop. I can feel the hard length of his erection against my stomach, and I swallow, trying to contain my reaction to him.

"Bring an overnight bag in case you want to stay. There are lots of rooms. Or I'll drive you home if you're not sure later."

Once again, he anticipated my concern. I'm still considering how he seems to read my mind when I come back down the stairs. Blake's dressed once again in his suit and white shirt combination, and my pussy clenches. His black hair is slicked back, and his grey eyes are intense.

Reaching out to take the bag from me, he carries it outside, capturing my other hand in his. He opens the door for me before throwing my bag onto the back seat. This feels big. I'm stepping out of my comfort zone and taking a chance. A big chance.

The drive is easy and the conversation flows. His hand rarely leaves mine, but as we get closer to his home, he seems increasingly tense. I squeeze his hand and his gaze drifts to mine. He looks worried.

"What is it, Blake? Tell me, so I'm prepared," I warn. I don't like being blindsided and I've had a rough few days.

"Mates are precious to wolves. I'm quite old to still be looking for mine without having chosen to just settle down with someone else."

I nod along cautiously. I think I'm following so far.

"Like Cooper, I run the pack. For me to find either my mate or to choose someone I would take as my own is a big deal. You might get a lot of attention. I'm worried you'll be uncomfortable."

He looks genuinely apprehensive, and I don't fancy being the object of discussion, either.

"Let's just say I'm here to see the clinic. If people want to read more into it, that's up to them. We'll just go with the flow," I suggest. He frowns and his grip on the wheel tightens. Even though I thought that's what he was angling at, he doesn't seem to like that idea either.

"Something else?"

"I won't cope well if anyone touches you," he admits with a wince, and I stare at him. I'm trying to work out if he's serious, but then I remember how he was after Matt spoke to me at the bar. Possessive and intense. Reaching out, I place my hand on his thigh and give it a gentle squeeze. He looks over, his expression drawn and pensive.

"Blake, it'll be alright. I'll make it clear I'm not available. I don't have to say I'm your mate to do that."

Something about that doesn't sit right with me, but I can't put a finger on it. If it makes life easier for him, I'm willing to do it. He whips his head around at my words as we roll to a stop at the front of a massive three-story property.

"Are you available?"

He asks, his eyes flashing, and his jaw clenched.

"Are you?"

"Fuck no. Angel, I have been yours every day of my life. The moment I caught your scent, that was it for me. There is no one else."

Wow. That's some statement.

"It's not quite the same for you," he says quietly, perhaps giving me an out from making the same type of dramatic declaration.

"No, but while we're doing this, I'm all yours."

Some people are good at playing the field and keeping their options open. Not me.

"We'll be *doing this* for a long time if I have anything to do with it."

He reaches across and grips my face in his hands, meeting my gaze with relief and gratitude all over his handsome features, before his lips fuse to mine in a scorching hot, passionate kiss. So much for being discreet. I'm breathless by the time Blake pulls away and presses his forehead to mine briefly before opening his door and coming to get mine.

As he walks around, I glance up to admire the massive house. It's incredible and intimidating all at once. I can't even imagine living somewhere this massive.

However, it's not the fancy steps up to the ornate doors that catch my attention. It's the beautiful young woman waiting at the top with a face like thunder and rage in her eyes.

CHAPTER 18

BLAKE

Opening the door for Zoe, I hold my hand out to help her from the car. She hesitates for a moment before placing her hand in mine. Following the direction of her gaze, I spot Jenna waiting at the top of the steps, wearing a scowl on her normally cheerful face. Hiding my annoyance, I give Zoe a reassuring smile as we walk toward the house. The fact that Zoe even agreed to come with me is a blessing. I want her to feel at home here. My assistant isn't exactly rolling out the welcome wagon as she continues to glare.

As we reach the top of the steps, I fix Jenna with a hard look.

"Is there a problem, Jenna?"

My sharp tone seems to snap her out of it, and she immediately turns to face me, a warm smile now spread across her lips and the icy look gone from her pale blue eyes.

"No Blake, sorry! The council is in the boardroom already. They're ready whenever you are."

I nod at her but don't smile back and she fidgets under my scrutiny, tucking her platinum-blonde hair behind her ears before twisting her hands together.

"Zoe, this is Jenna. Jenna, this is Zoe. She's staying overnight. Can you put her in the guest room on my floor?" I keep the introductions brief. My wolf is being extra protective of our mate and is angry at the less-than-welcoming reception she received. Zoe extends her hand and smiles politely as Jenna takes it.

"I'm sorry for staring," Jenna apologizes, looking genuinely remorseful. "You just look so much like Hayley, and then I saw you two kiss... I got a shock. I didn't know what was going on for a second!"

She laughs nervously, looking back and forth between us, waiting to see if she's still in my bad books, as well as trying to establish what's going on between us.

"Ah, you've met my sister." Zoe's expression softens as the reason behind Jenna's frosty greeting becomes clear. She smiles and walks along beside her as Jenna ushers us inside, her heels tapping on the hardwood floor. No matter how often I tell her there is no need, she continues to dress professionally, as though this is a five-star hotel she's managing, rather than a house full of crazy wolves.

"Briefly. Blake, why don't you get that meeting over and done with? I can show Zoe around." Jenna attempts to take the overnight bag out of my hand, but Zoe shakes her head and reaches for it first. I glance at her to check if she's alright with that and she nods, smiling brightly at me.

"Go on. I'm fine. I'll get settled and look around. You can show me the clinic when you're done." I pause for a moment, but she briskly shoos me away as she follows Jenna up the elegant, curved staircase. The growing distance between us makes my skin itch and I desperately want to follow her and steal one more kiss. As she exchanges pleasantries with Jenna, I get a glimpse of what life could be like with Zoe here all the time, and it warms my heart.

"You're so screwed," Max comments with a disbelieving shake of his head as he joins me, watching me admiring my mate. I can't help but smile.

"Yes, I am," I admit, and I'm thrilled about it. Max jerks his head towards the boardroom at the far side of the house and reluctantly, I follow him. The sooner I get this over with, the sooner I can go back to Zoe. Smoothing a hand down over my shirt and the lapels of my navy suit jacket, I suck in a deep breath and get my game face on.

The council is made up of former alphas and elder scholars of shifter customs and traditions. They usually support and challenge me in equal measure, but this visit is merely a smokescreen to see if Moon madness has claimed me. If I'm to keep my pack and my position, I must persuade them it isn't an issue - even if it is.

"Good afternoon," I say, greeting the council as I push open the heavy wooden doors and stride confidently to the head of the table. I unbutton my jacket and sit in the large leather chair, nodding to each member that meets my eye and accepting the glass of water that Will, my assistant, places in front of me. Murmurs of greeting reach me from the ten men and women sitting around the long table as they scrutinise me.

"So, to what do I owe this great honour?" I ask, getting straight to the point. They requested this meeting, but wouldn't say why because they don't really have a reason, or not a good one anyway.

"Alpha Weston says he met you recently and was concerned about your lack of focus. He said you were distracted and appeared to be unwell." Brett Wilson, a former Alpha in this region, states diplomatically. His gaze locks with mine; testing to see if there is any weakness in my alpha aura. I bite down the irritation of being tested and maintain my usual calm demeanour.

"You can tell Alpha Weston I lost focus because he insisted on giving a never-ending speech about the benefits of reinstating the Wolf Games, something I had already signed off on. He might find me more attentive in the future if he could keep his tirades to under thirty minutes."

Brett tries not to smile, but I see his eyes crinkle with amusement as he recalls his own dealings with the efficient but fastidious alpha.

Weston's pack is well run, but he's the most boring, self-important man I've ever encountered. That I excel at my job and find enjoyment in it seems to perturb him to no end. He had his eye on the top spot. If Moon madness took me out and cleared the way for him to assume my position, I doubt he'd lose any sleep over it.

"You didn't join the pack during the full moon run," Sharon says, her silver hair a testament to the extent of her knowledge of all things shifter, even if she herself didn't look much over forty. I won't bother wondering how she knows this. She's known for having her finger on the pulse of what's going on in the region. It would be foolish for me to worry about who told her. It would make it look like I have something to hide.

"I didn't," I respond.

"Neither did you come back last night," she continues, prodding for an explanation without directly asking any questions. All gazes shift from her to me, and I can feel their concern. This is the crux of it. This is why they wouldn't reschedule, why they had to meet with me now. They want to figure out what's going on with me, and if Alpha Weston's right in saying I'm starting to unravel.

"I did not." I pause deliberately, considering all the trouble this might get me into. "The truth is I had a date. Which you kind people are now preventing me from getting back to."

Brett chuckles, a wry smile playing on his lips as he looks around the table. Relief washes over the room in a palpable wave. Even though they don't know I've found my fated mate, the fact I'm involved in a relationship is enough to reassure them I will soon take a chosen mate.

"We won't keep you–" Brett stands to leave as though the entire matter is resolved and I'll be mated by tomorrow, but Sharon interrupts him.

"I'd like to meet her," she states bluntly, and indistinct whispers circle the table as the council members consider Sharon's demand. "Jenna generously provided us with rooms for the night. I believe I'll take you up on your kind offer so that I get the chance to speak to your special lady."

I don't know if she's genuinely interested in who I mate or if this is another attempt to test my control and observe the effects of my Moon madness. Either way, there's no way to say no and decline her request without looking like I'm covering something up. This is the council after all.

"You're always welcome here. I'll check and see if she's available for dinner. You understand that we're not mated, Sharon, so try not to scare her off."

I try to make my words sound light with a wink and a smile, but she gets the message. She knows exactly what I mean. I'm attempting to remain civil, but she's under my roof and pushing her luck by demanding to meet my date. I'll only be pushed so far. And there's no way I'll force Zoe to go if she doesn't want to. We barely know each other and she shouldn't have to be part of any drama.

I make some small talk for an acceptable amount of time before I excuse myself to find Zoe. My need for her is like an addiction and getting to her is the only thing that can break my current agitated state. I also need to break it to her the council has gate-crashed our plans for the evening. Following her scent outdoors, I find her with Jenna in the garage, looking at the row of high-end vehicles and motorbikes. Only one motorbike belongs to me and I frown at Jenna for assuming Zoe would be interested in seeing them. The idea of her showing off all we have makes me uncomfortable.

I take Zoe's hand and loop it through my arm as I kiss her temple.

"I hope Jenna took good care of you."

"Of course," Zoe nods, though her expression is uneasy. Jenna shrugs and hands me a water bottle before taking her leave with a wave. Moving into Zoe's personal space, I wrap my arms around her, yet she remains rigid, arms hanging stiffly at her sides.

"I don't think she likes me," Zoe murmurs into my chest. I trail a hand through her silky hair and breathe in her scent.

"Jenna likes everybody. It was probably just a shock when she thought I was kissing Hayley." It's a desperate attempt to reassure her, as I want so badly for her to be happy spending time here, but I'm not sure that's all it is.

"Maybe," Zoe responds, skepticism lacing her sharp tone. There's a glint in her eye, reminding me of the feisty attitude she had at the clinic, and it makes me wonder what has her on edge.

"Did she say something to you?" I lean away, taking hold of her shoulders and attempting to get a read on her mood. She shakes her head and draws me back to her body, burying her face in my white shirt and slipping an arm around my waist under my jacket.

"No, no. Don't mind me. Seriously, don't worry about it. How was your meeting?"

She isn't telling me something, but if she doesn't want to elaborate, I won't push it right now. But I will get it out of her later. Because if there is anything about being here that's bothering my mate, I'll do everything in my power to resolve it.

CHAPTER 19

ZOE

Blake's touch calms me, but I'm still irrationally angry. I can tell my visit is important to him, so I'll hold my tongue for the time being. We can talk about Jenna later. She hasn't done anything overtly hostile, but if she touches him once more, I can't guarantee how I'll react.

There isn't a doubt in my mind that she more than likes Blake and has designs on him for herself. Who wouldn't?

My initial suspicion was correct. When I first saw her staring at us, she looked jealous. After she explained it was merely shock at seeing her boss kissing a different alpha's wife, I gave her the benefit of the doubt. It was a mistake I could understand. After that, she acted friendly while taking me off for a tour of the property, but her body language transformed as soon as Blake wasn't around. That version of Jenna was clearly for Blake's benefit only.

The smile vanished as she took me to all the places meant to show me I didn't fit in — the swimming pool, the large gym, the extravagant ballroom — but not the kitchen or living areas that make up the heart of the lodge Hayley and Cooper live in. Those are the places I wanted to see, and where the rest of Blake's pack would be. Lastly, she takes me to the garage bigger than my house with its array of impressive cars.

Jenna obviously loves her role in Blake's life and has no desire to see me or anyone else come in and steal him away. When she showed me to a bedroom well away from Blake's, I got her message loud and clear. But I hate to break it to her. Blake's not hers.

He's mine.

He takes a long swig of his drink and I watch, enthralled, as his tanned neck works and he licks the moisture from his full lips. He nervously rubs a hand against the back of his neck, his uncertainty endearing. There is obviously something important he needs to get off his chest and is hesitating.

"I'm sorry, Zoe. I'm afraid I have bad news. The Council is staying, and they want us to have dinner together tonight," he says, wincing as he awaits my reaction. This isn't ideal, but now I'm determined to stake my claim.

"So what happened to not telling everyone that I'm your fated mate?" I whisper, stepping closer and running my hands over his shirt, up to his muscular shoulders, and around his neck seductively. As I lightly scrape his skin above the collar with my nails, he hums and closes his eyes.

He's so tense. He wants everything to be perfect, but that's not how real life works. I want to know the real Blake. I want to see his world.

"I'll shout it from the rooftops once you're absolutely sure you want me for keeps," he says in a mysterious tone, gazing at me before guiding me back against a black truck. The cool metal of the vehicle is a stark contrast to my burning skin as my back slams against it.

"Any idea when that will be?" he growls, his voice edged with something I haven't heard before. I frown at him, confused; this is the first time he's put any sort of pressure on me. Despite the enormity of what he is asking me to believe — fated mates and *happily ever afters* — he hasn't actively pushed his agenda. He simply laid his cards on the table and set about sweeping me off my feet.

This is not the same Blake as before. His eyes are glowing bright silver and his nostrils flare as he takes rapid, shallow breaths. His olive skin looks unusually pale and clammy, and his pupils appear peculiar. Reaching up, I place a hand on his forehead to check if he's feverish, and try to get a better look at his striking eyes. He catches my arm, pulling it away from his skin and pinning it roughly against the truck behind me, forcing his body against mine. I can feel his arousal - more aggressive than usual - yet my body still responds just the same.

"Blake? What's going on?" I ask, my nerves both thrilled and alarmed by this change in his mood. This dominance is a turn-on, but something in the back of my mind is screaming that this isn't right. He doesn't answer me, instead burying his face in my neck and shoving my hair back roughly to expose more of my shoulder.

I feel the sharp points of his teeth graze my delicate skin and I freeze. My body warms at the sensation, craving more from him and welcoming his attention. My pussy clenches, desperate for him to sink those teeth into my skin, but I'm also scared. Part of me wants Blake to take me right here, to fill me with his cock as he marks me with those dangerous teeth and makes me his forever.

But something is off.

"I could just take you right now," he murmurs, amused, as if he's seriously considering it, and fear slithers down my spine. "There's nothing you could do."

The Blake I know wouldn't do that, wouldn't even suggest such a thing. Is this his wolf taking control?

Is this a whole other personality that I need to contend with?

"*Blake?*" I nervously give him a little shove and he leans back, blinking at me in confusion. The hold on my arm instantly loosens. It's as if he's waking up from a trance.

"I… I…" He opens and closes his mouth, a look of utter

devastation on his face. Looking like I burned him, he jumps back and pivots on the spot as though he has no recollection of being here or how he got here.

"Are you alright?" I ask, stepping closer, but he moves further away and stares down at his fingers, flexing them in front of him. That's when I notice his hands trembling. Cautiously, I wrap my hand around his wrist to take his pulse. His heart is racing. Blake's wide-eyed gaze meets mine and I can tell he's as scared as I am.

"Okay. Come on." I loop one of his arms around my shoulders as he continues to look around, bewildered and unsteady. As we reach the door back into the main house, he shakes his head and pulls away from me, lowering himself to the floor and placing his head between his knees.

"Nobody can see," he grits out. "Get Max."

I nod, reluctant to leave him, but I know I can't force him to come with me; he's just too big. Bursting through the door back into the house, I'm debating which way to go when Max comes charging around the corner.

"Where is he?" he asks, worry etched across his features.

I point towards the garage entrance and follow him through. I stop in my tracks when I spot Blake hunched over, head in his hands, rocking back and forth. The pale walls of the garage are sterile and cold, and seeing Blake unwell in here makes it seem worse somehow.

"Shit," Max curses, watching as Blake's eyes roll in his head. Max springs into action, snatching a set of keys off the wall and yanking open the truck door. Carefully, he helps Blake climb into the back.

"It's okay buddy, I've got you," he reassures him, patting his leg as I climb in, kneeling beside Blake. Max slams the door shut and runs around to the driver's side.

"Max, what's happening? Do you know what's wrong?" I ask, taking Blake's pulse again, which thankfully seems slightly slower than last time. Max starts the engine, and we lurch as he pulls out of the garage.

"Unfortunately, I do," Max said tersely. "We need to get him to the clinic. The pack can't see him like this. And the council can't know or he's out of a job."

Max tears out of the garage and I throw out an arm to brace myself as he races across the property. The drive is bumpy but short and the next thing I know, Max has Blake under one arm and is helping him in through the doors of a pristine-looking clinic.

"Jeffrey?" Max calls out. "*Jeffrey!*"

A startled-looking man with a shock of white hair comes bustling out into the corridor and at seeing Blake, quickly rolls over a wheelchair for Max to lower him into. Without saying a word, they wheel him straight into an exam room, and it strikes me that this is not entirely unexpected if the doctor hasn't asked Max one single question. He doesn't even look that surprised considering Blake is a fit, healthy man in his thirties.

The doctor looks at me pointedly, and I step back from the doorway. Obviously, he doesn't want to say anything confidential in my presence and I respect that. Blake is lying on a bed now, eyes screwed shut, with a fist pressed to his forehead. He hasn't spoken a word since he asked for Max. As much as it kills me to leave his side, I need to let the doctor do his job.

"I'll get some water," I offer, then head out to the water cooler I saw near the entrance. After waiting as long as my anxiety will let me, I walk back toward the room.

"Will the symptoms disappear?" Blake asks, his deep voice sounding decidedly weak. My heart squeezes at the fragility in his tone. For someone so strong, being vulnerable doesn't come easy.

"I can't guarantee it, sir. I've seen it go both ways." Jeffrey's voice wavers. He sounds upset. Max goes to speak, but Blake cuts him off, dismissing him from the room with a wave of his hand. Both men leave with heads bowed as Blake closes his eyes and turns to face the wall. Jeffrey pulls the door shut behind him and releases a heavy sigh.

Max glances up at me with tired eyes and a haggard expression.

"What's going on? Is he okay?" I ask.

Max drags a hand back through the longer hair on the top of his head and casts his gaze around. His hesitation speaks volumes. *No.*

"He's been having some issues lately," he says. "I'm sorry if he frightened you. He mind-linked me, but I couldn't work out what he was saying, just that he was worried about you."

Max peers at me, scrutinising closely for any sign that Blake has hurt me. He clearly can't remember whether he did.

"What? No! I'm fine," I assure him, my gaze shifting to the closed door and a sudden feeling of being lost washes over me. Is it possible to miss his presence after such a short time apart?

"I don't think it would be wise for you to see him right now. I'm sorry," Max replies. "Jeffrey has everything under control. Blake just needs to rest. Come on, I'll bring you back to the house to get ready."

"Get ready?" I tilt my head in disbelief. He can't seriously mean what I think he means. Not today.

"For dinner." Max stares at me, his expression blank, as though the answer should be obvious.

"Are you frigging insane?! He's literally in a hospital. You can't seriously want us to go to dinner tonight?"

"The show must go on, Zoe. If anyone gets a hint of weakness from Blake, it could cost him his job, his pack, or his life."

Max's casual attitude shifts and something darker takes its place. He's protecting his friend and asking me to do the same. I have no idea what I'm walking into, but I already know that after what Blake has done for me, I'd walk through fire for him.

"Fine, but I want to come back here when he's getting out. I need to see him, for myself, in person, and make sure he's okay to leave."

Max smiles at my demand and holds out his hand to me.

"Deal."

I shake it, but my feet don't seem to want to move on their own, so he pulls me toward the front door. As we pass the room Blake is in, I linger, staring before finally allowing myself to be hauled outside.

Max stops shielding his eyes from the sun once we clear the door. His tattoos peek out above the neck of his t-shirt, winding their way around his forearms. His grey t-shirt and black jeans make him a stark contrast to Blake's immaculately suited style, yet they're clearly very close. Perhaps there's hope for me and Blake, despite our differences.

"I can't tell you what's going on," he says apologetically. "Just promise me this: remember what a good guy he is. That wasn't him, not the real him. Don't give up on him too easily, okay?"

"I can deal with anything once I know what's going on."

I'm not the type of person who scares easily, although when I think back to the garage and to the sudden shift in his personality, it still sends a chill down my spine. Like Jekyll and Hyde. Do I really know what I'm letting myself in for?

"I hope so."

Max's words hold an ominous weight. Whatever is going on with Blake is serious. And somehow, I'm now involved in covering it up.

CHAPTER 20

BLAKE

Just as I'm fastening my cufflinks, there's a knock on the door. Zoe peeks in, then pushes it open and steps through. Despite expecting her, the sight of her smiling face makes me melt.

Her toffee-coloured hair cascades over her shoulders, teasing the exposed skin of her chest and back as she moves. She's wearing a form-fitting red dress that shows just enough cleavage to take my breath away, but remains classy. The dress shows off her long legs to perfection, paired with nude heels that look like they could be lethal weapons in the right hands.

"You look stunning," I say as she enters.

Zoe steps closer to me, standing toe to toe before reaching for the cufflinks between my fingers, which I obediently drop into her hand. She turns my wrist over and fastens one, then the other, without looking up. My sensitive skin tingles from her touch and I watch silently, mesmerised, as she concentrates on the task. Her full lips press together and her eyes sparkle as she stares at where her nimble fingers make quick work of both sleeves. It makes me think of what it would be like to have her do this for every meeting, every event — never to go to one alone again. To have her support and her presence in my life. I can envision it all.

Once she's finished, she keeps one of my hands in hers,

rubbing her thumb back and forth over my exposed pulse point. I get a wave of her tumultuous emotions and guilt overwhelms me. Tilting her chin up with one finger so she's forced to look at me, I duck my head so that we're at eye level.

"I am so sorry, Zoe."

I cup her face in my hands and press my forehead to hers, savouring her dizzying scent and how soft her creamy skin feels under my fingertips. "Do you want me to drive you home? You don't have to stay if you don't want to."

Her brows draw together in confusion and she tilts her head to the side adorably.

"Why would I go?" she asks. "Do you want me to leave?"

"I never want you to leave, angel." It's the truth. I fight the urge to pull her into my arms and hold her forever. "But I lost control earlier, and I scared you. I hate myself for it. So if this is all too much, I'll understand."

Squeezing my eyes shut, I wait for her to tell me it's over before it's even begun. I could never blame her. She'd been right under my nose for so long. Why hadn't I noticed her a year ago when she moved into my territory?

I drag my fingertips along her chin and down the column of her throat. I pause as she takes a deep breath, feeling her neck muscles work underneath my palms before continuing with feather-light touches over her shoulders and chest.

My gaze locks on where my mark would go if I haven't wrecked things completely between us. I was moments away from marking her without her permission, taking away her choices, and ruining everything between us forever.

I can't express the terror that gripped me in those moments. The madness was the strongest it's ever been. Aggression and adrenaline flooded my veins. My head pounded as I fought a losing battle with my wolf and I was forced to concede control. For a man who plans every step carefully, to be unable to stop myself was unnerving. I can't even imagine what she thinks of me now. I really could have hurt her.

"Blake. Listen to me," she says, her fingers tightening around my wrists until I open my eyes. "I can feel it. I understand how torn up you are over what happened. Maybe I don't believe in this fated mates thing completely yet, but I can *feel* it."

Her pale grey eyes bore into mine. My bond with her might still be fragile, the strands that will keep us together only beginning to form and take shape, but I'm flooded with relief that she can sense it too.

"I was so scared I'd hurt you," I confess. Even through the clinging fog of my madness, my main concern was that I would do something to harm her. It was the only thing that allowed me to claw back control and send her to Max. I couldn't even establish a clear mind-link to my beta. That's how severely this Moon madness has affected me.

"But you didn't hurt me." She cuts me off before I can go down that road. "You need to tell me what I'm dealing with here, Blake. What happened to you? You can't hide things from me if you expect me to give this a shot."

I don't know what to say. All along, I had hoped to avoid burdening her with this, with the ticking time bomb that I am. How can I ask her to mate with me, and soon, knowing full well that I might not get better? Jeffrey said he doesn't know if my symptoms will go away completely or if they'll linger. Can I really ask her to commit to me, knowing I could snap and lose control at any moment?

Briefly, I debate giving her some phony story about a human physical illness, but she's too clever for that. And I don't *want* to lie to her.

"I'm sick, Zoe. It's called *Moon Madness*," I tell her reluctantly. "It happens to wolves when we get older and haven't mated. I don't know if I'm going to get better."

"But being with me helps?" she asks quietly. I can practically see the cogs in her brain spinning a mile a minute. I grit my teeth and take a deep breath, not wanting to put this on her.

"Being with you is *everything*," I say firmly. "And yes, it should stop me from getting worse, but I would never ask you to stay here just to help me."

Zoe nods along as I speak, and a thought occurs to me.

"You already knew that though, didn't you?"

"I did." She smiles up at me coyly and presses closer. "I had my suspicions, so I spoke to Hayley as soon as I left here. She filled me in on what it could be. But thank you for telling me. How are you feeling now?"

It was a test.

"Much better," I murmur as she wraps her arms around my waist and presses her cheek to my chest.

"I was so worried, Blake. I can't believe how much better you look now compared to earlier." She snuggles closer and breathes out a relieved sigh, her warm body fitting against me perfectly.

"I know. I'm sorry you had to see any of that."

I hug her tighter to me and savour her scent. She's still here - after discovering the truth. She knows everything, and she hasn't run away. For the moment, anyway. I run a hand down her back, over the dip of her lower back to the curve of her firm ass, gripping her hip and pulling her pelvis against mine.

"You scrub up well," she says, grinning at me. "It's a shame we can't have the evening to ourselves."

"And what would you do if you had me all to yourself?"

I slip on my jacket and take her hand in mine, leaving the hospital room together. If she hadn't insisted on seeing me before I left, I would have been home ages ago. I am touched that she wanted to be here to make sure I really am well enough to go. It feels like something a mate would do.

"I'd bring you straight up to your apartment and lock the door to keep everyone away. You still haven't given me the tour, by the way."

"And then?" I persist, heart racing as my mind gets carried away about having her alone in my space. The packhouse is beautiful, but it's shared. The idea of her being in my room, where no one else goes, is incredibly appealing. I want her scent to linger, so that even when she goes home - and I know that she will go home - it'll feel like she's still there with me.

"And then..." She slides gracefully into the passenger seat of the waiting car, allowing me to hold her hand and help her in. As I climb in beside her, she pretends to still be considering her options. "Then I would tuck you straight into bed and kiss you goodnight. You shouldn't be on your feet, let alone on your way to a work dinner."

I throw my head back and burst into laughter. It shouldn't surprise me; she is in a caring profession after all.

"I can assure you that I'm fully healed," I promise with a wink, and she rolls her eyes.

Even though it's a very short distance, she reaches out and rests her hand on my knee. She twists her body in the seat to face me, her long legs angled in my direction as I drive. She appears relaxed, and no longer uneasy in my presence.

"And if you think I could sleep after you tucking me in, you must not know how stunning you look in that dress," I add.

Zoe smiles shyly at me, before turning serious again. I guess our flirty banter is over for now.

"So, what am I walking into here?"

"The council suspects my illness - the Moon madness - is getting worse, hence the hastily arranged visit. Now that they think I'm choosing a mate, you, most will be satisfied with that. But I have an influential and powerful job. Someone will always have their eye on it. If they can create doubt, and convince the council that my health has declined further than they thought, they could push me out of office."

"So, it's all political posturing, really. There's no battle to the death or anything?"

"There used to be, but that's just a good way to kill off your strongest leaders. We try diplomacy first these days."

It does still occasionally come to a fight, but I don't mention that right now. This isn't the time or place to go into it.

"What will they think of me? I'm not a wolf."

"No, but you really are something." I lean over and give her a short but tender kiss before steeling myself and putting on my game face to endure what could be the most torturous evening of my life. A room full of stuffy old shifters grilling my mate when we've only just met will not go down well with my overprotective wolf.

Especially when we could be having much more fun elsewhere.

For the first time in my life, I don't care about the job, about my ambition, or about proving myself. I only care about Zoe.

"And to be honest, I don't really care what they think now that you're here."

And it really is the truth.

CHAPTER 21

ZOE

Blake looks much healthier than he did when I left him a couple of hours ago, but he's still not radiating the confidence I've grown accustomed to from him. Despite his attempt to hide it, he's still not well enough to be leaving the clinic.

As he parks the car, he rubs the bridge of his nose between his thumb and index finger, blinking hard several times.

"Are you alright?" I reach over to stroke the back of his neck. He should be resting. Blake tips his head back further into my touch and closes his eyes. He doesn't need to say anything. I know he's not.

"Just tired," he offers a tight smile, but it's forced for my benefit.

"Let's get this over with and go to bed," I suggest, and he perks up at that, raising an eyebrow and making me blush.

Shoving the door open, he climbs out into the fading evening and strides to my side to open it for me. I could get used to this.

Once again, I find myself entranced by his striking good looks. His dark hair is longer on top, pushed back off his face. His pale grey eyes stand out against his olive skin. He's broad, but his height gives him balanced proportions that the impeccably tailored suit enhances. Whenever I look at him, I want to reach out and make sure he's real.

He extends a hand to help me out and rests his palm gently on my hip as we stroll towards the house.

"You look good enough to eat," he murmurs against my neck, leaning in close, his soft lips brushing against my skin. When he inhales deeply and sighs, my flesh breaks out in goosebumps where his warm breath caresses me.

His scent is overwhelming when we're this close. Temptation pulls at me and I pause, reaching up to smooth the lapels on his navy jacket when he turns to see why I've stopped. Resting my hand on his chest, I feel his muscles move underneath, and the vibrations of low rumble behind his ribs. My body flushes with even more heat.

"Right back at you," I murmur, my gaze never leaving his as I stretch up on my tippy toes and press a kiss to his lips. His eyes darken and his expression is intense. Blake's hand tightens on my waist before drifting lower, squeezing my ass firmly and hauling me tightly against him.

Today wasn't the day either of us had hoped for. I came here in the hopes of getting to know him better and having some fun, yet I've only learnt about the difficult things going on his life. It shocked me how worried I was about him when I'm normally level-headed. If Max would have let me, I would have been back at the clinic fifteen minutes later. Even if he was only sleeping, I wanted to be by Blake's side.

This mate bond is insane. As soon as we're close, as soon as we touch, everything else drifts away. It's just us and this amazing connection.

"Fuck, Zoe… let's just go. Come on." As if he read my mind, he tugs my hand as he attempts to pull me away from the entrance, back towards the car, and I giggle.

I take hold of his wrist with both hands and pull, planting my feet firmly on the ground to stop him from dragging me away with ease.

"Blake!" I chastise, laughing loudly at his sudden playfulness. "We can't do that. Stop messing."

"I'm serious," he says, a mischievous expression stamped on his handsome face. Before I know what's going on, he tosses me over his shoulder and clamps his enormous hand firmly over my backside to keep me balanced. I kick and shriek with laughter as he hurries back to the car with his long strides.

"Leaving so soon, Alpha Steel?" A woman's voice carries to us from the doorway, and Blake's shoulders droop in resignation as he lets out a deep sigh, his back still turned to the front door. Lifting my head from my slightly compromising position dangling near Blake's ass, I spot a tiny, grey-haired woman standing beside Jenna. Jenna looks unimpressed at our display, but the beautiful woman seems amused as Blake slowly rights me and sets me down on my feet.

"No, Sharon," he replies. "We'll be right with you."

Sharon smiles and nods, violet eyes shining, then turns to go inside, reluctantly followed by Jenna. Blake adjusts the straps of my dress and smooths a hand over my dishevelled hair before giving me a tender kiss on the nose.

"To be continued."

The promise hangs heavy between us as we turn back toward the house. He takes a shallower breath while I'm grateful for the slight chill in the air. I need to calm down, and we need to change the subject before we race up the stairs to his room and blow off this stuffy dinner. When we walk through the door and into the elegant grand foyer, we're greeted by an exquisite flower arrangement in the centre of a circular table and more on the sideboards. Jenna clearly does a great job of managing the house.

"Sharon doesn't seem so scary," I comment, clasping his hand as we move towards an open door on our right where laughter and relaxed conversation can be heard.

"Appearances can be deceiving. Sharon's a hybrid; part wolf, part witch. Powerful. She seems to know and sense things that can be unnerving sometimes."

Duly noted and understandable if he's trying to keep a huge secret.

First wolves, now witches. Nothing should surprise me at this point, but I'm still wary about being in the presence of all these powerful beings. What kind of magic can she do? Can she read my mind?

As we walk into the dining room, where the council members are already seated, all eyes quickly shift to us, and a hushed silence falls over the room. Our linked hands, as well as Blake's arm grazing mine, draw immediate attention. I offer a polite smile to the room as I take my seat and Blake settles next to me. His hand takes mine, but when I pull away shyly and rest it on the table, he stubbornly places his on top of mine, slipping his fingers through mine and leaves them out in the open.

Sharon sits on my other side, her expression fixed on the two of us. Blake gives my hand a gentle squeeze, and it occurs to me that perhaps the need to stay physically connected is more for his comfort than mine.

"Zoe, it's a pleasure to meet you. I'm Sharon." Sharon gestures to her own place card and I find it strange that anyone present in the room would need them. Her silver grey hair seems at odds with her relatively smooth, unlined face.

"Lovely to meet you, too."

Sharon eyes our joined hands resting on the table and smiles before tapping her own fingers together, deep in thought while continuing with small talk.

"Alphas are a stubborn bunch," she murmurs, with a twinkle in her eye. "Looks like you'll be eating one-handed, dear."

Laughing at her own joke, she turns back to Max, who is sitting across from her. Jenna is directly opposite me and when I glance over, she glares at our hands with an expression of pure venom.

Blake stands and releases my hand, but his fingers linger lightly on my shoulder. I can feel his fingers trembling and a seed of worry plants itself in my stomach.

"I apologise for being late. I was unavoidably detained, but I'm yours for the rest of the evening," he says, inclining his head towards his guests in sincerity.

"It didn't look unavoidable," Sharon mutters and a flush blooms on my cheeks as everyone's gaze moves from Blake to me and then back again. Max shushes her, and she laughs, giving him a wink. They seem close. If she's as scary as Blake seems to think, I wouldn't have thought Max would play nice.

"Let me introduce my Zoe to you all. I'm sure you'll make her feel very welcome on her first visit to the packhouse and will refrain from turning this dinner into twenty questions. Let's just enjoy a delightful meal and good company. So, without further ado, let's eat!"

He sits back down heavily, and I notice his eyes appear somewhat glassy. The relief is clear on his face to have the introductions over with. I sip my wine, joining Sharon and Max in conversation as the first course is served. Blake hasn't touched his wine yet and pales at the sight of food.

Under the table, I rest a hand on his thigh but find it's bouncing away with pent up nervous energy. He's antsy and agitated, even though someone across the table couldn't tell. Charming conversation comes easily to Blake. He includes me where he can, and laughter flows around us, but I can see the signs. His eye movements quickening, breaths shallow and fast.

While there's a lull in the conversation, he excuses himself from the room. Sharon starts telling me an old story about life before Blake was the alpha of this pack. I focus my attention on her tale, keen to hear about teenage Blake, and doing what I can to help him out by making a good impression. But by the time I look up again, he's gone. Hopefully, some fresh air will do him good.

Sharon abruptly stops talking and reaches over to grab my wrists, her grip tight and unyielding. Pressing her thumbs down over my veins, her expression turns to one of concentration and she gets a distant look in her eyes. Max shifts uneasily in his seat and reaches out to intervene, but I give him a tiny shake of the head. Her hands are icy cold, and her painted dark purple nails dig into my skin, but she's not hurting me.

Without warning, she jerks away and emerges from whatever haze she was in. She narrows her eyes at me and purses her lips. Even though she's older, you can tell she was stunningly beautiful in her youth. There is something about her that's captivating when she speaks.

"I switched the place settings so we could have a chat. It was you I really came here to see. Not Blake. I know he's not well, but you are the key to that, Zoe"

Am I? The doctor said this might not be reversible, yet Sharon acts as if Blake's condition is inconsequential. His prolonged absence from the table further heightens my fear.

"It's remarkable, really. That both you and your twin sister are to be mated to alphas, considering there is no record of humans and alphas ever being paired before."

Jenna snorts from across the table, but quickly returns to her conversation with the man beside her when we look her way.

"And Leah," I add quietly. Her back straightens and twists fully in her seat to face me.

"Sorry, what did you say?" Sharon tilts her head in confusion, but there is nothing but intelligence shining in her deep violet eyes.

"My younger sister, Leah, is mated to Rex Jones."

There's no point in hiding it if, as Blake suggests, she knows everything already.

"Fascinating." Her eyes light up at this new nugget of information. "There must be something in your family tree. Something to explain it… I must do some digging."

Before I can interrupt and ask whether she really means she plans to research my family history, she glances meaningfully in Jenna's direction.

"Watch your back," Sharon warns. "You have a challenger."

"I'm well aware," I reply calmly. I'm reluctant to say any more.

This is a room full of shifters with excellent hearing. I know better than to be indiscreet. I'm aware they might be laughing and joking now, but Blake's tension was genuine earlier on.

"And I don't just mean metaphorically." She releases my hands and I see Max instantly relax. "Now, go find your man and make sure he's okay."

I don't need to be told twice. I'm out of my seat and half jogging towards the bathroom down the corridor when I hear the crash.

CHAPTER 22

ZOE

There's silence as I slowly approach the bathroom door, and I rest my fingers on the handle. This is where the noise came from, but none of the pack have come to investigate.

"Blake?" I whisper and push the door open gently. There's something behind it, so I use my weight to force it open far enough for me to slip in. My first thought is that Blake has fainted and knocked something over. Shards of porcelain and flowers from the shattered remnants of a vase on the floor suggest that I'm on the right track. Stepping over the mess, I close the door behind me for some privacy.

But as I turn, my mistake becomes evident. It's not Blake. Or rather, it is Blake, but not in his usual form.

"Blake, are you alright?" I'm now talking to this massive animal, who moments ago was my date for the evening. His immaculate suit lies tattered on the floor.

Glowing silvery eyes assess me as I reverse slowly, edging backward until I'm pressed against the sink. He's not exhibiting any aggression, but he's not relaxed either. I'm familiar with large animals, used to judging their behaviour, yet I can't help being intimidated by his sheer size and dominant presence. If I thought he was impressive when he was knocked out, seeing his wolf alert and on his feet is a different experience altogether. Wisely, I opt to put some distance between us.

"Did you get yourself trapped in here?" I ask gently, noting the scratches on the back of the wooden door and the bunched-up rug on the floor. Judging by the red smears everywhere, Blake sliced the pad of at least one paw open and is bleeding. I carefully squat down and lean forward to push the broken pieces off to one side, preventing further injury to his paws.

"Why did you shift, handsome? Is your body telling you that you need to heal like last time?"

Our gazes lock for a moment before he turns away and whines. He's not ready to accept that one just yet. Blake had mentioned before that's why he shifted in my clinic. The tranquiliser I shot him with made his human side relinquish control, and his wolf forced the change so he could heal faster.

Maybe, being so tired today, his wolf had taken control once more to force him to recover fully. If he didn't have a room full of people to entertain, I'd be on his wolf's side.

He takes a tentative step toward me and pauses, as if gauging my reaction. I nod and hold out a hand for him to sniff — but rather than acknowledge it, he pushes his muzzle up under the skirt of my dress and buries his nose between my thighs.

"*Jesus, Blake.* Stop it!" I push his head back with both hands, my fingers sinking into his thick fur, but he stubbornly refuses to move away. Instead, he keeps his cold nose pressed firmly against my thin panties and sniffs repeatedly before licking them. I blush. He doesn't seem very sick after all.

I am just beginning to process how messed up this situation is — and wondering how I'm going to get him out of here before someone sees him — when Blake jumps back sharply. He spins to face the small open window, ears pricked and alert. The fur on the back of his neck rises and a low menacing growl rumbles from within him.

Fuck. If the council hadn't heard the smashing vase, they're going to hear this. I need to calm him down, and quickly.

His attention suddenly shifts back to me, and he snarls, prowling forward to herd me into the far corner of the room. His body language exudes power and dominance. He's not to be trifled with.

"Blake?" I ask nervously, getting agitated now as his growls continue and his posture remains threatening. He inclines his head towards the door and continues to drive me further from it until I'm pinned against the wall.

"You want me to stay here? But open the door?"

I'm like Doctor bloody Dolittle here, attempting to decode what the barks and growls of my wolf-slash-boyfriend mean. This is insane. I reach out and open the door, and immediately he uses his muzzle to open it wider. At lightning speed, he vanishes, his grey tail disappears through the gap before I even process what's going on. I hear his nails on the hardwood floors as he runs through the packhouse and take a deep breath, trying to get my bearings.

What the hell was that?

"Zoe!" Max races around the corner and hurtles into the doorway. He pales when he sees the blood on my hands and debris strewn across the floor.

"No, no. It's not mine, it's Blake's. He cut his paw," I hasten to explain and ease his concern. "Where the hell did he go, Max? *And where were you?* You must have heard that."

"He ordered us all to stay away," Max grits out, apparently not impressed at his alpha's behaviour. "He's saying something about an intruder now. Everyone's been told to go indoors while the security team investigates."

Max extends a hand to help me across the slippery floor and once I'm clear, he closes and locks the door from the outside. He holds out the key for me to take, but I ignore him, still attempting to wrap my head around whatever is going on. Max radiates tension and I can tell he is keen to follow Blake.

"There's someone here? Who? Are they dangerous?"

Panic claws at my chest as I imagine Blake, already injured, out fighting another wolf.

"This is a master key. Go to Blake's room and lock yourself in." He presses a silver key into my palm and closes my fingers around it. "I'll find him and drag him back, but I can't bring him to the clinic. He's going to need you to stay with him."

"Because nobody will question us being holed up in a room together for twenty-four hours, but they will question a trip to the clinic," I surmise, and he grimaces.

"Something like that."

"But Max, I thought Blake is like the head wolf. Who would break in here?" I ask. "And with the council here? Blake told me some of them are powerful."

"You're right. Nobody would, Zoe. That's the point," Max says sadly, eyes downcast, as if he's ashamed and unable to look at me as he breaks the bad news.

Nobody would. Which means it's probably all in Blake's head. The madness is worse than Max thought.

"I'll help find him…" I say, but Max whirls on me, expression fierce.

"I need to track him before everyone else sees what a mess he is. I'm sorry to say it, but you'll slow me down."

Max's dark eyes plead with me to cooperate and so I back down. Dropping my hand away with the key firmly clasped in my grip, I turn toward the stairs, taking the first couple of steps as Max sprints to the front door. People cram inside, whispering anxiously, dismay clear in their murmurings at the prospect of an unknown intruder on the grounds.

Max pushes through the crowd before lifting his nose once and swiveling his head to the right. He has a scent to track.

I pause, one foot resting on the next step, uncertain of what to do. If I'm supposed to be his mate, would I really go to my room and barricade myself inside while he went out to face the threat head on? Hell no.

Fuck this.

If there truly is no intruder, I can't sit back and let Blake run in circles aimlessly until God only knows what happens to him. He'll come to me; I know he will.

Spinning, I jump from the bottom step and push my way back to the main entrance. Curious gazes follow me as strangers seem to wonder why their alpha's scent is all over me. I stay close to the wall, finding some space to slip through.

As I step outside and get a lungful of the fresh night air, a strong hand grips my arm and stops me in my tracks.

"Jenna," I murmur, trying to remain calm and composed.. "Let go of me."

She aims a sneer at me, digging her nails in deeper just because she can. The whole good girl act falls away whenever Blake isn't around to witness it. Her pale hair and sharp features are severe, making her look older than her years.

"Where do you think you're going? A human is no use against an intruder this close to the packhouse. Blake ordered the pack inside."

"Good thing that I'm not pack then," I shoot back, yanking my arm out of her grasp and continuing down the steps in the direction I saw Max disappearing.

Who does she think she is?

"Actually, go on and get yourself killed. Maybe then Blake will realise what a poor substitute for Hayley you are."

Her pale eyes gleam in sick amusement as she utters her parting barb. She's clearly enjoying the idea of me meeting my demise, but I won't dignify her with a response. I merely kick off my heels and dash across the lawn to the dark forest. This far from the packhouse, there's barely any light, only shadows and darkness. I have no sense of where I am or what the local geography is.

Still, I'm confident that I'll find him first. Or he'll find me. Taking a deep breath and mustering my courage, I remind myself that Max told me there is no intruder. Nevertheless, I pause about twenty meters in, where the scattered light no longer filters through the leaves and I can barely see my hand in front of my face.

Hugging my arms around my chest, I whisper his name. Praying that, despite the fact that he could be anywhere by now, he'll stop running and come back to me.

CHAPTER 23

BLAKE

Lights and colours swirl in front of my eyes as I try to get my bearings. I've lived in this territory my entire life. I know this place like the back of my hand, yet I'm struggling to get a grasp on exactly where I am. Disorientated, I stumble over a log and fall on my snout in the cold, damp leaves. Climbing back on all fours, I growl in frustration at being robbed of my physical prowess. I've taken it for granted.

Spinning around anxiously, searching for a clue to my whereabouts, I spot the old tree. The same one that had toppled over twenty years ago in the storm everyone thought had killed it. No longer lost at least, I take some comfort from the thought that things might not always be as bad as they seem. And right now, they look pretty fucking bleak. I know I saw someone outside the window.

Then why the fuck can I not find him now?

Could the madness have me so firmly in its grip that I'm hallucinating?

The swirling lights behind my eyes would suggest it's entirely possible. Mind-linking my security team, they confirm there's no sign of an intruder, no trail near the bathroom window, or anywhere else for that matter. I stand them down and tell them to return home, arranging a morning debrief before my slow, humiliating return to the packhouse.

Zoe. What on Earth will she think of all this? I wanted to get to know her and impress her, to show her that fate got it right and that we are compatible.

Instead, all I've done is show her exactly what kind of mess she'd be shackling herself to. The doctor's words ring loud and clear in my mind. *The symptoms might not reverse*. I can't imagine she's sitting in the packhouse, under lockdown, eager to commit herself to a lifetime of this. If fate is so clever, why didn't it deliver me to her door months ago?

And the council. I groan. That's a whole other problem for another day, but the wolves will pounce after this performance.

As the rushing of blood in my ears fades, I hear soft footsteps approach. I judge the size of the person creeping through the forest, unstealthily snapping twigs and cursing as they move deeper through the trees. I should have known Max wouldn't be able to keep her inside. After informing him he's failed miserably at the one thing I asked of him, I sit and watch her make her way closer to me, oblivious to my presence.

Zoe has her red dress hitched up, showing plenty of her toned, tanned legs. No shoes to protect her feet, I notice, annoyed that she's alone and taking such poor care of herself. She winces as she steps on something sharp and curses and it hits me.

She's only out here because of me. My fragile human mate, wandering alone in the dark to take care of her big bad alpha, who's become a volatile liability that might get her hurt.

Her blonde waves are dishevelled and her narrowed eyes focus intently on the ground in front of her, searching for roots and rocks in the near pitch-black darkness. She's breathtakingly stubborn, and I can't take it any longer. I make plenty of noise, emerging into a clearing in front of her so as not to startle her.

"Blake, oh thank god," she whispers when she sees me, and sinks to her knees in the dirt. She reaches for me, but I stay still, the sight of her tears tugging at my heart.

I did this. I made her cry.

My wolf whimpers and is just about to give up control and allow me to shift back when the faint sound of an exhaled breath from the dense vegetation behind Zoe catches my attention. I can't scent anyone, but I know what I heard. My nose seems to be malfunctioning. My mate is vulnerable with her back turned, and I won't take any chances where her safety is concerned.

A feral snarl rips from my throat, and Zoe lurches back in shock, eyes wide in fear. I want to reassure her she has nothing to fear from me, but there's no time. A shadowy silhouette emerges from the darkness of the trees, and a chill shudders through me.

It can't be.

He haunts my dreams so regularly that I know his face as well as I do my own. His very presence is threatening, and like when we were kids, I know when his intentions are wicked.

And what better way to hurt me than through Zoe?

I launch myself over Zoe's shoulder, teeth bared and snarling, toward the person poised to attack her. Zoe tries to grab me as I pass, but my momentum carries me through her grasp as I sink my teeth into the raised arm behind her. In my current state, I won't be much competition for someone in peak physical condition, but just like before, I'll fight till my dying breath to keep Zoe from harm.

"NO!" Zoe yells as the coppery tang of blood fills my mouth. Tumbling down with the attacker, I pin him beneath me. When he makes no effort to resist or fight back, my brain kicks into gear and I blink through the blurriness in my vision. Shrinking back, I realise who I've attacked as I clamber off an injured and bleeding Max. Instead of being angry, he looks completely stunned.

We cautiously stare at each other in silence as Zoe pulls up the sleeve of Max's shirt and examines the wound.

"Oh no. Jesus, Blake. What were you thinking? Max, are you okay?"

What have I done? I didn't recognise my own beta. I could have ripped his throat out.

"I'm fine, Zoe. Give me half an hour and it'll be good as new. It's just a little nip, really. I shouldn't have snuck up on you like that."

It's a nasty bite, and he's playing it down for my sake. Max will heal quickly. Physically, anyway. This is a crossed line, though, and we both know it.

My addled brain went on the attack, convinced he was someone else, a threat, and I hurt him. If it were anyone else, and they didn't have the sense not to fight back, one of us could have ended up dead.

Have I gone past the point of no return?

I shift back and Max tosses me the pair of shorts he thoughtfully stashed in his back pocket. Nodding, I pull them on, but I can't bring myself to look either of them in the eye. Max hauls himself to his feet and holds out a hand, pulling me to my feet when I take it. With a nod to me and a gentle squeeze of Zoe's shoulder, he turns and quietly leads the way back. He doesn't mind-link me, nothing. I'm sure he's having the same thoughts as me. Where do we go from here?

"Zoe, I..." I trail off when I catch the scent of her blood. "Oh goddess, you're bleeding. Did I hurt you too? I'm sorry. I'm so sorry." As I look at her and search for injuries, I'm frantic. At this moment, I don't trust myself to remember exactly what's happened tonight. And it's a scary place to be.

"No, no. It's just a scratch. I tripped in the woods. The blood is mostly yours from the bathroom," she says, turning her hands up to show me the smears on her palms.

We walk in silence for a few more steps before Zoe links her arm through mine, pretending to need help navigating through the trees. I know she senses my confusion and guilt over what I put her through today and what I've done to my best friend. Despite it all, she's offering me comfort.

"Who did you think it was?" Her voice is soft yet powerful. I halt and turn to face her, completely caught off-guard by her question.

"Pardon?"

"You heard me. In the bathroom, you looked out the window and freaked out. And you were fine earlier until you glanced over my shoulder. It was as if you saw someone. Who?"

Zoe gazes up at me with such concern in her eyes, her body language radiating caring and compassion.

"Goddess, I don't deserve you." I press my forehead to hers and close my eyes, afraid to touch her and pull her close. I don't know if I'm allowed to anymore.

"Who, Blake?" Her tone is serious now. I've put her through the wringer today. She won't take anything less than complete honesty, and I don't blame her.

"My cousin, Tyson. Or my half-brother, really, I suspect," I reply wryly. "Rogues murdered my uncle Ron and Tyson in the same attack that killed my mother. My father commanded me to stay in the safe room while they went out to fight."

"Oh, Blake, I'm so sorry." Zoe leans in closer, yet I remain rigid. It's not a topic I speak about often.

"I tried to convince Tyson to come inside with me, but he was older and determined to help protect the pack. He was disgusted that I was locking myself away with the women and children, but I couldn't disobey my father's direct order. And then he never came back."

Zoe's pensive as we continue to walk.

"Why would you think he was here? Or that he'd hurt me?"

"Other than because I'm losing my marbles?"

Zoe scowls at me, and I drop my self-pitying attitude. "Because we found out the year before that my father was having an affair with my aunt, Tyson's mother, for years. And everyone always told us we looked so alike that we could be brothers. If it was true, Tyson, as the oldest son, was the rightful heir to the pack. But Dad refused to entertain any talk of it. Tyson was upset at Dad and resented me, understandably. Felt like he was being cheated and ignored."

"But he died that day…"

"I think seeing Sharon put it into my mind. Right after the attack, when the council came to help, Sharon told me she was sorry I lost my mother and Ron. When I reminded her about Tyson, she just stared at me and said I'd see him again someday. As a teenager, I thought that meant in the next life, but as I've gotten older, it's played on my mind. She sees things. And I've often wondered if she knows something I don't."

"What does she say?"

"She stubbornly refuses to tell me anything. Says she can't remember the reason behind every little comment that she makes." I grit my teeth, my anger rising. She remembers well, she just doesn't want to tell me. Which makes me even more convinced that my suspicions are right. I never saw his body. I took my father's word for it.

What if he was wrong?

Zoe laces her fingers through mine and sighs, leaning in closer to me and rests her head against my shoulder as we walk. I cannot fathom why she's still here, listening to my sob story, as we walk barefoot and bloodied across the green to the packhouse.

"This was supposed to be a relaxing break for you after the robbery," I state, scarcely believing how badly it's gone. Zoe laughs, bringing a hand up to her face to hide her reaction. The whole thing really is absurd.

"How about we go to bed, and then tomorrow, I get to choose what we do? I don't mean to be rude, but this was the worst date ever," she teases as she yawns. I smile and shake my head, wrapping an arm around her as we enter the suspiciously empty packhouse foyer and climb the stairs, side by side. Even though Max must be annoyed, he's still looking out for me. Or maybe Zoe.

"Zoe, we need to talk about tonight. I'm sorry about all this." I pause at the door to her room and lean against the wall, looking down at her, feeling grim.

"I know, but tomorrow. I'm beat. And you must be too. Just let me grab my bag," she opens the door and waltzes inside, bending to grab the overnight bag waiting inside the door.

"Zoe, if you'd prefer…" I sigh, scrubbing a hand down my stubbled jaw, unable to believe that I'm about to utter these words to my mate. "If you'd feel safer here on your own, I won't be offended. I'm shocked you're still here."

"Blake, I'm not afraid of you," she says, jaw set stubbornly. "And I feel safer being close to you."

Bending down, I press a chaste kiss to her lips, expressing my gratitude, because I know she knows I need her. She catches me by surprise though when she pulls me closer and deepens the kiss.

"Zoe…" I groan as she backs us toward the door to my suite. "This isn't a good idea." Again, I can't believe these words are coming from my mouth, but here we are. The door swings open and she shoves me inside. Her mouth crashes against mine and her hands roam across my naked skin, leaving electric tingles in their wake.

My body makes a liar out of me as my cock reacts immediately to her, loving the way she takes charge and the reassurance that she still wants me. My shorts do little to hide the extent of my need for her, but I'm clinging to my self-control like a lifeline, because I cannot do anything else to ruin this.

When she wakes up and recalls the events of the day and night, will she freak out and run a mile? Will doing this make everything worse?

"Say that again," she dares, slipping the straps of her delicate red dress from her shoulders and letting it pool around her feet right there in the living room.

Fuck me. There's no way I'm going to win this fight.

Her sheer lace panties are soaked through and the scent of her arousal hits me like a freight train. My knees almost buckle as raw, primal need courses through me. I drop to my knees in front of her and press a kiss to her pussy through the material and she jerks as my hot breath reaches her skin.

Gently, I hook my fingers on each side and drag them down her legs. Noticing the dirt on her knees reminds me of exactly what went on this evening.

"Blake, please," she pleads, hands buried in my hair, and drops her head back to face the ceiling. I can feel her frustration.

"We're going to get cleaned up first, angel, and if you still want this, we're going to have a little chat about why you weren't waiting in this room for me as I asked," I warn.

Her thighs squeeze together, and she shudders. A small chuckle escapes me. This is going to be fun.

CHAPTER 24

ZOE

Blake stands, running his hands up my bare thighs before gripping my hips and turning me toward the open bedroom door and the bathroom just inside.

I take in his suite, and it's not decorated how I imagined it would be. I pictured dark, rich tones and masculine, oversized furniture, but it's not like that at all. It's bright and airy, with an enormous wall of glass that gives a view of the stars shining brightly, the almost full moon flooding the open plan space with plenty of light to see by.

Blake steps past me and leans into the luxurious shower, turning it on. The hot skin of his chest tickles mine as he leans in close. He rests a hand on my waist as he tests the temperature, and I tip my head back to rest on his shoulder, sighing contentedly. After today, I crave being near him.

He keeps his hand on me as he straightens and drops the shorts Max gave him in the woods. My head is spinning with it all, not just tonight and yesterday, but over the last three days. Just when I think I have my head wrapped around one thing, there's another bombshell to process. My poor brain is struggling to absorb it all, but my body is totally on board. This handsome, charming man wants me for his own?

Oh, hell yes.

When he was trying to be chivalrous, I'd never wanted anyone more. Except for maybe right now, because I know he's completely naked behind me and all I want to do is run my tongue over every inch of him. I go to turn around and face him, but his grip on me tightens as he forces me to stay facing away.

"Get in, angel," he growls, his lips close to my ear and the tip of his cock brushing against my lower back as he moves. A low moan escapes my lips at the feel of it and my empty pussy clenches, longing to be filled by him.

"In," he repeats, and my body automatically obeys, stepping into the double shower and waiting. My nerves are on fire with the anticipation of what's to come.

The click of the door closing and his presence behind me as he steps in is nearly too much. My nerves are alive with anticipation of what's to come. I hear the cap of a bottle open, and liquid being squeezed out into his hands. He rubs them together and I squirm, itching to feel them on my skin. This is torture.

"You were supposed to be safely locked in this room until I got back. Not wandering around the woods on your own in the dark." His voice is low and authoritative, and it sends a shiver down my spine. Soapy hands land on my shoulders, his talented fingers and thumbs massaging my tense muscles expertly. I sigh in relief at finally having his hands on my body.

"Why were you out there, Zoe?" he asks, stepping in close and moving so the spray from the shower reaches my hair. He tips my head back and runs his fingers through it as the warm water hits my scalp and flows down my back.

I groan as his thick, hard length pokes against my ass and I arch my back, pressing myself harder against him, granting him better access and seeking more. My nipples harden as I imagine him sinking into me. I moan, reaching around to grab his hips and press him tight to me. He's too quick though, and he catches my hands, holding them out to the sides, away from him.

My fingers flex in protest as I try to pull my hands free, an urgent whine escaping my lips as he thwarts my efforts. My head is spinning with my need to touch him.

"Answer me, Zoe," he growls. The vibration travels from his chest into my body and wetness floods my already soaked pussy. I am ready for him, if he would just put me out my misery.

"I wanted to make sure you were okay," I mumble absentmindedly, again trying to yank my hands back, but he holds me tight, his warm skin and erect cock against my back making my mind fuzzy.

"*You wanted to make sure I was okay?*" he asks in disbelief, his breath against my ear makes me shiver. I nod, unable to speak while my head swims with desire for the man who seems intent on torturing me.

"Hmm." Gently, he relaxes his grip on my wrists and places them against the wall in front of me. He adds more soap to a sponge and takes his time, washing across my shoulders, down my back and sides. He runs the sponge down my legs and back up to the crease at the top of my thighs. Next, he reaches around and cleans my chest and stomach.

"You look so pretty, all wet and soapy, that sexy ass ready for me to do with it as I please." His voice is low and thick with desire.

Oh, God. I'm not sure about that. I rock forward on the balls of my feet as the threat in his words filters into my brain. Nervousness flows through me, making me scared and excited at the same time. But his hand caresses my ass gently, soothing my nerves as he soaps me up, rubbing and massaging my ass where it meets the top of my thighs. He steps back and I immediately miss the contact, miss his presence. I'm dwelling on that thought when the first slap hits my ass and stuns my brain into silence.

"Blake!" I yelp, the surprise causing me to cry out. I lift my hand off the wall, but he covers it with his massive one and presses it back against the cool tile.

"Do you think I would ask you to stay here just to be bossy?" he asks. When I hesitate to answer, a second slap rocks me forward and I cry out once more. My skin under his hand is hot and burning, but Blake's tender strokes and the flowing water ease the sting.

"Angel?"

I pause again, my brain fighting to understand why I'm letting him spank me, and why my quivering pussy loves this so much. A third slap sends vibrations through my core, and if it's possible, I get even wetter. I moan loudly, my knees sagging, and drop my chin to my chest.

"No," I gasp. "I just…"

The words have barely passed my lips when his palm lands against my sensitive skin once more and I hiss.

"I might not be your alpha, but everything I do is to keep the people I care about safe. If I think there's a threat, I will do whatever it takes to keep you safe," he whispers, and my chest tightens.

I can feel his worry for me, can read his emotions like they're my own.

"But I was safe…"

Slap! He switches sides and this time my spanking is harder. I grit my teeth against the pain, but then it gives way to delicious warmth and pleasure. My eyes roll back into my head and I let the amazing sensations wash over me. I have no idea what's going on with me, and why I'm enjoying this so much, but I'm going with it. I'm perfectly content to let this delicious man have his wicked way with me. He seems to know what I like better than I do.

"You weren't safe! What if that hadn't been Max?"

His tone is sharp, but I recogonise it comes from fear. Protectiveness and possessiveness surround me like a warm blanket, and I feel his vulnerability. I'm his weakness.

"I don't know," I mumble. Right now, I don't know and I don't care. I just want more of whatever this is.

He soothes my tender ass with circles of his large soapy hands and I sigh. He brings down one more slap on my tender behind and I cry out, his hand coming around my waist to support me as I almost come from the dizzying desperation to be taken by him. My insides clench and pulse, begging to be filled.

"When it comes to your safety, angel, I need to know you trust me." He says it like it's an order, but I can hear the plea in his voice. Not only for me to do as he says in these matters, but to trust him and his judgement. To not believe that he's so completely lost to the madness that he's imagined what he saw.

"I trust you, Blake," I whisper, pushing myself away from the wall with my hands and reaching behind me to wrap them around his neck. He presses his face into my skin, kissing and nibbling my shoulder, squeezing my ass gently one more time before slowly trailing his hands around to my chest, cupping my breasts, and tweaking my nipples.

He rolls his hips forward and his cock slides between my slippery, wet ass cheeks. One, twice, three times. He moans loudly and presses his forehead between my shoulder blades, kissing my spine softly and trailing his hands back down my chest and along my waist, teasing and taunting me with his delicate touches.

"Thank you."

He spins me around, eyes burning into mine with a hunger I've never seen before, and crowds me back against the tiles. Cupping my face in his hands, thumbs caressing my cheeks tenderly, he leans against me, his cock settling against my stomach, impossibly hard. He rocks against me and I gasp, gripping his bulging biceps and biting my lip hard.

"You took your spanking like a good girl," he murmurs and his praise makes something inside me swell with happiness. He pulls my lip from beneath my teeth and kisses it softly.

"I think you deserve a reward. What does my good girl want?"

His hand slides lower, across my soft belly, and down between my thighs. He strokes softly through my lips, dipping slightly inside before dragging my wetness across my aching clit. A jolt of pleasure rushes through me and my legs wobble. Blake uses his enormous body to hold me up as he continues to tease and taunt me with slow circles and flicks. It's everything I want, yet not enough at the same time.

"Angel?"

I whimper as he presses a finger deep inside me, thrusting in and out in lazy strokes while his other hand holds me close to him, a thick arm banded around my waist. I bury my face in his chest and moan loudly when he curls his finger, touching me in exactly the right spot.

"Blake, please," I groan against his skin, the scent of him making my senses burn up. I want to drown in him at this moment. He's like a drug I can't get enough of.

"Tell me, Zoe," he asks, sounding as desperate as I am, his erection still standing tall and pressing hard against me.

"I trust you, Blake. Take me. I need you," I beg, finally able to admit exactly how much I want him.

This isn't just about a crazy physical connection, or about the concept of mates. It's about me and him together, and what I feel for him. And that's everything.

CHAPTER 25

ZOE

Blake growls quietly in approval. I reach between us and take his thick length in my hand, eliciting a grunt from him. I ache for him to be inside my body, one with me, but he shifts out of my grasp, picking up the speed of his thrusts, adding another finger, and using his other hand to rub my clit in sync. He's not willing to give me back control just yet.

I tilt my hips to give him better access, savouring the feeling of the warm water running over my heated skin as it continues to rain down on us.

"That's it, Zoe," he whispers, making my head spin with sensual kisses, his body pressed up to mine. He brings me closer and closer to release. I gasp and squirm, trying to escape the sensations washing over me. One of which is his overpowering desire for me. To own me and make me his. It makes no sense that I can feel it, but I know in my mind it's real. It's so intense.

"Stop Blake, stop," I call out and he immediately halts, pulling his head back and looking down at me with concern from under his disheveled wet locks. I try to catch my breath, reaching out to touch his chest, and he grips my chin, tipping my head up so he can see my eyes.

"What's wrong?"

Oh God, he looks so worried that he's upset me or pushed things too far, but that's not it at all. I grip his head and pull him down to me, kissing him passionately while I struggle to calm my racing heart.

"I want you inside me. I want to come with you buried deep in me," I whisper against his ear as I trail my nails through his dark, wet hair, down his neck, and along his back. I cling to him, unable to believe how much I need this. It's overwhelming.

"Fuck, angel. Are you sure?" he grits, jaw clenched. Every muscle in his body is tense, waiting for my response.

"I've never been more sure of anything in my life." I wrap my leg around his hip and press the full length of my slick body against him. My desire to be joined with him has me climbing him like a tree. This is crazy. I've never acted like this before, but I know what I want.

He sweeps me up and kisses me passionately, like it's the last thing he's ever going to do, before breaking away to make his way out of the enclosure. I cling to him, my legs around his waist, arms looped around his neck. My gaze remains locked on him in adoration as he carries me into his bedroom. We leave a trail of water from the bathroom to his bed, but neither of us could care less as we tumble down on the giant mattress. The sheets smell like him, and I groan, cocooned in his heady scent.

We lie on our sides on the bed, facing each other, both breathing hard. Blake wraps an arm around me, hauling me tight against his body with ease. He's so strong. I pant, stretching up to press my lips against his again. I grip his ass and pull his hips hard against mine. Or as much as I can. Blake is huge. He doesn't go anywhere he doesn't want to.

He rolls us over so that he's above me, using one arm to prop himself up as he gazes down at me intently. I reach up and run my fingers through his wet hair, pushing it away from his eyes. Smiling softly, he slows things down again, planting sensual kisses from my shoulder, up my neck, and to that spot behind my ear that drives me crazy.

I grind up against him, seeking pressure and contact to ease the ache there. With his thigh between mine, he nudges my legs further apart and settles between them. He strokes one hand from my knee to my groin, and takes hold of his cock, giving it a slow, firm pump before positioning himself at my entrance. I push my hips forward, taking an inch of him inside before he pulls back and hits my pussy with a light slap. A burst of pleasure-pain courses through me and I cry out in frustration and pleasure.

"*Naughty*," he chastises softly, a small smile playing on his lips as his thumb circles my clit to soothe the sting.

Fuck… I didn't even know that was a thing.

He strokes my cheek and cups my face, studying my expression intently before nodding in approval. Then he places an elbow on either side of me as he slides himself all the way inside me, inch by rock-hard inch, in one long, steady stroke.

I tense at the feeling of fullness and being stretched so tight. He's so big. Even though I'm extremely aroused and ready for him, I gasp and take a few deep breaths while I adjust to having him inside me.

"Shh, angel," he soothes. "It's okay. We'll go slow." I nod, holding his gaze as he rolls his hips slowly instead of thrusting, and the sensation is enough to lift me off the bed.

"Oh, God, Blake. I'm going to come already. I can't…" I shake my head and he kisses me tenderly.

"Zoe. Don't hold back. I want to feel you," he murmurs into my ear as he draws back then pushes in all the way to the hilt. My toes curl and I wrap my legs around his waist, as we both moan, this position allowing him to go even deeper.

"What about… protection?" I ask, some sense finally breaking through the heady fog of lust I'm totally lost within.

He pulls back further this time and drives home a little harder.

"You're not ovulating, I can tell," he states matter-of-factly. "And I've never slept with anyone else, so I'm clean."

His admission nearly makes my brain short-circuit.

"But I can get a condom."

He starts to pull out, almost all the way, reaching for the side locker, and I stop him by digging my nails sharply into his back. The thought of him leaving my body is unacceptable. The idea that he kept this moment for me is overwhelming, making me emotional.

"Blake," I whisper, and he stops, his gaze locking with mine in question. "I trust you," I repeat, and something in his expression shifts. It seems to break whatever thread of self-control he had left.

He moves his body up the bed slightly and rams home. This time, rocking us up the bed and pressing me deeper into the mattress. I reach between us and rub my clit, while touching where we're joined, loving the feel of him sliding in and out.

"Fuck... Zoe... I need to see you." He shoves my hand away and takes control, circling and stroking me in time with his powerful thrusts. His eyes are fixed to where he's pulsing in and out of me. We get wilder and faster until he's pounding into me, calling out my name as I arch off the bed, nails buried deep into the back of his neck, screaming in surprise as my orgasm rushes through me.

I fall over the edge of my climax, warmth spreading from my toes to my fingertips. Tingles radiate from my core, making my overwhelmed body clench around him over and over again until the aftershocks pass.

"Goddess, Zoe," he growls, shoving his arms up under my shoulders, holding me in place as he powers in and out of me, pushing me relentlessly toward another climax while he chases his own. He keeps me pinned, and I can do nothing but take it, digging my heels into his hips as I lose myself in his passion all over again. I wouldn't want it any other way. There's something so erotic about surrendering control of my body and seeing how he wants to use it.

"Blake, oh Blake!" I cry out as I come again, hard and fast, this time dragging my nails across his back, scoring his flesh while I bury my face in his chest to muffle my shouts.

"Zoe, fuck!" he yells, thrusting hard into me one last time and throws his head back with a roar as he stills, balls pressed firmly against me as he holds me down. I can feel his cock pulsing inside me. That's how tightly I'm wrapped around him.

Each jet of thick cum makes my body clench again, welcoming every drop. Blake falls forward, pressing his forehead to mine and dropping tender kiss after kiss to my lips.

Slipping from me, he wraps me in his arms and rolls again so that I'm sprawled on top of him. He drags his fingers lazily up and down my naked back, and I relax completely in his arms. I've never felt so blissful.

"That was incredible," I whisper, and I can feel him smile. "Was it worth the wait?" I don't know why I asked that, but it seems like his expectations must be sky-high after holding out for that long.

"It was perfect. *You're* perfect," he mumbles drowsily into my hair, and I can't help but grin. "Sleep Zoe, we both need it and I have a feeling it's going to be a long day tomorrow."

CHAPTER 26

ZOE

It takes me a second to realise where I am when I wake up. Stretching an arm across the cool sheets, I frown when I don't find Blake's warm body beside me. Gripping the bed sheet in one hand, I sit up and squint into the darkness, listening for him in the ensuite. Silence.

I swing my feet over the side of the bed and stand, wrapping the sheet loosely around myself as I tiptoe out into the living area. It's not as dark out here. The silvery moonlight streaming through the massive windows gives enough light to see by. I can make out Blake's tall silhouette, leaning against the glass, his head resting on one forearm. The plains of his taut body are on full display, only hidden by the dark pair of boxer briefs he's put back on.

As I walk up to him, with the sheet trailing behind me, he wordlessly extends his arm to the side for me to slip under before drawing me close to his side and dropping a kiss on the top of my head.

"Did I wake you?" he asks quietly, even though we're alone. It feels right to whisper in the dead of night. Nothing stirs outside. A handful of lights twinkle in the distance, but everything is still and quiet.

"No. I was just wondering where you went." I relax into him and stretch my free hand up to rub circles on his back. "Can't sleep?"

"I never sleep much," he answers. "The last couple of nights have probably been the best I've had in a long time." He goes back to staring out the window and my heart goes out to him. It's as if he has the weight of the world on his shoulders. His job holds a lot of responsibility and, with no family to support him, it must be lonely.

"It must be all the fresh air," I say, innocently smiling up at him with a wink. Blake laughs, deep and carefree. He needs more joy in his life.

"That must be it."

He presses a soft kiss to my lips, then turns his attention back to the view outside.

"What are you looking for?" I enquire, following his gaze. All I can see are the dark shadows where I know the forest surrounding the pack house begins. In the inky night, it looks sinister and uninviting. I can't believe I was traipsing around out there in my little red dress only a few hours ago.

"Him. He's out there. I'm certain of it." His tone is steadfast and certain, without an inkling of doubt. "But how can I differentiate between what's real and what isn't if I can't rely on my own mind? And how can anyone else trust me if I am no longer confident myself?"

He turns to face me, genuinely looking for me to give him an answer. The cold moonlight gives his features a more chiseled look and highlights every rippling muscle in his Adonis-like torso. In another life, he really could have been a male model.

"I don't know enough about Moon madness for the scientist in me to answer that. But I'm a big believer in trusting your instinct. What does your gut tell you?"

He frowns and takes his time, considering his response.

"That he's still alive," he repeats. I nod and give him a squeeze.

"Then I think you're probably right," I say, having absolute faith in this man. "Although I never felt like I was in any danger out there. Maybe his reasons for being here aren't as dark as you think."

I genuinely didn't. Even if his half-brother was lurking out there in the woods, I'm not convinced he meant any harm. At least not to me, anyway.

"Good," he rumbles. "Because if he touches a hair on your head, I'll kill him." He says it like it's no big deal, but my breath catches. He can't really mean that.

"But... he's *your brother*."

"Exactly. He knows what the consequences would be."

I fall silent, realising how little I know about wolf shifter culture. I know nothing, actually. Blake might have me sold on the fated mate's thing, but there's still a lot for me to learn.

"So being with me helps with the Moon madness symptoms," I state, keen to broach the topic he has told me the least about. He grimaces, but nods.

"Apparently. It didn't seem to work last night, though," he scoffs, looking frustrated with himself once again.

"Will spending more time with me stop your progression?" I find it both fascinating and ludicrous at the same time. How can my mere presence do anything to help?

"Not exactly," he hedges, but doesn't elaborate any further. Interesting. He doesn't want to tell me, which means it's something important — something I need to know, even if it's bad.

"*Blake?*" I press, not willing to let it go. It's his health. It's too serious to let him get away with hiding things. He sighs and pulls me to him, wrapping me up in his warm embrace. It feels like home, even though we've only known each other for a short amount of time.

"Marking you will. But I can't promise that I'll go back to normal completely." He rests his chin on the top of my head, swaying from side to side ever so slightly. I'm not sure if it's to comfort me or him.

"You mean 'normal' for you," I remark without thinking. "Normal for me doesn't involve turning into a wolf."

He chuckles softly but then turns serious again at my next question.

"Is that why you wanted me to come here? To mark me?"

Blake tips my chin up so I'm looking him dead in the eye. He looks completely horrified that I would even ask such a thing.

"No. Zoe, I invited you here so that we could get to know one another. I can understand why you'd think that, but marking is for life. I would never expect that of you so soon. You have a choice in this, angel. It's not something to do out of pity or obligation. There's plenty of time."

"I'm not the obliging type, unless it suits me," I quip, thinking back to the spanking I got in the shower last night. That had been electrifyingly hot. Any other man would have lost an arm for trying something like that, but Blake… I trust him completely. His chest rumbles and his nostrils flare. He knows my mind is in the gutter.

"I wanted to show you my life, what being a member of a pack is like. To see if you could ever picture yourself being a part of it. That didn't exactly go to plan, but…" Blake steps back and runs a hand across his lightly stubbled jaw.

"You mean your plan wasn't to end up in the hospital and turn into a wolf in the bathroom on our date?" I tease and he grimaces. He clearly isn't amused. It's clearly too soon for jokes.

"No," he says tersely, his jaw clenching and the tendons standing out on the sides of his neck. Is it wrong that I think he looks sexy when he's angry?

"What was your plan, Alpha?"

Still clutching the sheet to my breasts, I steer him backward with one hand on his hip. When his legs hit the armchair behind him and I topple him into it, he groans.

"For you to meet some of my pack — Jenna, Will, Max — to take you on a tour of the house and the gardens and to see the clinic. I had reservations for us at a new, amazing restaurant nearby. I thought we could go dancing after or come back here for a drink…"

At the mention of Jenna, I purse my lips but then decide not to let her ruin my fun. Standing in front of him in just the thin sheet, I twirl a strand of my blonde hair around my finger and pout at him.

"Why, Blake, that sounds suspiciously like you were planning on seducing me?"

"Damn straight."

He stretches out those long legs in front of him, his muscular thighs flexing, and holds my gaze with an intensity that takes my breath away. As I struggle to breathe, he reaches forward and runs his hands up the backs of my thighs under the sheet. I watch in fascination as his erection grows bigger, straining at the thin material barely containing it.

"Goddess, you look so hot, all freshly fucked in my sheets."

"And what about out of them?" I ask, dropping the sheet and letting it fall in a pile on the floor next to us. Blake's hungry gaze roams my body, illuminated by the moonbeams streaming in through the large window right beside us. He frees his cock from its confines, lifting his hips to shove his boxers all the way down and off. I lick my lips at the sight of him in all his glory, reclining in the buttery soft leather chair.

"Fuck, Zoe," he hisses, as I let my hands drift over my body. He grips himself firmly and bites his bottom lip, beckoning for me to come to him as I cup a breast with one hand and let the other slide from my hip down between my legs. His eyes dart to the expanse of glass and then back to me. "Do you want me to close the blinds?"

"Do *you* want to close the blinds?" I bat the question right back to him, an eagerness in me to know what's really going on behind that calm facade.

There's something about being safe here in his suite, with the wilderness right outside, even in the darkness, that's both exciting and comforting all at once. He shakes his head slowly and I step towards him, climbing onto his lap, and straddling him with one knee on either side of his hips.

"Open it is," I whisper against his ear and he moans. I feel the tension in his shoulders and arms as he resists taking control.

Biting his earlobe, I lift my body, tickling his chest with my pert nipples as his cock finds its position at my entrance. He can't seem to help himself as one big hand comes to my backside, grabbing me hard as he waits. His entire body is taut as I tease and taunt him with kisses along his neck and jaw before I take his mouth, both hands buried in his thick hair as our tongues tangle. My core is drenched, my arousal coating the tip of his cock, ready for him as I torment us both.

"*Zoe,*" he gasps into my mouth as I sink down onto him by an inch, before lifting back up and repeating the movement, using my hands on his broad chest for leverage.

"Fuck, woman. Stop teasing me." His hands settle on my hips, a clear warning that he'll take control of the situation if I don't put him out of his misery.

I reach back and cup his balls as I sink down further, tickling and teasing. His head falls back against the cushions and his grip on my hips tightens. He groans in despair as I lift off of him again, fighting my natural instinct to plunge myself all the way down on top of him.

"No, no, no. You're killing me, Zoe. *Please.*" Blake lifts his hips off the chair, seeking what his body craves, chasing me as I rise higher and away from him.

"Nuh-uh, Alpha. Right now, I'm the boss," I purr, dragging my nails down his pecs and the top of his stomach, loving the sight of the faint red lines that appear in their wake.

Grabbing his hair between my fingers, I tip his head back roughly, watching the fire in his eyes as he lets me have my moment. I kiss up his throat from the hollow at the base and feel it work against my lips when he shouts out as I sink down all the way, joining us completely at last, and clench around him hard.

As I move, I roll my hips and brush my clit against him, sending jolts of pleasure through my body.

Up and down, up and down. I move, gripping his shoulders and using my thighs to set a steady rhythm. He doesn't try to dictate anything, just relaxes and exhales deeply while his hands trail along my sides to my breasts. Rather than squeezing or pulling them, he caresses and touches them tenderly.

I rest my forehead against his, and his gaze locks onto mine, neither of us wants to look away. The moment is insanely intimate, and the slow pace only intensifies it. We aren't frantic or desperate. All our walls are down, souls bared without needing to say a word. We both feel it.

Our lips part a scant inch apart, our breaths and hushed moans mingling with every whimper that escapes me. I can feel my orgasm looming closer, and I'm overwhelmed by it. My entire body tenses as I'm almost there. I can already tell it's going to be powerful and I'm not sure I'm ready for it. For what it's going to give away. I almost start to panic as my pleasure peaks and I know I'm about to tumble down the other side.

"I'm yours, Zoe. I'm all yours. Let go," he whispers against my lips, and that does it. My climax surges through my body just as Blake claims my lips in a desperate kiss, and I moan my pleasure into his mouth. I've never felt anything like it as my body clamps down around his rock-hard cock as waves of pleasure continue to wrack my body.

"Zoe, fuck Zoe," Blake grits out as I fall forward and rest my forehead on his shoulder, overwrought and spent. He lifts me with his strong, sure hands and powers into me from below. It's enough to trigger another mini-climax, and I cry out as he calls my name, holding me tight onto him as comes, spilling his hot seed deep within me.

I feel every pulse, every twitch of his cock as he fills me completely. Clinging to him, I barely notice when he stands, wrapping my legs around him and draping the sheet over me as he carries me back to the bedroom.

He gently places me down on the bed and lies down beside me, our gazes meet. Nothing needs to be said between us. We both know how deep we've gone. He's changed me, irrevocably, and ruined me for all men now.

It feels like I'm floating on cloud nine, but I can't ignore the worried thoughts lingering in the back of my mind. I'm not sure if it's his or mine, or both. There are lots of logistics to work out, and I need to find out more about treating this moon madness.

But one thing's for sure, for me anyway, there's no going back.

CHAPTER 27

BLAKE

"Maybe I can come and work for you?" I joke with a grimace, leading Zoe downstairs, reluctant to leave the bubble of my suite.

It was torture to leave my bed. I long to steal away and hide away with my mate, enjoying every inch of each other's bodies as a normal wolf pairing does. She looks stunning, dressed in a simple cream jumper that sets off her golden tan, and fitted jeans that show off her delicious curves.

Zoe seems self-conscious, as if she thinks she's underdressed, but it doesn't take much to polish a diamond. Her beauty doesn't need flashy clothes or layers of makeup — she's radiant without them.

Zoe grips my hand tighter as we walk into the pack dining hall, and I lead her toward the table at the back where I usually sit. Max is there, along with senior wolves from my pack, and some of the council members.

At first, I think it's because she's nervous about us potentially getting a grilling about what went on last night. Or intimidated by being surrounded by an entire room full of wolves. But when Max gets up and gives Zoe his seat at my right-hand side, placing himself on my left next to Jenna instead, an uneasy feeling settles over me. It's something else completely that's bothering her. I watch Zoe closely as she greets the rest of the table warmly, but her gaze skims past Jenna before coming back to me with a tight smile.

Blake: Did I miss something?

Max: I'll let Zoe fill you, but I wouldn't blame her if she didn't want to sit beside Jenna right now. I thought it best to avoid any unnecessary tension this morning.

Jenna's avoiding eye contact with Zoe by focusing intently on her food and she's looks both guilty and sullen at the same time. When she catches me studying her, she flashes me a charming smile, but for the first time, I'm not happy to see my old friend. That catches me off-guard. I've relied on Jenna for years to keep the packhouse running smoothly while I focus on my role as both Alpha of this pack, and the other Alpha's within my region. Right now, though, my wolf is feeling protective of Zoe, who remains quiet.

"Everything okay, angel?" I ask Zoe quietly, tilting my head so I can see her expression clearly. She nods a little too brightly and smiles a little too quickly.

Hmm.

Bringing her hand up to my lips, I press a kiss to the back of her knuckles, and she gives me an embarrassed grin before tugging her hand back from my grasp and picking up the freshly poured tea in front of her. She raises those pale grey eyes to heaven, teasing me, but I can tell she liked it. This is a tense situation I've thrown her into. Some reassurance is the least I can do.

The pack members clearly notice us and exchange wary glances. Having Zoe here is sure to have them intrigued, but the council always makes everyone nervous. Normally, they only deign to visit when there's trouble. Like in the aftermath of the rogue attack that took my mother and devastated my family. Or when I finally had to challenge my father, his behaviour turning erratic after losing his mate.

Standing, I decide to kill two birds with one stone and try to put everyone at ease so they can eat their meal in peace. Extending a hand to Zoe, I see the realisation on her face as she sees what I intend to do. Much to my relief, she places her hand in mine, once again putting her trust in me, and gets to her feet at my side.

"Good morning. As you may have noticed, I have some guests with me here today. First, I would like to introduce Zoe Walker, my fated mate. Zoe will hopefully be spending a lot more time with us, so please make her feel welcome."

Jenna stifles a gasp and Max fixes her with a stern look. The stunned silence in the room quickly fills with cheers, whoops, and applause as I wrap my arm around Zoe and press a kiss to her temple. Murmurs of congratulations flood my brain via the mind-link. Jenna's already pale skin has turned ghostly white as she stares up at Zoe unblinkingly, lips drawn into thin lines.

The council looks equally shocked. They all thought Zoe was my intended chosen mate. I'm hoping that giving them this nugget of information will be enough to keep them off my back for at least another moon. When the chatter dies down again, I continue.

"We had an intruder last night, and I know it was unsettling for all of you. I thank you all for jumping into action as quickly as you did. But please don't worry. This person has been to the pack before and was always welcome here, but seems to have forgotten proper manners."

I pause and a few chuckles go through the room as I try to ease their concerns.

"We know who it was, and I assure you I will speak to this individual. In the meantime, please stay vigilant and let us know if you see anything out of the ordinary."

"Thanks for the warning."

Zoe elbows me in the ribs as we sit back down at the table, just as Will arrives with coffee. I smile at her, loving how comfortable she is despite the craziness of the situation. She wouldn't have stood up if she didn't want to. Her willingness to go public as my mate so soon fills me with pride. Reaching out to touch her arm, she winces and jerks it away from me.

"Just the scratch from last night," she says, rubbing her hand up my arm to reassure me. The council members are paying close attention, so I don't push it. I try to remember seeing a wound last night, but I wasn't exactly paying attention. It must be tiny, either that, or I'm a terrible mate for not noticing.

Appeased by the knowledge that I've found my fated mate, and assuming I will mark Zoe in the very near future, the council announce their intention to depart after breakfast.

"We'll be back after the next full moon," Brett warns. So that's my timeline. They're giving me until then to claim my mate or I'll have to answer more questions. I feel a surge of annoyance at being pressured, but I push it away and nod politely.

"Of course. It'll be our pleasure to have you back." After last night, I have to play their game. I sense Zoe stiffen at the word 'our'. It's a loaded word. I'm sure she's wondering exactly what I mean by '*our*'.

Sharon appears at our side and smiles warmly at Zoe. I'm not sure I've ever seen her be so nice to anyone. It makes me anxious.

"Come. Let's leave the boys to chat."

She phrases it as if she's merely tagging along like a bored wife, rather than being one of the most powerful members of the council. Zoe gives my forearm a squeeze before excusing herself and following Sharon. I itch to accompany her, and not just because I don't trust Sharon. Not having her with me already feels strange. I don't like it.

As I turn back to the table, where they all offer their best wishes, joking and teasing that they now understand why we were so late to breakfast, Jenna anxiously wrings her napkin in her lap before reaching out via the mind-link.

Jenna: Blake, I apologise. I spoke out of turn to Zoe last night when she followed you outside. I didn't realise she was your fated.

Blake: Would it have been okay if she wasn't?

Jenna: No, that's not what I mean. I... I'm just sorry.

She trails off, shaking her head, obviously assuming that Zoe has told me the details of whatever altercation they had last night. I won't contradict her. Zoe and I will always present a united front. Right now, all I care about is making sure she really is alright.

Blake: That's twice that you've been sorry in two days. There won't be a third time. Understood?

Jenna nods, wide-eyed at my tone. We've been friends for a long time. I've never had to speak harshly to her before, but my wolf is furious.

Blake: Anyway, it isn't me who needs to hear your apology.

Jenna: I'm going to make things right with Zoe. I'd like us to be friends.

Blake: See that you do

"Your fated mate, Blake. Just in time to save the day," Brett comments, moving over to sit in Zoe's vacated seat as the rest of the council drifts out of the dining hall, preparing to depart. "Alpha Weston will be delighted for you," he adds with a smirk. Right. Weston will be fuming.

"I wouldn't say just in time. But I will admit that I'm feeling pretty lucky," I agree with a grin and the older wolf smiles back at me. Every mated wolf knows how special this time is and how amazing it is to meet your mate.

"Now it's definitely time for us to get out of your way. I'll be expecting an invitation to the mating ceremony." Brett winks, folds his napkin, and places it down on the table.

I stand and move to the back of my chair as he pushes up from the table and we shake hands. He nods to Max and Jenna before leaving the hall and I relax now that it's back to just my pack.

The knowledge that Jenna said something inappropriate to Zoe, and that she chose not to tell me, is making my blood pressure shoot up the more I think about it. Abnormally so. I need to leave.

"I better find Zoe before Sharon turns her into a frog or

something," I mutter, excusing myself from the table and following her delicious scent into a lounge off the main hallway. As I push open the door, Sharon is rubbing a green ointment onto her skin, while Zoe appears to be leaning away to avoid the overpowering smell.

"What the hell do you think you're doing?" I bark, suddenly not one bit happy that this mysterious hybrid is administering her potions to my delicate mate.

"Blake!" Zoe chastises, frowning at my rudeness. It's not a great way to address a member of the council, but my wolf is on edge. Something has his hackles up. With the moon madness coursing through my veins, it's not a brilliant combination.

"What is it?" I ask again, striding forward and snatching the brown glass jar away from Sharon, holding it up to my nose to get a good whiff.

"Relax. It's just some herbs to fight off any infection," she says to placate me, tugging down Zoe's sleeve and hiding the scratch before I can see it. Zoe glares at me, unimpressed with my attitude. "I'll leave you both to it. Congratulations, again. And, Zoe, remember what I said at dinner last night."

Zoe nods politely as Sharon leaves, pulling the door shut behind her. I immediately grab Zoe's arm and pull it toward me, shoving the material up to her elbow so I can see the wound clearly. Zoe gasps but doesn't try to stop me, knowing it's futile.

My gaze lands on the small puncture wounds near her wrist. They're not bad, but they look red and angry. Staggering back, I stare down at her wide-eyed, as the enormity of it sinks in. Zoe is my mate. I should be the last person in the world to hurt her. It's not a scratch.

"I bit you?"

CHAPTER 28

ZOE

"Did I bite you, Zoe? Did I do that?" Blake repeats impatiently, eyes blazing and jaw twitching, as he grits his teeth.

Swallowing apprehensively, I try to buy myself some time before answering. Blake's already vibrating with rage and his hands are trembling by his sides. His nostrils flare as he takes a deep breath to steady himself. My Blake is slipping away. I watch cautiously as he raises a jerky hand to his face and pinches the bridge of his nose. No matter what I say, I expect him to overreact. Aggression pours off him in waves.

Max appears in the doorway and freezes, glancing back and forth between the two of us. He hesitates, reluctant to interrupt, but senses in an instant that something is very wrong.

"*TELL ME RIGHT NOW!*" Blake roars.

It should terrify me, but I can see the despair in his eyes. The guilt. I steel myself against the overwhelming desire to blurt out the truth. Max, however, grimaces, looking pained as he tilts his head to the side, baring his neck to Blake.

"Yes. Fuck. You caught her hand when you were going for me."

Blake's chest heaves as he continues to drag in ragged breaths.

Max looks tortured as he glares angrily at Blake from his cowed position. Hell no. He doesn't deserve to be treated like that.

Walking over to Blake, I poke him hard in the chest to drag his attention back to me.

"Stop it! Are you doing that to him?" I shout. Blake's attention turns to me, but he doesn't look any less intimidating, his handsome features dark and brooding. "Did you just try to force me to answer your question? To *compel* me? I'm supposed to be your partner! And he is your friend!"

Pressing my finger deeper into his muscular chest, I move closer, holding his gaze, challenging him. Something like admiration flashes across his face and he relaxes ever so slightly, his features softening. In a movement so fast that my eyes don't follow it, he captures my hand where it touches him and pulls it up to his face. He holds my wrist to his nose and breathes in deeply, before brushing his lips across the small wound.

"You *are* my partner. More than that, you are my mate and I am yours. I live for you now. My entire purpose is to protect you."

"It was an accident. No big deal. It's my fault for putting my arm in the way."

Blake ignores my words and continues to fixate on my injury, kissing it softly again as I stretch my fingers out to cup his cheek. He leans into it and closes his eyes briefly.

"Zoe, the only bite you should get from me is when I'm buried deep inside you, and you're screaming my name as you come. Milking my release with your tight cunt as I fill you up."

His voice is soft and belies the filthy words he's just spoken. I gasp and he lifts his gaze back to mine. I see the heat there but also the sadness. Coughing to regain my composure, I continue trying to brush off what he did and convince him it's not the disaster he thinks it is.

"In my line of work, do you really think it's the first time I've been bitten? This one time…"

I don't get to finish that sentence as Blake steps into my space and growls.

"I'm not some random dog, angel. This is different. This is unforgivable. Why didn't you tell me?"

He's hurt that I kept this from him, but this is exactly why. It's barely more than a scratch, but he's catastrophising. I can see his brain making the leap from this to him being a threat to me.

"Blake, I know it wasn't really you out there, and I didn't want you to feel bad about it. You have enough on your plate." Snapping his gaze back to mine, he scoffs.

"You mean you didn't want to upset me because I'm unstable?" He seems to be struggling to keep his voice calm and even.

"No! For fuck's sake. I'm not afraid of you."

"Maybe you *should* be. What if this is the new me? Even now, I just want to tear this place apart." He glances around the room and shakes his head as if trying to clear the thought from his confused brain. "I'm not in a good place, Zoe. I don't think you should be here."

His words are like a kick in the gut, and I recoil, feeling each syllable like a slap in the face. I step away from him, but his grip on my arm tightens, and he uses my momentum to pull me back into his solid body.

"It's because I love you, Zoe, and I'll never forgive myself if anything happens to you because of me," he whispers against my hair, his voice thick and cracking at the end. His masculine scent surrounds me, and I bury my face against his shirt, relishing the cool feel of the material against my skin.

"I can help you, Blake. Don't push me away," I plead, and he wraps me tightly in his arms. The thought of leaving him makes me anxious. This bond is doing crazy things to me.

"Just for a few days," he lies, pressing a kiss to my head. "You need to get back to your clinic. And Leah's wedding is next weekend. I'm sure you have a lot to do."

My eyes sting at the clear dismissal, but I knew he would freak out over this. Trying not to take this personally, I disentangle myself from him and re-establish some space between us. I have things to check up on. Hiding out here forever was never the plan.

"Max, can you drive us back?" Blake asks without taking his eyes off me. Max nods and walks away in silence. I'm sure he's desperate to escape this conversation.

"You don't have to come," I say, summoning all my strength and lifting my chin to maintain my dignity. "You have work that needs your attention. Max can drive me home on his own."

"Angel…" Blake warns, looking hurt, and goes to move closer, but I hold up a hand to stop him in his tracks, needing to keep some distance from him. He won't change his mind and I won't beg him.

"No. Go, run, work, do whatever you need to do."

Exhausted after the emotional rollercoaster of the last few days, I long to be alone. As I turn to leave, suddenly in a hurry to pack and get out of there, Blake falls into step beside me, his head bowed.

"I'll meet you out front," I say quietly, without looking at him. His eyes burn into my back as I climb the stairs to his suite alone. I can almost taste his longing. As I turn down the landing and disappear out of view, I hear him stride quickly across the foyer, a frustrated growl filling the air as he slams a door behind him.

My temper flares as I gather and pack my things. He's the one sending me away and shutting me out. After bringing me here, showing me what life could be for us, convincing me fated mates are real. Then he has the audacity to act like the wounded party. I know he's doing the over-protective alpha male thing. I have an older brother so I get it. But if us being together helps him, sending me away makes no sense.

My anger builds as I exit the building to find Max waiting in Blake's shiny SUV. Flinging my bag onto the back seat, I stomp to the passenger side, wrenching the door open before Blake has a chance to do it for me.

"Let me know how the repairs at the clinic are going," he says, leaning against the open door. "And that the CCTV is working. My guys should be finished by now."

"Don't..." I snap, giving him a withering look as my irritation gets the better of me. "Don't pretend like everything is okay and you're not kicking me out of your house like some kind of fucked up one-night stand."

He growls, stepping away from the door and crowding me back against the side of the vehicle. Despite myself, my body reacts, my pulse racing, and my core heating. I curse my weak willpower with this man. When he touches my cheek, my eyes drift closed, savouring his touch.

"*You. Are. Mine*," he asserts, the deep timbre of his voice vibrating through me where our bodies touch. He's using the bond against me, knowing the effect he has on me.

"Really? It doesn't feel like it. Maybe Jenna's right."

I roll my eyes as I slip in through the passenger door and into my seat, grab the handle, and slam it shut. When Blake knocks on the window, Max, the *traitor*, lowers the window to let him talk to me again. I scowl at him, but he shrugs, his loyalty to his boss clear.

"What happened last night? What did she say to you?"

"It doesn't matter." I never should have brought it up. He doesn't need to hear about Jenna's bitchy comments. I shouldn't lower myself to her level.

"It fucking matters to *me*." He grips the door so tightly that his knuckles turn white, and the leather interior creaks under his fingertips.

"That I was just your poor replacement for Hayley. And since you're getting rid of me, maybe she's not the only one who thinks that."

It's a low blow and I know it.

"Max, can we please go?" I ask, my voice wavering as I

struggle to avoid looking at Blake's stunned expression. It's only when the SUV starts to move that he releases the door. He looks as if I've stabbed him in the heart. Being angry at him for acting like a fool is one thing. Pretending I don't know what his true feelings are is another. It pulses through whatever tenuous bond we have. The words he uttered earlier are true.

He loves me.

And I'm afraid to admit that I might feel the same way.

"He's trying to protect you. He's crazy about you, Zoe," Max says softly, as we pass the large wrought-iron gates at the end of the long driveway. The man standing guard at the small building on the side bows his head in respect and I smile. What the hell is Blake thinking, introducing me to the pack one minute and then sending me home the next?

I turn to look at Max for a moment in silent contemplation before sighing softly and going back to staring out the side window at the lush forest lining the road. He can't tell me anything else, his loyalty is to Blake.

"I know that. He's being an idiot, but I can *feel* him somehow. He's trying to do the right thing," I admit begrudgingly.

"What do you mean, you can feel him?" he asks curiously. We're not mated. It shouldn't be possible, but I shrug, struggling to put it into words.

"It's like I'm sitting here with my own emotions. Annoyance mostly, yet I can already feel how much he misses me. How conflicted he is about letting me leave, and how worried he is that he'll hurt me if I stay. Or that I'll see him at his worst and reject him. It's all in here."

I rub my sternum to ease the physical ache there. Max looks stunned at the idea we could be so connected after less than a week in each other's company. He grits his teeth and shifts in his seat.

"Blake is bombarding me with questions about how you are."

"Tell him I'm alright," I say, touching his arm to get his attention. "I'll call him tonight."

"I will." He nods and gives me his most sympathetic smile. Even though I'm hurting, I don't want him to worry unnecessarily. Pulling out my phone, I tap out a message to one of the few people I can confide in about this. I need to unload. My mind is churning. I need a distraction and some answers.

CHAPTER 29

BLAKE

Blake: Is she okay?

Max: How could she be okay? She's mated to an asshole.

Blake: Watch yourself, Max.

Max: No. You announce your future Luna to the pack and then kick her out? What the hell, Blake? How do you expect her to feel?

Blake: I am hanging on by a thread, Max, and this is not helping. Do you really think I don't feel terrible already? I do, let me assure you of that, but I can't mark her... not when I might be a danger to her. She'll spend the rest of her life worrying about what will set me off next. I need to fix this first... I have to.

Max: What if you can't?

I don't answer him and he knows what that means. I've dedicated my entire life to taking care of others. And Zoe is my mate. As long as there is a threat to her, I won't mark her.

I'm getting worse and the longer I leave it, the riskier this gets. I sigh and twist my hands around the steering wheel in frustration, trying to hide my agitation. What I want to do and what I should do are completely different things. I have the perfect mate, a chance to stop the madness from getting worse, but I need to be cautious regarding her welfare. I'd rather lose my mind than hurt her.

Max: I'll stay with her tonight. Make sure she's safe.
Blake: Thank you, friend.
Max: She said she'll call you later. Go to the elders and tell them what's going on. There's no time left. Keeping it a secret isn't an option anymore. They might have an idea we haven't thought of yet. But you're hurting Zoe by staying away, remember that. Her bond with you is stronger than you think.

He shuts down the link before I respond. Normally, I would never stand for such rudeness, but although I'm his alpha, he's also my best friend, and he's worried about me.

We haven't properly discussed what will happen if we mated with everything that's been going on, but we need to. Fast. It doesn't seem fair. We're so lucky to have met. But with a ticking clock and my illness added to the mix, it has the potential to all blow up and go horribly wrong.

Max continues to block me as I repeatedly attempt to reach him throughout the day. Creative solutions for revenge flicker through my mind, only to be dismissed in the end. Nothing he said or is doing was wrong. He's my beta, and he's sticking up for his Luna. It's what I would want him to do if it was anyone else treating her this way. Still, I'll make my point when he returns. He might be part bear, but it doesn't give him immunity from the normal pack hierarchy.

My anger is much better directed toward someone who truly deserves it. Stalking through the pack house in search of my target, my aura is clearly sending out *'don't talk to me'* vibes as wolves scatter in all directions when they see me coming. Even Will backpedals into my office as I pass. He's here to give me the debriefing I asked for on this week's schedule.

Knocking loudly on the solid wood door, I wait impatiently for Jenna to open it — surely she would have picked up my scent as I approached.

"Jenna, open the door right now or I'll smash it in," I warn, perfectly prepared to do exactly that. I usually prefer to use my words and alpha aura to encourage compliance within the pack.

They know what I can do if provoked. Most of the pack saw me take down my father. The stories of that night are enough to keep most people from testing me.

This is different. This is someone attacking my mate and I won't stand for it.

The door swings open and a sheepish-looking Jenna stands there at the entrance to her quarters, blinking up at me with tears glistening in her eyes. I march past her, closing the door behind me, gesturing for her to sit. She perches herself on the edge of a cream-coloured velvet chaise and it's only then that I realise she's wearing only a thin nightgown and a silk robe.

"Sorry, I was about to hop into the shower," she explains, crossing her legs and lifting the hem of her gown even higher, revealing a not-too-subtle expanse of skin. She fiddles with her blonde bob, dragging her perfectly manicured nails through the ends.

"Zoe told me what you said." I stand further back, uncomfortable for the first time in my old friend's apartment. Would I be happy with Zoe in another male's home if he was wearing only his boxers? Absolutely not. Jenna bows her head before glancing up at me from under her long lashes.

"I didn't mean to say I actually wanted her to get killed. She wasn't listening to Max's order to stay inside and I got frustrated with her. It was wrong of me to speak to her like that, but, Blake, she needs to understand that what you say goes," she blurts out in a rush and I can smell the fear rolling off her. She looks chastened, but something about it doesn't ring true. My wolf isn't impressed, anyway.

"*Interesting*," I say tightly, as my rage notches up to another level. I pace, needing to move before I explode. Not only did she tell Zoe she was a mere replacement for Hayley, suggesting she's second best in my mind, but she told her she wished she was dead. If Zoe was Luna, this would be treason.

I'm silent, but Jenna takes it as an invitation to keep going.

She doesn't understand the precariousness of her situation. The ice she's treading is paper thin.

"Blake, you're not well. I know you're trying to hide it, but I know you. A human can't understand. I know you're drawn to her, but if you mark her, she's not physically strong enough to deal with you if you lose control."

The thought has been consuming me, gnawing away at my insides ever since I found Zoe. But to hear someone else question my mate, to suggest that she's weak, makes my blood boil and my temper flare. It forces me to realise that I may have been underestimating Zoe, too.

"Zoe is stronger than you think, and you must show her the respect she is due," I growl. Jenna nods and rises, stepping closer to stand in front of me. As she goes to touch me, I capture her wrist and hold it away from me. My wolf doesn't want any female other than Zoe near me. I'm on the brink of lashing out. Getting into my personal space could push me over the edge.

"I'm not saying you shouldn't have her, Blake," she murmurs, licking her lips in a way that makes me feel physically sick, "and I should never have spoken to her as I did, but maybe you need to take a different mate. A wolf who understands and is strong enough to handle you. You and your needs."

She pauses and her words take on a vile quality. "Zoe could still be in your life once you get control of the madness."

Nobody with any respect for the mate bond would dare utter such words. With sickening clarity, I realise what she's suggesting. I toss her hand back toward her and create some much-needed distance between us.

"And let me guess, Jenna," I growl, disgusted by her. "You're volunteering to mate with me, to be Luna, so I can have my fated mate as some kind of little pet concubine?"

"If you so wished," she spits out. Her expression betrays her disappointment that I didn't jump with enthusiasm to accept her proposal.

"And what if I can no longer feel my bond with her? *What then?*" I challenge.

"She's human. She'll get over it and continue with her life. She'll be safe. Isn't that what matters?"

Her logic is twisted. In one sense, she's right. Leaving Zoe alone might be the best thing for her, but I could never take another mate. The mere thought of touching another woman makes my skin crawl. I only want Zoe.

"Jenna, the only reason I am going to pretend you never suggested something so horrific is because we've known each other since we were pups."

"You didn't think it was so horrific when I had your fingers in my pussy and my hand wrapped around your cock, Blake," she purrs seductively, as I feel the bile rise in my throat. *Has she been harbouring these feelings since then?* "I could be Luna with my eyes closed. You know it's true. I've basically been doing it for years."

"I was twenty-two, drunk and lonely. That was a long time ago, Jenna, and we both agreed it was a bad idea. If something was going to happen between us, it would have happened already."

Anger and humiliation flash in her eyes. That's why she has such a problem with Zoe. It has nothing to do with mistaking her for Hayley. Jenna's jealous. Jenna thinks she's already Luna and Zoe is encroaching on her territory.

"Give me your word, Jenna. This stops now, do you understand? No more. This is the last I'll hear of this. If you can't get this ridiculous notion out of your head, we will not be working together anymore."

Her jaw is set stubbornly, but she dips her head in submission and nods. Disappointment courses through me. I had genuinely believed Jenna was my friend, but it turns out she was just another person looking for something from me. Max and Zoe are the only people I can truly count on.

Zoe.

Fuck. I'll have to tell her about my history with Jenna,

eventually. It was nothing. I had just taken the pack by force from my father; I was overwhelmed and on my own. Thinking a release would help, I'd sought comfort from my friend, but my wolf hated it and we never went further.

I give Jenna one last stern glare before storming out. She can't manage the packhouse anymore, that's for certain. I'll need to find a suitable replacement. Jenna will be furious. I'll need to make sure she's really past this before I decide if she can even stay in the pack at all. Although none of this matters if I'm going to descend into madness in the next couple of weeks. It will all be Max's mess to deal with.

Maybe that can be his punishment for blocking me. I have bigger problems to deal with.

CHAPTER 30

ZOE

For the rest of the drive, Max and I travel in companionable silence. It lets me mull over everything in my mind as I consider all that's happened in the last few days. From the break-in to finding out shifters exist; to the sexiest man I've ever met claiming to be my soulmate, then finding out he's ill. The wheels in my head are spinning so much, it's making my head hurt. I massage my temples, trying to ease the pain that has been building steadily since we left.

I take some paracetamol from my purse and swallow them down with a sip of water from a lukewarm bottle sitting on the console.

"Leah's coming over. You don't have to babysit me. I won't be alone." I wave my phone at him as the screen flashes with message after message from my overly-excited baby sister.

"All the more reason for me to stick around and keep an eye on you. You Walker women attract trouble wherever you go."

"Not me," I argue and it's true. The other two tease me non-stop for having no life. Max scoffs and shakes his head.

"Not buying it. But don't worry, I'll stay out of your way."

He turns down the winding driveway and I feel a surge of pride as the clinic I scrimped and saved to buy comes into view.

As we get closer, I can see the new doors have been installed, just as Doc said they would be. All arranged by Blake.

Max begins to drive past the clinic, heading straight for the house. Right now, though, there's nothing I want more than to go in and see with my own eyes that everything is back as it should be. Work grounds me. It's all I've had in my life for a long time.

"Stop, please? I want to go in and check things out."

Max frowns but complies, slowly rolling up to the side door and parking as close as he can. He shifts in the seat and turns to face me as he kills the engine.

"You look tired, Zoe. Why don't you rest for a few hours and come back? I have a feeling Blake didn't let you get much sleep."

He gives me a cheeky wink and I blush furiously, but there's no hiding the genuine concern in his eyes. I smack him on the arm with the back of my hand and immediately regret it because it's like hitting a rock. Shaking out my aching hand, I curse, but I don't argue with him. Blake has been wearing me out in the most delicious ways imaginable. I'm bone tired, though I won't admit it to Max.

"Hmph. How on Earth did I survive before you boys came along to tell me what to do?" I roll my eyes and climb out, walking straight to the door and punching in the security code. Max is right behind me as I walk in. I stop and stare up and down the corridor. In my mind, I recall how it looked the night of the break-in, supplies strewn everywhere, Blake's blood splattered on the walls. It's immaculate now. Not a trace that anything untoward has happened. Again, all Blake's doing. He had someone come in and clean it all up as soon as the crime scene technicians finished their work.

As I push open my office door, I remember Blake on the security feed standing in front of it, protecting me from the intruders. Putting himself between me and the danger, even as the tranquilliser kicked in and he knew he could be at their mercy any minute. I pause at the threshold, recalling how he laid down across it, as if his sleeping body could somehow prevent someone from getting to me.

A knot forms in my stomach at the memory of how he was wounded and how vulnerable he was because of the drugs. Yet, he was only concerned about me, in the same way that he is now.

"Shh. He'll be okay." Max comforts, stepping up and wrapping me in a tight embrace as tears well in my eyes and a stifled sob escapes me. There is no way I could ever go back to my life here and forget him, no matter how sick he is. He thinks he can deal with the Moon madness on his own, but by turning up here that night, he changed my life forever. Blake saved me and I'm going to do my utmost to do the same for him.

"Stubborn man," I mutter, wiping my eyes on my sleeve and taking a steadying breath. Max grasps my arms and bends down, so we're eye to eye.

"This is only a quick pit stop, Zoe, then you're getting some rest. This will all be here in the morning." He isn't asking, he's telling. Maybe that is what I need right now. There's a stack of paperwork on the desk, but it's nothing too daunting. Max is right. I won't be able to concentrate, anyway.

"Doc just left. I'll check on the animals and then we'll go," I offer. Max nods, leaning against the wall and waiting while I go to check the two dogs. Dressed head to toe in black, he looks every inch the intimidating biker. The tattoos and muscles add to the dangerous aura he exudes. Even if he wasn't partly wolf, I wouldn't blame the dogs for being wary. It's better he stays out here.

Both dogs are unusually subdued. Turning to the Golden Lab whom I've met many times before, I expect a warm welcome, but nothing. In fact, it's as if he's intimidated by me. I give him a gentle pat before moving on and making sure everything is in order. I have no reason to doubt Doc, but I wouldn't have been able to relax without making sure everything was alright.

"Alright, let's go." Max pushes off the wall and holds the heavy door open for me. As I duck under his arm the bright light and rush of fresh air disorientates me for a moment. The toe of my shoe catches on the doorjamb and I stumble forward. Max shoots out an arm and prevents me from face-planting into the concrete. As I straighten, he frowns at me and puts a warm hand on my forehead.

"Home," he orders, walking me back to the SUV and making sure I'm in before returning to the driver's side.

"I'm fine," I argue half-heartedly, falling quiet and all but admitting defeat when he raises a dark eyebrow at me. I really don't feel too great. A nap will do me a world of good.

Once we get to my tiny house, Max carries my bag inside and points to the sofa, refusing to let me help as he makes two mugs of tea. Handing one to me, he directs me toward the stairs, his expression stern and leaving no room for argument.

"I'll send Leah up when she gets here."

I nod and stretch up to give him a kiss on the cheek, holding my steaming mug out to one side.

"And, Zoe, we'll work this out, okay?"

Nodding, I blink away the tears that appear again, grateful Blake has a friend like Max. Feeling emotional and slightly dizzy, I climb the stairs and head straight into my room. Diving under the covers, the scent of him, still lingering on my sheets, swallows me up and my chest tightens. It's ridiculous, but I miss him already. Not being with him aches like physical pain. It doesn't seem normal. I must ask Leah I think to myself as sleep pulls me under.

* * *

"*NO WAY!* Can you turn into a bear *and* a wolf?!"

I wake up to my sister shrieking at Max about his half-bear, half-wolf heritage, and chuckle to myself. Leah is never one to shy away from asking questions. Walking to the ensuite, I turn on the shower and jump in. I figure Max can cope for another ten minutes. Feeling refreshed, I throw on the softest jeans I own and an oversized hoody before wandering downstairs.

Leah has Max cornered in the kitchen, where he's rummaging through the almost bare cupboards, trying to ignore the non-stop stream of questions Leah is throwing at him about being a hybrid shifter.

"Not everyone wants to tell you their life story, Leah," I tease, only half joking as she practically invades his personal space and appears to be comparing thigh size.

"Are all bears big like you and Marcus? Or is it just because you're both alpha types?"

Is it intrusive to ask questions like that? I'm not sure but I keep my mouth shut, because I'm curious about that myself.

"Most are bigger," he mumbles distractedly, pulling out a box from one cupboard and grimacing when he checks the use-by date. "Zoe, you have no food."

"Doc was staying here. And you guys ate everything the last time you stayed." I feel like I need to justify why I live like a poor college student. He grunts in response and turns, snatching his keys up off the counter.

"I'll leave you to catch up. I'm going to hit the diner and I'll bring you both back some dinner." He doesn't look back as he slams the door behind him, the engine of Blake's SUV roaring to life a second later.

"Hangry," Leah comments, as if her inquisition couldn't possibly have anything to do with his surly mood.

"Hmmm. I'm sure that's it," I say sarcastically as I move past her and pull a bottle of wine from the rack and shove it into the freezer.

"You're not supposed to do that," she comments absently as she pulls out two wine glasses and sets them on the counter, before wandering out to the sitting room. She pats the cushion beside her, and I flop down onto it with a groan, tipping my head back against the couch.

"Come, dear sister, and tell me all about how your wolfman

has been driving you crazy. The good and the bad. Because I know there's bad, too. You're not marked yet. I swear all that testosterone and sex scrambles their brains!"

She wiggles her eyebrows and I smile. This is exactly what I need. If there's anyone who can understand what I'm going through, it's my sister.

CHAPTER 31

ZOE

"He just kicked you out?" Leah shoves a hand all the way to the bottom of the bag of chips, scooping out the last remnants. Telling her my sorry tale doesn't seem to have fazed her at all. I thought at least the part about Blake shifting in the bathroom and racing out into the woods would get a reaction, but she barely blinked.

"Kicked me out is... harsh, but, basically, yes." I retrieve the well-chilled bottle of wine from the freezer and pour her a glass.

"Eh, what about you?" She waves the other empty glass in the air, and I shake my head. Her eyes narrow.

"No, I'm not feeling well and I'm on call tonight. Doc was here all day and he's working again tomorrow."

Leah doesn't look convinced.

"*Are you pregnant?!*" She claps her hands with glee; her eyes dance with excitement.

Cola sprays past my lips as I cough and choke. "*What?!!*" I sputter, gobsmacked. "Leah, I just met him! Besides, you're not supposed to ask people that!" Scoffing at my stunned expression, she hands me a tissue to wipe my face as she moves to sit cross-legged facing me.

"You're not 'people'. These alphas move fast. They find the one they want and they go all baby crazy. I wouldn't leave your birth control lying around." I blush and bite my lip. Leah picks up on my non-answer and leans back on the couch, laughing her head off at me.

"You're not on birth control? Oh, Zoe, you're every breeding-mad shifter's wet dream." She wipes her eye with the back of her sleeve and her gaze drops to my stomach.

"Stop it!!" I scold, jumping to my feet and waving my hand in front of my belly to stop her from staring. She ignores me and continues to chuckle. "Anyway, he can't *breed* anyone if he's not even here."

I know that I'm sulking and feeling sorry for myself, but it feels wrong being away from him. I'm restless.

"Did you know Rex had a mate when I met him?" she whispers, her expression serious and her hands clasped together in her lap. Shocked, my mouth drops open as she nods with a wry grin, understanding my disbelief. "She rejected the bond with him, but he never got the chance to accept it; he was stuck in limbo. It was painful for him and completely messed with his head."

"But you're mates now?" My gaze darts to the silvery marks on her neck to confirm what I thought I knew and she reaches up to touch them, carefully brushing over them with her fingertips. They're definitely teeth marks.

"We are, but he tried to stay away from me at first. He wouldn't sleep with me until he'd broken their bond completely. Then it turned out that we were second-chance mates and the rest is history. But it was torture." She's complaining, but she's smiling at the memories just the same. I've seen her and Rex together. They're so in love. Bunching her blonde curls into a pile on her head, she leans forward and hugs me.

"My point is you are the most important thing in the world to him. More important than his job, his pack, and more important than his life. He doesn't want to be away from you, Zoe. I'm sure he's miserable, but he cannot cope with the idea that he might hurt you."

Sighing, I pick at the bandage on my wrist and her sharp gaze follows the movement. Taking hold of my arm, she pulls it close to her and runs a thumb over the plaster.

"What's this, Zoe?" she asks. Her voice is perfectly calm, but I know Leah too well. She doesn't look at me, just continues to look at the small square of gauze. Yanking my arm back, I tug down my sleeves and hide my arms. Leah sticks her chin out defiantly and waits. She'll sit here all night if she has to. Even though I'm older, she's protective of me. She's always been the feistiest of the three of us.

"I got a scratch from his teeth…" Even to my own ears, it sounds pathetic. I can't say he bit me. "He hasn't gone mad. I promise you, Leah, it wasn't like that. Someone was sneaking up behind me, and he went to stop them, and I shoved my arm in the middle."

"Hmm." Leah rolls her eyes and the blood in my veins boils. How dare she insinuate he did it on purpose? Blake would never intentionally hurt me.

"Stop it. You don't know him," I snap, surging to my feet, and she raises an eyebrow at me. I rarely lose my temper. Leaning back on the sofa, she takes another long sip of her wine and watches me intently.

"Wow. The bond is already strong. If you're so grumpy, I bet he's an absolute delight. Lucky Max." I stick my tongue out at her as my phone buzzes in my hand. Welcoming the distraction from Leah and her little tests, I open the message and sigh.

"Matt," I say his name out loud as I text him back. He has a small farm nearby and apparently has a sick foal. With Doc getting some much-needed sleep, I'll have to go take a look.

"Matt. As in *'we went on a couple of dates, cute, but it just kind of went nowhere'*? That Matt?"

Ignoring her, I fire off another message to him, informing him I'm on my way. With a groan, I shove my phone away. I was really looking forward to dinner.

"I have to go. Hopefully, I'll be back soon. Max is bringing food... I'm sorry, Leah. I didn't mean to drag you up here and then run off."

Moving to the door, I pull on a pair of knee-high riding boots and shrug on a warm jacket. It's almost dark outside and the evenings are getting cooler. Leah hesitates for a second before launching herself off the couch.

"Wait for me!"

"What? Leah... you'll be bored out of your mind," I warn, but she shakes her head vigorously. Reaching past me, she steals another thick coat and puts it on before shoving a woolly hat down low over my eyes.

"I really don't think I will. Come on. You're tired. I'll keep you awake while you drive and you can put me to work." Her expression is all innocence, but Leah loves mischief. I bet she's just tagging along to get a good look at my *kind of* ex.

Sighing loudly, I let her follow me outside, knowing there's absolutely no point in arguing. I don't have the time or energy and I'm tired.

She's practically bouncing with giddiness as she hops up into the passenger seat beside me. When she puts the radio on full blast, I let out an exasperated groan, but smile despite myself. Maybe this is a good idea. It'll be nice to have some company and she can drive home.

BLAKE

Sweat drips down my forehead into my eyes, stinging, and I push myself harder. The branches whip at my bare chest as I run in my human form, afraid to give my wolf control. He's almost feral, furious with me for pushing away our mate and making her leave. But he's the one that bit her, so I'm not exactly thrilled with him either. Our trust in each other hangs by a thread. He's a formidable beast. I'm no longer certain that if I shift and let him have control he'll give it back. He doesn't trust me to complete the mating bond and claim our mate, so he'll try to take charge. It's a dangerous impasse.

"Fuck!" I roar, punching a tree beside me and splitting open the skin on my knuckles. Numb, I watch as the ruby-red blood drips down my fingers onto the forest floor. A breeze tickles the cool skin on the back of my neck, and I go still. Tensing, I glance around me, hackles raised.

"I know you're there. Come out, Tyson. Or are you too much of a coward? Are you watching and waiting for the fucking madness to do your job for you?!" I yell, spinning around in a circle and taking a deep breath. To anyone who might witness my odd behaviour, I would definitely appear to be losing it, but on this, I'm certain.

He's here.

The lights dancing in the periphery of my vision, the trembling in my hands, and the palpitations that make it impossible to sleep are all the madness. Not this. I know this is real. Tyson is still alive. What he wants after all this time is another matter.

Despite my fear that I might never regain control of my body, I can't hold back my shift any longer. Rage drives my wolf, pulsing through our veins like hot lava. Anger at Tyson. Anger at the goddess for not giving us Zoe sooner. And anger that I'm not asshole enough to mark her without considering what that might do to the rest of her life.

I shake out my thick grey fur. Damn, it feels good to run free. We tear through the forest, searching, tracking, and chasing. We can sense Tyson lurking, but again, can't find any trace. There's no sign of him. How the hell is he doing it?

We come to a stream and drink our fill from the fresh, babbling mountain creek. The water is ice cold, and my heart rate settles as I pause, flopping down on the soft grass in the last rays of the evening sun. As it warms my body, this is the most peaceful I've felt since returning from Zoe's. Allowing myself this moment of rest before I head back, I can't help but reach out to

Zoe via the bond. I attempt to convince myself it's because I want to make sure she's okay, but deep down, I know it's because I'm not. Missing her already, I realise I didn't think this through at all.

She's in good spirits and, for some reason, that makes me feel worse. I imagine her laughing and I long to be with her, to be the one making her smile instead of making her sad.

What the hell am I doing here? I feel better when I'm with her. While I still have time, I should spend all of it with her.

Jumping to my feet, I race back to the packhouse for a quick shower and change, bursting with excitement now that I've decided how ridiculous being apart is.

Driving down her lane, I'm so excited to see her I can barely contain myself. As I park, Max pulls in behind me, stepping out with two brown paper bags filled with a variety of takeaway foods. Excellent, I'm starving. But then I glance back towards the house and register that Zoe's Land Rover is gone. She's not with Max. She's not home. *Where is she?*

Max realises this at the same time and strides toward the front door, pushing down the handle and wincing when no lock stops him from pushing it wide open. Ignoring the irritation I feel at the fact she left her house completely unlocked less than a week after the attempted robbery, I barge past him. Leah's scent here is recent, but she's gone, too. At least Zoe's not alone. Marching to the kitchen table, I snatch up the note left there, and my heart seizes. I ball it up in my fist and pinch the bridge of my nose to calm my raging temper.

GONE ON A CALL OUT TO MATT JACOBS'. BACK SOON X

CHAPTER 32

ZOE

Matt chats away as I pack my bag and stand to leave, putting a hand against the rough wooden rail beside me to keep my balance. The foal is fine, but very nervous, and it has made me feel off my game. I'm still feeling a bit light-headed. I must be coming down with something. Peeking over the side of the stall, I spot my sister. Leah's still sitting on a hay bale, petting Matt's old sheepdog. She was no help at all. Why did she bother to come?

"Thanks again for coming out, Zoe. I'm way behind on chores. Is it okay if I head out?" Matt asks, lifting his hat and wiping his forehead with the back of his hand. His smile is warm and friendly and I'm reminded of what a genuinely nice guy he is. He'll make someone a great husband.

"Of course. I'll call you in the morning to see how the foal is doing."

He tips his hat to me and pushes the stall door open before slipping through. My heart jumps into my throat when I hear Leah's laughter and a deep rumble that I would recognise anywhere. Without thinking, I run out, swinging around a post, just so excited to see him.

Blake stands next to me as he stops to greet Matt, apologising for turning up unannounced. Impeccable manners, as always.

Max lingers at the door, hands shoved deep in his pockets, ever vigilant. There's no mistaking his anxious expression. He's watching Blake's every move.

"Blake, good to see you again," Matt says affably, rubbing his hands on his jeans before offering Blake one for a handshake. "I was at Earl's yesterday. It was Mandy's last day. It's a good thing you did. She deserves a break."

What's that about? Blake nods in agreement, and Matt tilts his head, clearly wondering why he's not more eager to discuss his good deed further. Then the penny seems to drop.

"Sorry, did I ruin date night?"

"No," I quickly assert, giving Blake a pointed look. Matt's eyes dance with amusement. Blake clenches his jaw and takes a deep breath. As excited as I am to see him, I want to know what the hell he's doing here on someone else's property? Judging by the way he's behaving, he hasn't come to help me.

"No, I wanted to surprise her," Blake explains with a wink, but it's a lie. He's not fooling me. He's checking up on me. When he meets my gaze, I see the jealousy and possessiveness there. I've missed him. I long to go to him and touch him, to wrap myself around him and breathe him in, but this isn't right. We need boundaries.

Matt raises his eyebrows, picking up on the tension, but says nothing. He obviously thinks that it's strange as well that Blake would turn up at his place unexpectedly. Leah is the only one who looks completely unsurprised. Her head swivels back and forth, taking in all the unspoken interactions with an enraptured smile on her face. All she's missing is a bowl of popcorn.

"Well, we're done. She's all yours again." Matt gives a casual wave over his shoulder as he strides out, a busy man with work to do and no time for drama.

"Yes, she is," Blake whispers, not directed at Matt but straight at me. My pussy clenches at the possessive tone in his voice. Matt's sheepdog bolts from his spot at Leah's feet and follows closely at his owner's heels, keen to escape these dominant predators.

"Leah, come on," Max says, bending down to offer her a hand. Leah pouts and frowns, reluctant to miss whatever fireworks are coming.

"Aw! It's about to get good," she sulks, pushing to her feet.

"I'm sure you'll get the blow-by-blow tomorrow. Come on, I'll take you home. I'm sure Rex is looking for you anyway."

She blows me a kiss before following Max to the open barn door. Blake tosses the keys to Max without a word and continues to stare at me. I glare right back at him.

"How's Matt?"

"Great," I sneer with forced sweetness. Who does he think he is to come here and act all possessive when he tossed me out of his home just this morning? Not to mention, he's living under the same roof as a woman who's clearly madly in love with him.

He stalks forward and my bravado falters as I'm forced to walk backward to maintain some distance between us. God, he looks so sexy when he's all brooding and pissed off. I have to remind myself that I'm angry, not turned on.

"This is my job, Blake. I get calls in the middle of the night all the time. You can't follow me around checking up on me. Where is the trust?"

"I trust you. I don't trust him. He's the one who called his ex, my unmarked mate, out to his house late at night." His chest rises and falls, his voice deathly calm. But his pupils are normal. I don't see any tremors. This isn't Moon madness. This is jealousy, plain and simple.

"He's the client who called his veterinarian out to his farm, Blake. It's not the same thing."

"Same thing to me. How do I know what his intentions are?"

"You don't, but you should know what mine are. If memory serves me correctly, it was you who put an end to my visit. If you can't trust me, if you can't handle me doing a job I love, that, yes, sometimes involves long hours and working with a lot of men, then this will not work."

I say the words in a much more confident tone than I feel, but this is important. He looks like his head is going to explode if I even dare to suggest we wouldn't be deliriously happy together. As much as I love his dominance in the bedroom, I can't be with a man who tries to control my life.

"Perhaps you'd prefer a mate who's happy to stay home and look after the house." I hold my breath as I watch him closely, attempting to gauge his reaction. As much as I hate to admit it, Jenna's comment about Hayley has stuck in my head. Maybe deep down he'd like a mate who's as good at networking and building relationships as my sister.

Something flashes in his eyes that looks suspiciously like guilt. I narrow my eyes at him and study him closely. He takes too long to answer and I curse. We never really talked about what a future would look like. Is he really like all the other men who thought I'd quit my job once they put a ring on my finger?

"No! No, Zoe, stop. That's not what I want."

"But you imagined you'd have a mate who would be the perfect hostess. Who'd be happy to plan parties and travel everywhere with you..."

Again, he hesitates, as if he's debating whether to tell me something.

"Maybe. I won't apologise for liking the idea of you working alongside me. Of coming with me on business trips, so we're never apart for even one night. It's much more appealing than tracking you down and finding you in stinking barns with strange men."

Oh no he didn't.

I'm sure flames are shooting out of my eyes. I can't even describe the white-hot fury licking along my skin and coursing through my veins.

How dare he?

For a second, I think I see a flicker of amusement on his face. Is he just trying to provoke me? Well, it's working.

I react without thinking. It's only when I see the handful of manure that I've thrown at Blake smack him right in the middle of his pristine white cotton shirt that I realise what I've done. It hits with a wet splat before rolling off his chest and landing on one of his shoes. His gaze drops slowly, first to the greenish-brown stain on his shirt, then to the pile of manure on his shoe, then back to me.

"Mature," he grits out, his fists clenched at his side. Something tells me that in all his years as Alpha, no one has dared to throw anything at him, let alone a ball of shit.

"Manure, actually," I retort, with a cheeky grin, because apparently, I'm not in enough trouble already. His expression is completely blank and my heart pounds in my chest as a wicked grin appears on his lips. It's unnerving. I swallow hard as he raises his eyebrows. Oh, shit.

"What do you think you're doing, angel?" he asks. I'm completely confused. His voice is soft, but there's no doubt he's wound up like a coiled spring.

"What do you mean?" I ask tentatively, regretting my impulsiveness and backing away toward the door at the back of the barn. Perhaps I've gone too far. I feel the weight of my keys in my pocket as I consider my options here. I can't hide from him, but if I can get enough of a head start, I might be able to make it to the Land Rover before him.

He never takes his gaze from my face, but I blink when his eyes drop to my lips, which I lick involuntarily. His hand twitches at his side and excitement rushes through my body, my core aching in anticipation of the punishment I know is coming.

"What are you doing still standing there, Zoe? *Run.*"

CHAPTER 33

BLAKE

I grin as Zoe turns and bolts for the back of the barn. A human can never truly understand the thrill of the chase for an apex predator like me. Her wavy curls bounce as she runs, laughing as she races away from me, knowing she has no chance of escaping. In the interests of fairness, I wait a few seconds before letting out a menacing growl. As I expect, she shrieks and glances behind her to see how close I am. When she sees I haven't moved, she looks disappointed. That's all the confirmation I need to know she wants to be chased. She wants me to catch her and punish her. And show her I really do want to make her mine.

Ever the gentleman, her wish is my command.

Adrenaline pumps through my veins as I take off after Zoe, keeping my pace to a slow jog. I force myself to remain in control as she entices me to chase after her. I can hear her footsteps and light panting as she runs. My instincts scream at me to catch her and sink my elongated canines into that soft, pretty neck of hers. But that's not going to happen in a dusty old barn. The cabin I use as my retreat is nearby. I want to take her there and show it to her, because it's my sanctuary. I hope she loves it as much as I do.

Hopefully, once I've reminded her exactly who she belongs to, she'll still be willing to come with me.

"Crap," she mutters to herself and I grin. She's trapped and she knows it.

As I round the corner, she backs away, her hands spread out wide, her gaze darting around, looking for a way to get past me. It's not going to happen. I let out a victorious chuckle as a pink blush spreads across her pretty cheeks. Zoe pulls her plump lower lip between her teeth as that amazing brain of hers works overtime, trying to find a way out of her predicament. My rock-hard cock stands at the ready and twitches as I long to be the one to suck her lip and kiss her sensual mouth again. The little temptress has no idea what she's doing to me.

"Finders keepers," I growl and her eyes sparkle with excitement. The scent of her arousal is thick in the air. I can taste it. She wants me as much as I want her, even if she is still angry with me. The bond is already so strong that I swear I can feel her desire inside me, fueling my own.

But I won't be too complacent. I know my girl is a fighter and won't give up easily. Judging by the state of my shirt, she has no problem playing dirty. She pulls off her gloves, rolling them together inside out, and shoves them into the pocket of her dark green wax jacket. It's as if she's getting ready to tussle with me. I have no problem taking a tumble in the hay with her.

"I'm not going to give up my job," she declares, a stubborn set to her jaw. I know without being told that this is her list of demands. Listening with keen interest, I pay attention to what she wants for this to become a permanent thing. She thinks she's negotiating when, in fact, I'll do anything she asks of me. She's the one with all the bargaining power here.

"I would never ask you to do that," I counter, easing slowly and quietly closer, like the predator I am. "I love that you have your own business and I know you've worked hard for it. I'm proud of you."

I mean every word. Would life be easier if she stayed in the packhouse and was available to travel with me? Yes, it would. Would it fulfill her? No. And she wouldn't be Zoe if she wasn't doing something she's passionate about. There's no quicker way to kill a relationship than with resentment. Look at Tyson and me. We were as thick as thieves before he realised my father was his too, but he would never treat him that way.

"And I don't want to go to endless boring parties and dinners. With the hours I work, I wouldn't be able to, anyway."

I can barely tolerate most of them myself, and now that I'm settled in my High Alpha role, I can probably afford to miss a few of them.

"Fine. Max needs to find himself a woman, anyway. He can go."

She stifles a smile and continues to add more requests.

"I want you to let me investigate what's going on with you."

As I start to speak, she holds up her hand to cut me off.

"You say it's Moon madness, but I'm not convinced. You're completely fine sometimes, but then off your rocker at others. There's no in-between. When you're here, you have no problems. And all your symptoms are physiological, not psychological. Blake, this is what I do. Let me try."

I nod because after hearing the anguish in her voice, there is no way I can deny her.

"And last, but not least..." she hesitates, reluctant to say what's on her mind. I decide to put her out of her misery and give her the thing she feels bad for asking of me.

"Mandy is going to replace Jenna in running the packhouse. If she can help run a bar and a diner, she can run my packhouse in her sleep."

Relief washes over Zoe's expression and I could kick myself for not seeing it sooner. Jenna had been nasty to her and obviously had an ulterior motive for being my friend all these years. Zoe must have picked up on it. "Actually, Jenna's moving out as we speak."

"What happened?" She leans back against a barrel and rests her hands on her thighs, scratching nervously at some mud on her jeans.

"Nothing happened. She just wanted something she can't have." Something no one else can have. Zoe is it for me. "And no one disrespects my Luna. I won't tolerate it."

"Thank you."

Her thanks are genuine and I nod. It's what any mate would do.

"This isn't going to be easy, Zoe," I warn, referring to both my life as a shifter — a powerful one at that — and my illness, which is a completely unknown entity. It could get worse. It could get better. We just don't know.

She nods, accepting all of me with that one simple movement. My heart soars as we stare at each other and an understanding passes between us. This is it. With no more obstacles, we both know what comes next.

Zoe's lips move, but her voice is so soft, I strain to hear it. When I step forward to listen, I'm completely caught off guard as she ducks under my outstretched arm, sliding across the dirt floor before scrambling to her feet.

She barely makes it two steps, her giggling slowing her down, before I grab her by the waist and toss her over my shoulder. Clutching her ass with one hand to keep her in place as I stride out of the barn, I run the other up her leg to the top of her thigh, teasing her lightly through the stiff denim.

"Naughty girl," I murmur and she laughs, pinching my backside as I walk. I give her a gentle slap on the bum and grin, loving her playfulness.

"Blake, I..." Zoe moans and at first, I think it's in frustration because she wants my touch. The urge to mark her right now is overwhelming. My wolf doesn't understand the need to go somewhere private and make it special.

"Blake, I feel... I feel." But she doesn't finish her sentence before she slumps and goes limp against me. It takes me a moment to realise she's fainted. Panic as I've never felt before surges through me as I slip her off my shoulder and cradle her in my arms, tight against my chest and rush outside to her SUV.

Setting her carefully into the passenger seat, I brush her hair off her face and buckle her in.

"Zoe. Zoe?" I repeat and she groans, her eyes rolling in the back of her head as she struggles to focus.

Blake: Max, Zoe's not well. She passed out.

Max: Shit. She wasn't feeling well earlier. I made her go to bed, but she still looked pale.

Blake: What do I do?

Max: I don't think she's eaten much. Get her into bed, give her some food and water, if she can stomach it, and get a doctor to come to check her out. It's probably just exhaustion and stress.

Guilt floods me. She's been through hell in the past week and I certainly haven't helped. I should have taken better care of her.

Blake: I'm taking her to the cabin. I'll keep you posted.

Pressing a hand to her head, I check her temperature. She's not feverish. If anything, she feels a little cold to me. I pull a blanket off the back seat and tuck it around her, taking her keys from her pocket at the same time. I mind-link our pack doctor and ask him to come to the cabin as quickly as he can. He can hear the fear in my voice and he promises to leave immediately.

It's only a short drive, thankfully, and by the time we get to the cabin, Zoe's a little more coherent, but still looks pale, although she reassures me she's fine. My nerves won't recover until the doctor looks her over and tells me everything is alright. I hold her close as I carry her inside, opening the door with the thumbprint scanner and kicking it shut behind me.

"This place is beautiful," she whispers, resting her head on my shoulder. Trying my best not to jostle her, I take her straight to the main bedroom and sit her on the edge of the bed. She's so weak she has to brace an arm on the mattress to stop herself from slumping over. Stripping off her mucky clothes, I press a kiss on her forehead as I tuck her under the covers. I run to the kitchen briefly, returning in a few moments with something for her to eat and drink. She silently complies, drinking deeply as I press a glass of water to her lips, but only takes two measly bites of a banana before pushing it away.

"I just need to sleep, Blake. I'll be alright." Forcing myself to appear calm, I nod and smile, but her reassurances mean nothing to me. Not when I can sense exactly how terrible she feels through the bond. As she rolls over, something catches my eye and I grab her arm, lifting it carefully to inspect it. The puncture wounds on her arm look red and angry, with a spiderweb of dark lines stretching out across her hot skin.

"Zoe, this looks infected. Could this be the reason you feel so ill?" I ask and she glances at her arm, looking totally taken aback at how bad it looks.

"Maybe," she mumbles, losing the battle to keep her eyelids open.

Moving to the large windows, I absent-mindedly pull the blinds shut as I contact the doctor again. I ask him to bring some human antibiotics with him, explaining what I saw on her arm. My mind drifts to Sharon and the image of her rubbing something onto Zoe's skin. If she did this, if she hurt my mate with her magic and potions, I'll kill her with my bare hands.

Blake: Max, find Sharon. Ask her what the fuck she put on Zoe's skin.

Max: On it.

Pacing, I watch my mate toss and turn restlessly. Her skin looks clammy now, so I rush out to find some clothes, feeling completely helpless. She is my world. Nothing can happen to her. Just as I get back to the room, the door to the ensuite slams shut. I pace, and linger just outside the bathroom, reluctant to go in if she wants privacy. When she retches and vomits, I clutch handfuls of my hair, on the verge of pulling it out. I press my head against the door that I'm desperate to break down, pretending to be far more civilised than I feel.

"Zoe... Do you want me to come in? Can I get you anything?"

"*No!*" she yells with a groan. The toilet flushes, and I hear her moving about before she vomits once more. I can't stand it.

Forcing myself to stay on this side of the door and respect her wishes, I shove all the snacks I brought for her into my mouth. Something is seriously wrong with her and I'm freaking out, but I need to keep my emotions in check until we discover what's going on.

Suddenly, the door flings open and a wide-eyed, wild-looking Zoe stumbles out of the bathroom and races straight toward me on unsteady feet. I don't know what's going on as she knocks the bottle of water out of my hand before collapsing on the floor at my feet.

"Zoe!" I drop to my knees beside her and pull her into my arms. Her heart is racing dangerously fast, and she's trembling all over. She's rapidly declining right in front of my eyes, and I feel completely helpless. Goddess, I cannot lose her.

"The water... it's... *poisoned*..." she whispers, squeezing her eyes shut as pain racks her body. "How much did you drink?" We both glance at the bottle that's rolled to a stop against the bedside locker. Not a drop spills from the open top.

"All of it."

CHAPTER 34

BLAKE

Poison.

The instant Zoe says the word, I know she's right. As I look at her writhing on the floor, I know with devastating certainty that this is no stomach flu. If it's been making me sick, even with my accelerated healing and fast metabolism, then Zoe is in real trouble here.

There's only one person who could be responsible for this. Three people have access to the cabin: Jenna, Max, and me. This is my private sanctuary. Most of the pack doesn't even know it exists, let alone know where it is.

Jenna wants to be Luna. She made that perfectly clear. I never thought she'd go this far, but after her recent behaviour, I'm ashamed to admit I was naïve. And now my mate is paying the price.

With my age becoming a topic of conversation among the pack and the council, Jenna would have known what everyone, including me, would assume when I became unwell. Moon madness. Shifters rarely get sick. Especially an Alpha like me. What else could be wrong with me? Especially when the symptoms were so similar. Tremors. Elevated heart rate. Mood swings. No one would question it.

No wonder my health has deteriorated rapidly since meeting Zoe. Jenna may have been playing the long game initially, hoping I'd give in to the pressure to take a chosen mate. She would have been the obvious choice if not for the fact I was completely determined to find Zoe. I never would have settled. But she must have panicked when I brought Zoe home and concentrated on scaring her off by exacerbating my illness, making me seem like a lost cause. And then, when that didn't work, she tried to make her feel intimidated and unwelcome.

Little did she know she was messing with the wrong woman.

I scoop Zoe up and carry her to the massive bed, resting her head in my lap, attempting to use the calming presence of a mate to soothe her. She tosses her head and writhes on the rumpled sheets, moaning and struggling to focus. My wolf howls long and sorrowfully in my head. He can't bear to see her like this.

"Blake," she whispers through dry lips, her voice hoarse, her throat raw from vomiting. I lean in close to hear what she's trying to say, but as soon as I'm close enough, her hand darts out and she grabs my hair with remarkable strength, considering how sick she is. "What are you still doing here? Make yourself sick... vomit. You need to get it out of your system!"

"But —" She shoves me as hard as she can to get me moving.

"Go, Blake... *Please*." Her eyes are wide and watery as she begs me to leave her and take care of myself. Reluctantly, I nod and stand. My stomach clenches as cramps rip through my gut. I'm beginning to feel it. It seems wrong to leave her side for even a moment, but I won't be able to help her if I'm incapacitated, too. Cupping her face in my hands, I press a soft kiss to her lips. I'm about to step back and do as ordered when a faint creak from the front porch catches my attention. Pressing my forehead to Zoe's, I squeeze my eyes shut, trying to push down the crushing despair that washes over me before Zoe picks up on it.

"I love you, Zoe. Never forget that. I'm so sorry." I barely get the words out and a tear threatens to fall as I back away slowly. She blinks up at me, her pale grey eyes shimmery and wet. It takes all my willpower not to rush back to her side and comfort her.

"Blake. What are you doing? Come back. You need to empty your stomach," she pleads, frowning, and attempting to grab my arm as I back away from the bed. She realises I'm going in the wrong direction, heading for the hall instead of the bathroom.

"She's here, Zoe. I can't let her hurt you. I'm sorry, angel. Max is on his way. He'll know what to do."

ZOE

Every bone and muscle in my body aches. The effort of struggling to get to Blake has me exhausted and I collapse onto my side and curl up in a ball as pain radiates along my arms and legs. Even the slightest movement has my stomach churning.

Ice-cold dread washes over me as I realise what he's saying. Jenna is the one that poisoned him and now she's here. My mind screams at me to stop him from walking out the door, but my body won't cooperate or move. He hesitates at the door but never turns back around. Before I even hear his footsteps reach the bottom of the wooden stairs, I'm sobbing. Hauling myself to the edge of the bed, I drop to the floor and force myself to sit up. Even that requires a monumental effort.

Inching and sliding my way along the wooden floor, it takes all my strength and energy to get to the open doorway. Leaning against the jamb to rest, sweating heavily as I pant raggedly. Blake's deep baritone carries up the stairs, but my relief is short-lived. Hearing Jenna's saccharine voice making small talk with my mate — the man I know she loves — makes me feel sick to my stomach. As they move into the hallway, I can just make out the back of Blake's head while Jenna remains out of view.

"What was your plan here, Jenna? Kill me for not accepting your offer?" he asks. *What offer?* I wonder as red-hot possessiveness scorches its way through my body. Trying to suppress my emotions, which won't help anyone right now, I focus on Blake, who is swaying on his feet and clutching the sideboard to keep himself from falling over. From what I can tell through our bond, he doesn't feel as sick as he looks.

"Now why would I want that, darling?" she purrs, moving closer and placing a hand on his chest. His broad shoulders tense, but he doesn't pull away, still appearing unsteady and frail.

"I can't believe you're doing this, Jenna. I thought we were friends. You're hurting Zoe, too? She has nothing to do with this. Your problem is with me."

Jenna lets out a shrill, hysterical laugh, and I cringe. This woman is unhinged.

"She has everything to do with it, Blake. Don't you see? At first, I thought she was a threat. But now I see that this is an opportunity. You never would have marked me knowing she was out there somewhere. I can see that now. But if mating with me is the only way to save her, well, that's another story altogether. Isn't it?"

Jesus Christ. She's blackmailing him. "And once that pesky fated mate bond is gone forever, ours will take its place, and you'll realise just how perfect we would have been together all along."

Jenna holds up a syringe and a small vial, which I'm assuming she is suggesting contains an antidote for the poison I've ingested. Blake's head half turns in my direction and I know he is aware of my presence, listening.

"You'll give her that? Do I have your word?" he asks and I whimper. "Because if you don't, Jenna, I'll rip your head off. Mate or not."

Jenna looks terrified for a second before the smug expression is back on her pretty face. She knows she has him. Blake will do anything to save me, including destroying us.

"I promise." She winks and he snarls at her, low and menacing enough, despite his weakness, to still make the hairs on the back of my neck stand up. Jenna doesn't seem concerned, though. As a shifter, too, she's obviously confident that she can overpower him if he tries to attack her. He looks like a strong breeze would knock him over.

"Don't mistake this for willingness, Jenna," Blake warns. "I would do anything for the woman I love. You're gambling with your life here that the chosen mate bond will be enough to save you from me. Because right now, I can't imagine any scenario where I don't want to tear your heart out."

My chest feels as if it's being torn open at the thought of him with another woman. Touching her. Kissing her. It's excruciating. Blake's gaze lifts to mine and I can feel his heartbreak as strong as my own.

"Say goodbye, Zoe," Jenna calls out wickedly as she moves in close to him, pressing her body against his. That was purely for my torment and she has the nerve to laugh as Blake recoils from her touch.

"Let's go. I know just the spot where our wolves can *consummate* our arrangement without Max interrupting the fun."

Pressing my nails hard against the floor in rage, I'm about to scream obscenities at her when Blake shakes his head and tips his head toward the door just a fraction. He's trying to get her outside and away from me.

As soon as they cross the threshold, he slams the front door shut behind him, and she curses. The door handle rattles as she shakes it violently.

"Just in case you get any clever ideas about coming back to hurt my mate, I already had Max reconfigure the security to block your access," I overhear Blake explain, his voice sounding strong as he puts an end to any other plans she may have had for me. "So even if you get rid of me, you, or anyone else you have with you, can't hurt her."

My eyes well up again. This can't be happening. I can't let him go with her. Determination surges through me but when I try to stand, my aching limbs won't support me. I slump to the floor once again, stabbing pains causing me to twist and curl up, attempting to escape the agony.

I'm vaguely aware of slow, heavy footsteps approaching along the landing behind me. I can't move, can't summon the energy to turn around and look at Max even though I'm relieved he's here so fast. Blake's words echo in my mind once more.

Max will know what to do.

I need to tell Max what's going on, that he needs to look for Blake, not babysit me. I can't let him do this when the doctor will be here soon.

Rolling over, I lift my head a few inches off the floor and go to speak. But it's not Max who's squatting down beside me, hands dangling casually between his massive thighs. An eerily familiar face tilts to the side as he scrutinises me closely. My breath catches in my throat when he lifts his dark eyes to mine. The red line circling his iris is bright and startling. It doesn't feel like a good thing.

Despite his non-threatening body language, I can tell this man is a stone-cold killer. His aura is terrifying and every cell in my body is telling me to get away from this guy.

"Where on earth did Blake find you?" He's speaking to himself rather than to me as he brings a large hand up and trails a knuckle down my cheek. I suppress a shiver as I try to work out whether he's merely toying me with or actually being genuinely friendly.

"Tyson," I whisper, and he nods, looking apologetic that I am, in fact, correct. Sighing, he stands, hands on his hips, and surveys me, zoning in on the burning red rash spreading across my forearm at an alarming rate.

"How did you get in here? Have you been here the entire time?"

My brain hurts as I try to work out how he could have slipped past Blake. Did Jenna let him in?

"No. Blake just never removed my access. Suppose he never thought he needed to since I was dead."

He shrugs, extending a pale hand toward me and waiting patiently for me to take it, pretending I have a choice.

"Come on," he says almost cheerfully as he helps me to my feet and allows me to lean on him, taking my weight as we edge our way downstairs.

"Where are you taking me?" My voice comes out shaky as I try to pull away from him once we hit the bottom of the stairs. He holds me perfectly still as I tug and twist, a neutral look of complete calm and patience on his face.

"To get your mate back," Tyson answers like it's the most obvious thing in the world. As though there would be no reason to doubt his intentions after disappearing and letting everyone think he'd died, only to come back and stalk Blake, messing with his head.

"But why?" Afraid to hear the answer, I close my eyes and wait.

"Because Zoe, when I win my pack back from Blake's lying cheating clutches, and I will, I want it to be a fair fight. I don't want to just finish him off when he's already been weakened by someone else. Where would the fun be in that?"

CHAPTER 35

BLAKE

Jenna's holding the vial out at arm's length like it's a hand grenade, ready to explode at any second. My instincts are telling me that there is no antidote, and this is a ruse, but I'm happy to play along and put as much distance between her and my mate as I can. Zoe needs to be treated immediately with no disruptions from crazy she-wolves.

"Where are we going?" I ask, slurring my words, making myself sound weaker and more downtrodden than I feel. It doesn't come naturally to me. But I need to get her talking.

"The old hunting cabin." Jenna continues to march forward, pushing back a low-hanging branch and letting me pass. I nod. That's miles away from Zoe. Perfect. Because when I kill this bitch, I don't want Zoe to witness how much I'm going to enjoy it. Killing her won't be enough. My wolf is going to tear her to shreds.

"Anyone joining us there I should know about? Maybe Tyson?"

My voice is breezy, like I'm just asking who's joining us for brunch and not whether there are any others within my pack willing to commit treason against their Alpha and future Luna. Provided I have enough power left in me, I could force it out of her, using my alpha command to make her tell me what I want. But experience has shown me you catch more flies with honey. If forced, she'll tell me the bare minimum. The important information is often in the details.

"Tyson? Blake, Tyson's dead." Genuinely confused, she's looking at me with concern, her voice soft. Jenna was around back then. She knew how badly I took his death. The guilt I felt. "I shouldn't have given you so much in that water, but Zoe just wouldn't go away. I thought she'd get scared by your behaviour and leave. But even after you bit her, she came back for more."

Jenna shakes her head violently, almost like she can't believe her plan didn't work out how she wanted. She looks unhinged.

"She's my mate. Of course, she'd stick by me. I'd do the same for her." It's that simple. I was overthinking it before, but when it boils down to it, we're better together. "I know your heart was in the right place, Jenna. You've gone too far, but you can still stop this. Tell me what you gave us."

Jenna ignores my question and launches into a tirade.

"A human can't be your mate. She'd be a weakness, a liability to you, Blake. You need someone fearless, who can stand by your side and tackle your foes head-on."

"What foes, Jenna?" She stiffens. That was more than she planned to give away. And I'm not stupid enough to think she's done this for altruistic reasons. That might be what she had to use to convince herself so she could do it, but I think getting a permanent position as head of my household was number one on the list of priorities.

"There will always be people looking to steal your power. I would never let them," she mumbles before picking up the pace and driving us forward.

Power. It always comes back to the same thing. The council, Tyson, and Alpha Weston who longed to get the head alpha role. There's always someone waiting in the wings to see you fail. Maybe they did a little more than wait this time around. Max mind-links me to tell me the doc is almost there, and I'm nearly overcome with relief. Zoe is going to be okay.

As the old broken-down hunting cabin comes into view, I take a deep breath. Coming out here in less than peak health is a gigantic risk, but I couldn't stay at the cabin and risk drawing whomever else might be involved in this plan closer to Zoe. Groaning and gripping my side in pain, I follow slowly.

ZOE

Tyson supports my elbow, keeping me steady as I slowly descend the steps of Blake's porch. Slipping on the last one, I land on my ass with a thud, scraping the back of my ankle and banging my elbow. Shivering from head to toe and gritting my teeth against the pain, I attempt to push back to my feet, but the stabbing pains in my limbs force me back to sitting.

"Oh, for goddess' sake." Tyson stands hands on hips in front of me and looks up to the heavens as if my agony is a major inconvenience for him. The family resemblance is clear, but Tyson's skin has less of an olive tone and his pale lips are fuller. And the put-upon attitude is nothing like Blake's.

"Where is she taking him?" I pant, struggling to get in enough oxygen when my entire body is shuddering and my chest is tight. *And why is Blake following?*

It doesn't make sense.

"Does it matter? We'll never catch them if you don't get a move on." He frowns down at me disapprovingly. Dark, almost-black hair falling into those creepy, red-rimmed eyes, he points towards the ominous-looking trees creeping onto the edge of Blake's property.

Tyson seems to think this is a mind-over-matter type of situation, which it clearly is not. Assuming the poison was meant for Blake, the dose Jenna has been giving him is likely to be massive. Even though I only took a few sips from the water in his car, that's when I started to get unwell. Mentally, I kick myself for not putting it together sooner. Maybe I never would have if that drink in the cabin wasn't so strong. When it instantly made me vomit, my suspicions were raised.

Sighing, Tyson bends his back and hefts me over his shoulder like a bag of coal. Just as tall as Blake, he's less bulky but every bit as strong. He makes it seem easy.

"This is exactly why alphas aren't supposed to be mated to weak little humans. At least Blake had the good sense to turn you. Didn't think he had it in him," Tyson sneers, adjusting my weight and causing every joint in my body to jar. I cry out and almost forget what he just said.

But then a niggle starts somewhere in the back of my mind, and I repay his last words. *Blake had the good sense to turn you.*

"What?" I whisper. Tyson huffs out a laugh.

"Mr. Boy Scout didn't tell you? Sounds about right."

Unceremoniously, he dumps me on the ground. My back hits the dirt hard and knocks the wind out of me. Aware he's done it to reinforce the fact that I'm weak and he is strong, I refuse to stay down. He raises an eyebrow as I glare defiantly at him and roll onto my hands and knees.

I'm vaguely aware of the cold soil between my fingers and the pine needles sticking to my hands. A cool breeze feels wonderful against my overheating skin. I don't get to enjoy it for long as my foggy brain once again forces me back to reality.

"Didn't tell me what?" I groan as pain so awful wracks my body that it has my back arching and cracking. Tyson kneels in the muck beside me and lowers his big body down so he's on all fours beside me. Leaning his face close to mine, I shrink back as an evil grin spreads across his nearly handsome face.

"Interesting. So, it wasn't Blake then." For a moment, he regards me with pity, reaching out to push a lock of my hair back behind my ear. "I hate to break it to you, *angel*, but you're about to turn into a wolf." He spits out Blake's pet name for me like it's a curse word and then laughs cruelly when he sees my horrified expression.

"Not... possible..." I grit out, shaking my head emphatically. He's just messing with me, trying to scare me. As if I could be any more scared than I already am. Tyson scoffs and the red in his eyes becomes even more prominent. Shrinking away from him, I gasp when his icy fingers grip my chin like a vise and he moves closer, so our lips are only centimetres apart.

"And it's going to hurt like hell. You can feel it already, Zoe, can't you? The stretching, the cracking." Staring into his eyes, I can't move. Despite his good looks, he's terrifying. But I can't argue with him. The pains are in my bone, and my body is twisting and contorting with each shudder that wracks my body. I've already thrown up whatever was in my stomach. Why am I in so much agony? What did she give me that is making every joint scream?

Whatever he sees in my eyes makes him move back, giving me room to breathe again. When he runs his tongue over his teeth, I glimpse razor-sharp canines. I blink and swallow hard. His gaze is laser-focused as he waits, watching me scramble to put together the information in my brain.

"What are you?" My voice is weak and wobbly, primal fear taking over as I finally realise just exactly who I've let lead me into the woods. Away from Max and the doctor, who must be near the cabin by now.

"Oh angel, I wouldn't worry about what I am so much as what you're about to be." He strokes a hand over my hair, along my shoulders, and leaves it resting on my lower back. "We need to hurry this along. It's too soon for me to make a public appearance, but someone needs to help that brother of mine."

With a cruel smirk dancing upon his lips, he rocks back on his heels and into a squat beside me. I'm still shaking my head, refusing to believe this could be true when Tyson tilts his head to one side and smirks.

"Shift!"

CHAPTER 36

ZOE

Tyson never breaks eye contact as he gently rests a hand on my shoulder and waits.

And waits some more.

Finally, he sits back on his heels, a confounded expression on his face as his order doesn't have the desired effect. If I wasn't in so much pain, it might be funny.

"You two really are brothers. Don't try to pull that crap on me," I huff, shrugging away his touch as his suspicion turns to amusement. His lip twitches in an almost smile.

"Now I get it." Tyson whistles, looking impressed. Rather than looking at me with the same pity and borderline disdain he had before, he's curious now. I don't appreciate the implication that only now does he deem me good enough to be fated to a wolf like Blake.

"Alpha commands don't work on you," he states incredulously.

"Apparently not."

Squinting at me, he taps his index finger against his lower lip as he considers me. His assessing gaze rakes over me from head to toe, and I feel intensely uncomfortable. Tyson's personality keeps switching from almost friendly to predatory, and it's making my head spin. I don't know what to make of him.

"Is it because you're human or because of your wolf DNA?" he ponders out loud and I cough, sputtering, and choking in surprise at his words. He glances at me sideways, taking in my reaction, and narrows his eyes further.

"What wolf DNA? Why do you think I can shift?"

"You will be able to soon, angel. That little love bite Blake gave you started it. Wolves are told that it's not possible for a human to be changed, but that's not strictly true. It's rare, but it can happen. Not usually this fast, though."

Tyson is loving the fact that he's getting to explain this to me. That he perhaps knows something Blake doesn't.

"Have you met any witches lately, Zoe? Did you get any treatment for that bite?" His eyes dance as his meaning hits home with me and I groan. My misery and confusion are clearly entertaining for him.

"*Sharon.*"

The name tumbles from my lips as I slump onto my side and tuck my knees up to my chest. He chuckles as I curse, recalling how much interest she paid to my injury. I thought she was being nice to me. Looks like I was too naïve. Telling him who it was might not be the right thing, but if she played any part in making me feel this awful, she can deal with the consequences.

"Maybe she didn't and you're wrong. It could just be the poison."

He stops and stares at me, eyebrow raised as if to say, *are you really that stupid?* Even I don't really believe that. She zeroed in on the bite immediately and insisted on applying her ointment.

What did she do to me?

Shaking his head absentmindedly, still tapping that finger against his lip, he pushes to his feet and stalks away, considering something. Pacing back and forth on the far side of the clearing, he's not in any great rush to help me or go after Blake, or maybe he doesn't really care.

"Blake bit you in wolf form. The great Alpha of all Alphas." His voice is mocking, dripping in disgust. How much he despises his step-brother comes through loud and clear. "For it to work, you needed to be his mate and have a powerful wolf somewhere in your lineage. The genes were latent, but his bite has awakened them, and Sharon has sped the process up for some reason."

Nodding to himself as he pieces it all together, he mulls this over in his head, circling me and then squatting again to examine me like I'm a fascinating science experiment. It's unnerving.

I squeal when his hand darts out and snatches my leg. He's terrifyingly fast. Watching in horror, I try to kick my foot free as he swipes a thumb over my cut ankle and raises it to his lips. Pausing to make sure I'm watching what he's doing, Tyson angles his thumb toward me so I can see the streak of bright red blood on the pad before he pushes it into his mouth.

Tyson's eyes drift shut, and I freeze, my heart pounding so hard that I can hear my pulse in my ears. A sensual moan comes from deep within his chest and he tilts his head to the side, sighing in pleasure as he savours the taste.

When his eyelids finally open, the red in them has expanded, and darker shadows have formed underneath, making his eyes look sunken. A chill runs through me as he continues to look at me like I'm a meal instead of a person. Tyson has gone from a scary man to a monster in a heartbeat. My suspicions were correct.

"You're a vampire," I whisper, horrified, scrambling back on my ass to put some more distance between us. He stands again and moves at an alarming speed until he looms over me.

"Not *just* a vampire, angel. A hybrid. The best of both worlds." His cocky smirk falters for a second, and he peers over my shoulder and stares into the distance. His attention is being pulled back in the direction we came. Back towards the cabin.

What can he hear or see that I can't? Is help coming?

Sharp white fangs extend from under his top lip when he turns to face me again. Inhaling deeply, and sighing in satisfaction, his broad chest rises and falls. He looks as though he's struggling to maintain control.

"What are you doing, Tyson?"

My body is trembling, adrenaline coursing through my veins as my fear ratchets up to another level. Frozen to the spot, I'm unable to bring myself to move or run. I wouldn't stand a chance even if I could.

"We've wasted enough time. If you want Blake back, I'm going to have to do this the hard way. Sorry, Zoe."

He definitely doesn't look sorry. In fact, he looks like he's having fun. Once again I scream as a cold white hand grips my wrist so hard I'm afraid it will snap. Pulling and twisting my arm to escape his clutches does nothing.

Tyson drags me to him easily, his other hand reaching out to brush my hair back from my shoulder as he pins me against his body. As my panic rises, something else stirs deep within me. Blake is in danger and I need to get to him. He saved me. I can't just roll over and let his monster stop me from getting to my mate.

With a roar, I stop trying to pull away and escape, and lunge at him instead as rage erupts from me. I squeeze my eyes shut and lash out blindly. It's only as my teeth sink into his arm and I dig my back feet into the ground to get enough leverage to topple him to the ground that I realise something weird is going on.

Leaping back, I dance in circles and look down.

White fur. Paws. Claws. Tail. *Oh, God.*

"Shh, Zoe, it's ok."

Tyson falls to his knees in the dirt, hands extended, palms up. A growl fills the air as I turn my attention back to him. Then I realise with a fright that it came from me. My shout of surprise comes out as a yelp and Tyson laughs, his threatening demeanour completely disappearing once again. Edging backward, I make sure my back is to a tree and I can keep him directly in front of me as I drop to sitting and try to absorb what is going on. At least I'm not in pain anymore.

Everything is sharper. My vision, my sense of smell, my hearing. It's overwhelming. I shake my head to escape the barrage of new information bombarding my brain.

"Zoe, are you okay? I didn't want to scare you, but I needed to trigger your shift. Fear seemed like the quickest way."

If he thinks I'm going to forgive him for making me fear for my life that easily, he has another thing coming. I snarl at him and he smiles at me with affection.

"Good girl."

There's only one person I want calling me a good girl, Blake. I need to get to him. Jumping to my feet, I press my nose to the cold ground and sniff. I know where he has gone. His delicious scent floods every cell in my body as I inhale.

"That's it, Zoe. Use your senses. Find him."

I ignore Tyson as I follow Blake's trail, tracking him further into the dense forest and away from the clearing. Tyson doesn't follow me, but that's fine. I'll find my mate all by myself. Jenna's scent irritates my nose and my hackles raise in response. Speeding up to a jog, I dart around trees and over roots and branches as I get more confident sticking to the trail.

Instinct completely takes over as I single-mindedly search for my partner. An all-encompassing need to be by his side and make sure he's safe consumes me. I might not understand how to be a wolf or how I ended up like this, but I'll figure it out once I have my mate back. And I will. No matter what I need to do.

That bitch doesn't know who she's messing with.

CHAPTER 37

BLAKE

As we near the cabin, I hang back, scouting out the immediate surroundings for any out-of-place scents or disturbances. The woods are silent. The smaller animals and birds have the sense to leave the area. They steer clear and go into hiding, knowing that something dangerous is in their presence.

The effect of the drugs on me is getting stronger. My legs feel weak and I'm sweating, despite the shivers wracking my body. Zoe's symptoms were instant. I've likely built up a tolerance if this has been going on for months, but this is the worst I've felt.

Stopping, I look up at the sky above and the way the branches overhead sway in the gentle breeze. Feeling detached from my body, I stare, just thinking about how much I love this land. This territory has been my home my entire life. When I was a child, I spent my days roaming, often with Tyson, learning every path, rock, and tree. Every hiding place and each swimming spot. I knew it like the back of my hand.

As a teenager, after my mother was killed, I stayed closer to home. Everyone felt a little less safe in the far corners of our land. We all stayed near the packhouse and other wolves. Dad struggled in the aftermath of her loss and continued to get worse as time went on. In hindsight, I think he suspected Tyson's mother might have been his fated mate and felt guilty about straying when he realised she wasn't. Tyson probably bore the brunt of that; a living, breathing reminder of how Dad had hurt the woman that he loved before she died over some misguided belief.

More and more of the pack responsibilities unofficially fell on my shoulders when he couldn't cope at all. Until, eventually, I couldn't ignore his descent into madness any longer and had to take the pack from him by force. The guilt was indescribable and I never thought I'd experience anything like that again.

Until today.

Thinking Zoe might be on death's doorstep because of me is tearing me apart. Stalling for time, I'm praying I'll get the reassurance from Max that she's getting treated before I deal with Jenna and her co-conspirator. My prayers don't get answered.

Max: She's not here, Blake. We're tracking her, but she left the cabin. She's following you.

Goddamn it, Zoe. Inwardly, I curse her stubbornness, but hope it's a good sign. If she's moving, she may not be as bad as I thought she was. But unease trickles down my spine. How would she even know where to go?

Max: She's not alone, Blake. How or who, I don't know. I can't pick up any other scents, but there are definitely two people on the move. I'll find her, I promise you.

Shifting my attention back to Jenna, my aching brain is spinning. My plan had been to come here to see whether Jenna's partner in crime would make an appearance. To keep them away from Zoe and kill them if I can for what they've put her through. Simple. Now, though, I don't care about revenge. All I care about is making sure Zoe is safe. If by leaving her I've made things worse, I'll never forgive myself.

Jenna turns, sensing a shift in my mood.

"Keep the antidote. It's bullshit anyway, isn't it?" I ask, and she nods weakly. "I'm leaving."

Without knowing what intentions the person with Zoe has, I

can't be here, away from her. I thought she was safe inside the cabin, with help on the way. I wanted to draw the danger away from her, not leave her exposed. This changes everything.

"You can't," she cries out. "Blake, you can't. He'll kill me." Her voice drops to a whisper, and I grit my teeth to stop myself from shouting at her.

"And why should I care, Jenna? You almost killed my mate. You almost killed me. It's no less than you deserve."

"He promised I would get to have you if I did what I was told. That was our deal. I'd be yours and you'd be mine. That's all I've ever wanted. I did it because I love you, Blake."

She comes close and tries to grip my hand, but I pull away. Her touch repulses me. She's blaming someone else and taking no responsibility for her actions.

"Then when the time came, I'd help him. To weaken you, so he could take the pack."

"Enough!" I roar and her mouth slams shut. I can't bear to listen to another word from her traitorous lips.

Tyson. He must be with Zoe right now. That's why Max can't scent him.

Whatever problem my stepbrother has with me, I can't believe my own flesh and blood would hurt my mate. Growing up, I considered him my best friend. We played together, lived together. I loved him and mourned him. This is unforgivable.

Grabbing Jenna by the arm, I drag her to the cabin and fling her in the door. There's nothing but a cot bed and a small stove in the sparsely decorated one-roomed building. Glancing around, I spot a length of rope hanging on a hook on the wall. She clearly thought I'd be in worse shape and Zoe's presence has thrown a spanner in the works.

My head is buzzing with an impending migraine and there's a rushing noise in my ears that's disorientating. I'm dizzy, weak, and pissed off, and I just need to get out of here. Zoe is my priority. Dealing with Jenna can wait.

"Sit."

Jenna's ass hits the bed instantly and her pale eyes follow me as I reach for the rope. Impatient to get out of here, I'm completely focused on tying Jenna up. Max can come back and get her later. I never want to look at her again. I should have banished her when she suggested we get together before. My hand wraps around the coiled length and pain shoots up my arm, sending me to the floor. I fling it away from me, scorching skin coming away with it, and glance down at the burning skin on my palm.

What the hell?

It's been soaked in wolfsbane. Jenna had a backup plan, after all. Before I can get back to my feet, Jenna runs out the door and slams it shut behind her.

"Jenna, open this door." My powers are weak, but she still has to obey my command.

"I can't, Blake." She's crying on the other side of the wooded barrier. "You should have just listened. If you just marked me, then you and Zoe would be safe."

Looking down, I realise there's no handle on the door. I can't get out. There are no windows and this is the only entrance.

"Oh goddess, he's here," she whimpers, and I hear her footsteps backing away from the door, still sniffling and sobbing.

"I didn't take you for a coward, Tyson. Not willing to face me in a proper fight? You want *your* pack back? Prove you're man enough to deserve it."

Throwing myself at the door, ramming it as hard as I can with my shoulder again, and again, in my drastically weakened condition. I'm desperate to get to my mate. I can't scent her outside. But if Tyson's here, he must have brought Zoe with him.

"I've met my mate, Tyson. If you'd come back and spoken to me like a man, instead of skulking around, I might have given it to you and retired to the beach somewhere."

I wouldn't have, but right now, I would do anything to keep Zoe safe. She must be terrified. Sun and sand seem like a pretty decent alternative to this. Anything would be. I'll give him whatever he wants if he'll just leave her alone.

I look around, desperately searching for something I can use to escape from this wooden box. Max is on his way, but he might be too late. And I want to get us out of this mess without endangering anybody else. As I scan around me, I'm distracted. My attention gets pulled to the collective consciousness that is my pack, always humming steadily in the background of my mind. Something has changed unexpectedly, and I had been trying to ignore it. It's not the time to worry about who just had a baby. A new member has joined the overall bond, but my wolf is telling me to pay attention. As I zone in, I realise this is no infant.

Zoe? It can't be. How would she join the pack without being marked?

Oh goddess, no. I force myself to calm down. The bond would have broken. I would have felt it snap if someone had forced their mark on her. One thing is for certain, whatever is going on, I need to be out there and not trapped in here.

Blake: Zoe?

Testing the mind link, I hold my breath. This isn't how I imagined our first link to happen. I had pictured something much more romantic and intimate, but I'm desperate to know she's safe. What happens to me doesn't matter once I know she's not hurt.

Zoe: Oh my God, Blake! Are you okay?

Blake: I'm fine. Just temporarily detained. Did Tyson hurt you? How do you feel?

Zoe: I feel great!

Blake: Angel, I'm so sorry. I'll get out of here and come find you. I promise.

Zoe: Don't worry, I'm coming to get you.

Her breathing is heavy. She's running. She really must feel better. But none of this makes any sense if Tyson has her with him here. If she escaped, why would she come back?

Blake: Zoe, Max is on the way. Just hold tight and stay where you are. He'll find you.

Zoe: Hold on? No way. I'm nearly at the cabin.

No! She can't be here. This is exactly why I tried to leave her back in the cabin. This woman is going to be the death of me.

I can't see outside, but I hear a howl and the hairs stand up on the back of my neck. My wolf howls back, recognising the call of his mate and answering her immediately. I don't know how it happened or what is going on, but there's no denying that's my Zoe. Pressing my head to the cool wood, I fight to regain my composure. He wants out. He wants to burn down the world to get to his mate. But as I hear a low growl and a snarl from right outside, I fall to my knees, head in my hands.

There's going to be a fight. And there's nothing I can do except listen and pray.

CHAPTER 38

ZOE

The further I run, the steadier I become on four legs. At first, my balance was off, but I'm getting the hang of it now, increasing my speed as I gain confidence. I'm pushing my new body to see exactly what it can do.

All my senses are heightened. At first, I found it disorientating. I'm getting used to tuning out the background noise, leaves rustling in the breeze, the water rushing in the distance, and focusing on what I want to hear.

Voices. Footsteps. A door slamming shut.

Already slowing down to concentrate, Blake's deep voice slips into my brain and I skid to a stop. Spinning around to see where it's coming from, I'm startled and confused when I can't find him. He sounded so close. But then I remember mind linking. I've seen Blake and Max use it countless times, but to experience it is incredible.

The giddiness at hearing him speak takes over for a second before I realise it still doesn't mean he's safe. It just means we can communicate. Listening patiently, he tells me to wait for Max, and my heart warms that he is still trying to protect me above all else. I love him for it, but there's no way I'm not going to help him if I can.

Just as Blake did when he shifted to his wolf form in my clinic, my body seems to have practically healed itself. The effects of whatever poison Jenna put in that water are almost gone.

Moving forward at a trot, I skirt around the clearing, nose to the ground, taking in as much information as I can. Blake, Jenna, and someone else that I can't place have all come this way. My intention was to be cautious, to see who else is here and what their plan is. But when I step forward and see Jenna, standing a few metres back from the cabin, her platinum blond hair looking a little less perfect than normal, uncontrollable rage surges through me. Something inside me drives me forward and I bare my teeth as I race toward her, growling and snarling.

Mate. She dared try to take *my mate*.

I take great pleasure in the look of pure disbelief on her face as she pivots on the spot and sees me as a large white wolf barrelling straight for her. I'm not just a weak human anymore.

"Zoe!" Blake worriedly calls out my name, just as I plough straight into Jenna. The two of us roll along the grass, landing in a tangled heap right up against the wooden porch with a thud. One second I'm snapping my powerful jaws close to her face and the next I'm toppling forward. She's shifted underneath me into a pale brown wolf and rolled away. Leaping straight to my feet, I spin to face her as she shakes out her fur and lowers her head, growling. Her blue eyes are ferocious. She hates me as much as I hate her. To her, I'm stealing the man she loves, stopping her from having the life she envisaged with Blake.

But he's not hers. He's mine. That's my life, and I've had enough of this.

Zoe: He's mine, Jenna. We're fated mates. You know that.

Jenna: You don't deserve him! I've spent years, YEARS, taking care of him. Helping him become the Alpha he is. And then he falls for your pathetic damsel in distress act?!

Zoe: Let him out!

Jenna shrinks back, hind legs bent as she cowers, stunned at the urge to submit to me and looking even angrier than before. I might not be Luna yet, but clearly, my wolf is more dominant than hers.

Jenna: No! This doesn't make any sense. How can you be a wolf?

While she's distracted, I leap toward her, throwing her on her back. I might not have any fighting skills, but I have a strong desire for revenge on my side. Twisting around, I get a firm grip on her side and bite down hard, her fur and the metallic tang of blood filling my mouth. Jenna yelps, a pitiful sound that has me releasing her flesh and jumping back out of the reach of her snapping jaws. My wolf is telling me to hurt her, to take our vengeance, but deep down, I'm a healer. Violence doesn't come naturally to me.

Dragging herself to her feet, she falters, glancing back at the wound on her side that's dripping bright red blood onto the ground underneath her. She whines, limping and moving gingerly as she edges away from me. When I lunge for her again, she turns tail and runs, crying out when my teeth sink into her hind leg to stop her escape. She whimpers, trying to roll over onto her back, and I release her once more.

"Open this door!" Blake's voice booms out through the shut door and I struggle to stay on my feet under the weight of his order. Jenna dips her head and bares her neck, the need to submit overpowering.

Jenna: I told you I can't!

Her voice is whiny and irritating, and she's making this a lot less fun than it should be. Pressing her belly to the ground as Blake's energy pulses out around us, her eyes dart to the side, to the dark edge of the trees on the opposite side of the clearing from the cabin. She's not telling us everything. I look all around. Someone else was here.

Are they still here watching and waiting?

Sniffing the air, I can't pick up any scents, but I'm new to this wolf stuff. Maybe the breeze is blowing in the wrong direction and they're clever enough to know I can't detect them. I growl and prowl closer to Jenna. She shrinks back, not even trying to put up a fight.

Zoe: Who's there, Jenna?

She stares defiantly at me, unwilling to take me on, but still unable to hide how much she despises me. With one last snap of my teeth, I leave her cowering on the ground and run to the cabin. Blake can do what he wants to her when I get him out.

Blake: You were amazing.

His soft whisper in my mind is a soothing caress, and my heartbeat slows down. He's so close. I need to see him so much my body is shaking. My wolf craves him and I'm desperate to get the door open.

Zoe: How do I change back, Blake? I need my hands.

Blake: Imagine reaching out with your hands, using them to open the door. Imagine the feel of your feet touching the floor.

I try to picture my hand around the door handle, but nothing's working. Getting frustrated, I huff and growl, but then an image of Blake's hand reaching for mine fills my mind. We're leaving the diner and he's trying to pull me closer to him, leaning in to press a kiss to my temple. It takes my breath away and I melt, pining for him. All I want is to see him. I imagine reaching out a hand to take his and before I know it, it really is my hand stretching out in front of me and settling on the cool brass handle.

But it won't budge. It's locked. Groaning in frustration, I thump the door with a fist.

"It's okay, Zoe. I can't force it open from this side. I'm too weak, but you're a shifter now. You'll be strong enough."

Laughing at the notion that I can kick a locked door down, I shake my head in disbelief.

"Zoe. You've got this."

Blake's so certain it makes me pause. He's right. I might not have the same rage that pushed me into overpowering Jenna, but my body is different now. Strong. Capable. I can do it. Moving back, I steady myself before taking two big steps and aiming a kick right below the lock. Then another. And another. After the next one, I suck in a deep breath, hands on my hips, considering whether to even bother trying again. It's cracked, but it still looks solid to me. Maybe there's something around here I can use.

"Again, angel," Blake insists. "You can do it."

I'm concentrating hard on where I'm going to place my next kick. So hard that I almost don't hear what my subconscious is trying to tell me. Sharon's voice trickles into my mind, delivering her warning from the packhouse again and making the hair stand up on the back of my neck.

Watch your back.

I spin just in time to get my hands up in front of my face as Jenna's tawny wolf pounces on top of me. Crashing back against the wood, I hear Blake going crazy on the other side to get to me. He can't shift to heal because he needs his hands to open the door, but I his human form, the poison is still affecting him. I'm on my own.

Raising my feet up, I wedge them between her body and mine and push with all I have. For a moment, I think I'm gaining some ground, but that space just gives her the opportunity to claw me down my thigh as she falls back, and I cry out. Her eyes are wild as she fixes me with an evil glare before launching herself at me once more.

This time, as I tumble back against the door again, it gives way and I land on my ass with a heavy thud, knocking the air from my lungs. Jenna comes with me, teeth bared only an inch from my neck. I'm fighting for my life, pushing her with all my strength, but I'm exhausted. It's been a hell of a day.

From the darkness, a terrifying growl fills the air as a hand grabs her by the scruff of the neck and lifts her up like she weighs nothing at all. Blake. He tosses her out the door and follows, hesitating for a split second to take in the gaping cuts on my legs. Teeth clenched; he storms outside and picks her up once more by the throat.

"Don't look," he whispers, and I do as he says, covering my eyes. I hear a pitiful yelp and then silence before Blake howls, both angry and mournful. His regret at being forced to take a life is clear and my heart aches for him as his pain travels to me through the bond. She betrayed him, but for years they were friends.

Sniffing the air and tensing, he jogs to the treeline, checking the area exactly where Jenna had been looking earlier. Where whoever was helping Jenna had been lurking. Frowning, he turns back to me just as a blur of movement to my right catches my attention. A strangled cry escapes me as Tyson appears and stands between me and my mate, his broad back blocking my view of Blake. It's unnerving how fast he can move. And how quietly.

"Get away from her." Blake's voice is calm as he strides forward, but he looks deadly. Those pale grey eyes of his glow bright silver and his features have darkened. His lips pull back into a snarl as he nears, crouching and preparing to shift.

"Relax, brother. Zoe and I are old friends now. Well acquainted. Aren't we?"

"Tyson, don't," I warn. Blake is not a man to be messed with at the moment, and Tyson is trying his hardest to provoke him. Thanking the heavens, more movement in the trees announces the arrival of Max and Jeffrey, both still in wolf form. Hopefully, they'll stop this from turning into a challenge right here and now.

"She's beautiful, Blake. That scent." Tyson makes a show of sucking in a long breath and groaning. "And that taste." He dips his knees and puts a hand to his heart. I can tell he's smiling by the way Blake roars.

"If you hurt her, if you even touch her, I'll fucking kill you. What did you do to her?"

"Nothing, brother. But I think I've decided something. When I come back to reclaim MY pack, MY birthright as the firstborn son, I think I'm going to keep her. She doesn't deserve to be a young widow. The pack gets to keep their Luna, and I'll enjoy showing her what pleasures she could have with someone a little… darker."

Tyson chuckles to himself, enjoying watching how his words hit home. Blake shifts, but by the time his paws have hit the floor, Tyson is already gone. Not a trace left behind.

My eyes lock with Blake's and I moan, gripping my leg as the pain flares back to life. He's by my side in a second, pulling me into his arms and cradling me close to his massive body. Stretching across me, he snags the blanket off the bed and places it over my naked body just before Max and Jeff come into view at the doorway. They look around, completely shell-shocked.

"Blake?" I whisper, pressing my face into his chest. His hand smooths my hair and rubs my back, comforting me. Back in his arms, I sag, leaning on him for some strength that I definitely don't feel in myself.

"Yes, angel?" he answers, pressing soft kisses to the top of my head, my forehead, and my shoulder.

"I was a wolf."

It sounds ridiculous to say the words out loud. If it weren't for the evidence of the fight with Jenna throbbing and bleeding down my battered body, I'd think the whole thing was just a hallucination. Now that the fight is over, all the energy leaves my body as my adrenaline bottoms out and I droop, sagging against him. He scoops me up in his enormous arms and stands, striding out the door.

"Yes, you were, Zoe. And a magnificent one at that."

Blake presses a tender kiss to my lips as I close my eyes and let the tiredness pull me under.

CHAPTER 39

BLAKE

"She's strong, Blake. After a good rest, she'll be fine. Think of how exhausted you were after your first shift. I know I slept for two days." Jeffrey places a reassuring hand on my arm before leaving the cabin, waving over his shoulder as he goes.

"Call me if you need anything." Jeffery was the only other pack member who saw how truly unhinged my father was becoming. When I needed it most, he was straight with me and told me things weren't going to get any better. Something needed to change, and I was the only person who could do it. He's not a man who sugarcoats things, so his confidence means a lot to me.

Erring on the side of caution, and after all my pestering, he's given Zoe strong antibiotics and had her on a drip to get her fluids back. But we both know that her wolf will have healed her by now. The physical changes and injuries will not be the problem. When she wakes up, she'll have to deal with the emotional trauma of being attacked, but potentially more life-altering: the implications of becoming a shifter.

Little more than a week ago, she didn't even know shifters existed. Now she is one. Not only that, but she's also part of a pack. My pack, no less. Zoe didn't ask for any of this. Her world has been turned upside down and she's been put in danger more times than I care to think about.

Sighing, I return to the kitchen island and sit on one of the high stools, resting my elbows on the smooth wooden countertop. Covering my face with my hands, I breathe deeply and try to get a grip on my emotions. Without talking to Zoe, I still don't know what went on out there. The idea that Tyson might have touched her, *tasted her*, scares me to death. I saw the unmistakable red rim around his eyes. I know what that means. Vampire.

When my father returned to the packhouse after the attack that claimed his mate, he listed out the dead, including Tyson. Dad was devastated, describing how he found Tyson torn apart in a pool of blood, deep in the woods and far from the house. The pack took over arranging the burials and my father locked himself away, a broken man with the loss of his mate. I always thought the guilt he felt for not accepting Tyson while he had the chance played a part in his breakdown. As a young teen faced with so much death, I never questioned his loss. I had no desire to see the bodies.

It's clear now that someone or something found him while he was still barely clinging to life and turned him into the walking undead. I shudder to think of what he went through or how he could have been saved if they had brought his body back as soon as they found him.

And what he has been doing since that day.

I've heard stories of recently turned vampires and how bloodthirsty they can be in their early years. How am I going to deal with him? And when do I tell the council?

"Say nothing until your mate is fit and strong again," Sharon answers my unspoken question from where she stands in the doorway. Her hands are clasped behind her back and she holds her head high, but I can feel the nervous energy radiating from her.

"Sit," I command, standing to drag out the stool beside me for her. As usual, she knows more than the rest of us, but the powerful witch doesn't have to tell me a damn thing if she doesn't want to. Losing my temper won't help me here.

"I didn't know exactly what would happen, or when, just that Zoe would need her wolf sooner rather than later," Sharon admits. Her gaze shifts to the stairs, towards the main bedroom where Zoe sleeps.

"You knew my bite was changing her. She had a right to know what was happening to her own body," I snap.

It hurts me to think I sent my mate away from my home, in pain, to endure the transformation by herself. Everyone's first shift is agony. She was already feeling the effects when she got to the clinic. It's hard to know how much of her sickness was poison and how much was the changes taking place inside her. Goddess, she must have been so scared.

"I did. When I heard that all three Walker sisters have been mated to wolves with alpha lineage, I knew there had to be a reason for it. But I needed to be certain. And I am. I found out what that reason is."

The temptation to ask is overwhelming, but Zoe deserves to know first and then decide whether she wants to tell me.

"Then why the fuck didn't you tell us instead of sneaking around behind our backs? We could have prepared. I'm assuming that balm had something to do with this."

Sharon nods, her expression tight with tension. She knows I'm a man on the edge.

"I like Zoe and I wanted her to be able to protect herself. And you needed her to stick around. I couldn't risk scaring her away. You would be no match for Tyson if your mate left you. He'd take the pack, and we'd be stuck with him and Alpha Weston to lead the region. No good would come from that."

She has no idea how right she is. But that's for another day.

"How is this any better?" I throw my hands up and gesture in the general direction where Zoe lies still unconscious in my bed. "She had nothing to do with any of this. *Nothing.* But we've taken her choices away and ruined her life. Can a wolf even be a vet? Fuck!"

Standing suddenly and gripping the back of my head in my hands, my stool topples to the ground behind me as I push away. I'm desperate to fight someone or something. I need to work out this frustration and anger, but I can't bear to leave my mate. Just being in another room is tough.

"When she's ready, call me and I'll come to answer whatever questions she has." Sharon hands me an envelope and stands, bending slowly to pick up my stool. "I know you're angry with me right now, Blake, but I promise I was trying to help. She's alive and you're alive, so I'll take that as a win."

Silence falls over the cabin as she lets herself out, the soft click of the front door letting me know we're alone once again. Max is dealing with Jenna's body and seeing if he can find any more evidence at the cabin. I doubt it, but it's worth a go.

Climbing the stairs to the enormous suite that takes up the entire right side of the cabin, I'm dragging my feet, almost afraid to see Zoe. My wolf longs for her. His simple way of reasoning allows him to be thrilled about this unforeseen turn of events. He would wish no harm on his mate, but in his mind, if Zoe's a wolf now, this makes things even better. She'll be stronger and better able to defend herself and our pups, as she showed yesterday. But I know the reality is much more complicated than that.

Tucking Sharon's envelope into the back pocket of my jeans, I push the door open wider and pause in the doorway before walking inside. The soft evening sun shines through the blinds and falls across her sleeping face. Her beauty takes my breath away and my feet carry me on autopilot to her side, the urge to touch her too great to resist.

The bed dips as I sit on the side and reach out to stroke her silky blond hair. Her skin is glowing and her thick, dark lashes fan across her cheeks. The sight of her chest rising and falling with each shallow breath calms me. She's here. She's okay. Anything else will be a bonus.

Stripping down to my boxers, I climb into the bed behind her and wrap an arm around her waist, tugging her close to me. Burying my face in the back of her neck, I hold her close and thank the goddess nothing worse happened to her.

"Blake, are you okay?" Zoe's voice is slightly raspy from sleep as she stretches a hand back over her shoulder and cups the side of my head. I lean into her touch and swallow down the lump in my throat.

"Zoe. I'm so sorry." I press a kiss to the back of her neck and another between her shoulder blades, before leaning my forehead there and inhaling deeply.

"Hey, hey." Zoe rolls over to face me and places her hands on my shoulders. "Less of that."

Burying herself into my chest, she snuggles in close, fitting against me perfectly, and just stays there, holding me. Soaking in every second of this, my body relaxes, and the hell of the last few days slowly ebbs away. This feels so right and I allow myself to imagine what it would be like to wake up like this every morning.

"You smell amazing," she murmurs, her lips brushing across my skin. My breath hitches and I groan, my body reacting to my mate, but knowing I can't do anything about it.

"Zoe," I warn through gritted teeth. She runs her arms from my shoulders, down my arms, squeezing my biceps and I catch her hands and hold them away from me. She meets my gaze defiantly, a wicked glint in her eye, before casually glancing down between our bodies at the evidence of my arousal. It's pressed hard and aching against her soft belly and she rolls her hips, moving purposefully just to drive me crazy.

"Your scent, Blake. Was this what it was like for you, every second we were together? I just want to *eat* you." Her tongue darts out and she licks my pec, struggling to pull her wrists free from my grasp as she throws a leg over my hip and uses it to pull my pelvis flush to hers.

Fuck. Her sense of smell is off the charts now compared to what it was. She's like an over-enthusiastic teenager, except with adult hormones and her fated mate right in front of her. My hands pin hers over her head, against the crisp white linen, and I roll us so I'm on top of her. I slide down her body, pressing ragged kisses over her collarbone and across her chest, my hands caressing every curve and dip.

"Goddess, I can't believe I'm going to say this, but we can't. I'll make you feel good, though, I promise. And then we're going to talk."

Zoe begins to voice her disagreement with my plan, but as I move lower and my palm drifts up her bandaged thigh, from her knees to her hips, she shivers in anticipation. Slowly, carefully, I loop a finger into each side of her panties and drag them lower. She raises her bum off the mattress to make it easier and wriggles as I pull them down past her ankles.

Stroking my hands from her instep, up her shin, brushing her calf with my thumbs, over her knees, and all the way to the apex of her thighs, she sighs contentedly. I nudge her legs wider as I move back up, positioning myself there and raising my head so I can meet her eye. Gripping her ass in my two hands, I tilt her hips up to get better access, growling just at the sight of her beautiful pussy.

"I love you," I whisper. "Whatever you want, I'll give it to you. Do you want this, Zoe?" I lower my face to her and suck her delicious clit into my mouth, savouring her taste and scent as I lick and tease. She grinds herself against my mouth as I drive her quickly toward the edge. This is no time for messing around. She needs me to work her hard and fast. Pushing one finger, then two, deep inside her as she clenches tight around them, I thrust them in time with my tongue stroking her clit. Her hands tug at my hair as she presses my face harder against her, riding me, desperate to race toward her release.

"Come, angel; let it all out." The vibrations of my voice through her core tip her over the edge and she comes almost violently, her shoulders lifting off the bed as she grasps at me and then the sheets, searching for something to cling to. When she slumps back against the pillows, chest heaving with exertion, I rise up above her and kiss her gently, ignoring the raging desire that's consuming me.

I try to ignore all the plans I had for when I finally got my mate back in my arms, because this isn't about me. It was Zoe's wolf's desire to connect with her mate, her reaction, and her needs after scenting her mate properly for the first time. But now we need to have a rational conversation about everything that has happened and what comes next.

And I'm afraid that isn't going to go nearly as well.

CHAPTER 40

ZOE

My gaze drops to Blake's crotch, where an impressive bulge is pressing against the front of his boxers. Running my tongue over my bottom lip, I pull it between my teeth and moan. All I want to do is to shove him down on the bed and yank those trousers off, tug his cock free and taste him. I want to take him deep down my throat and drive him wild so he's completely at my mercy. To stare up at him from my knees, with his dick in my mouth, and know that I own him, that he's mine.

"Goddess," Blake groans like he's praying for strength. "Zoe, whatever you're thinking about, stop. You're killing me here."

"I can't stop, Blake. Is this what the mate bond has felt like for you this whole time?" It's the truth. I can't stop myself. Just his scent is enough to make me want to jump his bones right now, combined with how he looks, how he moves, and even his voice. I feel like one giant raging hormone. Now I appreciate how much he has held back his natural urges in order to give me space and time. But he doesn't have to do that anymore. I feel amazing. Strong and powerful. I can't explain why being together feels so right either, but I know I could never have this with anyone else, and I wouldn't want to. Blake is it for me.

"It's amazing, isn't it?" Blake gives me the biggest grin, and I sit up to cup his face and kiss him. Pouring my love for him into that moment. His hesitancy fades as I don't push things further and he relaxes, cupping the back of my head with one hand and holding me in place. Without realising, he's slipping back into taking control. He doesn't know how to be any other way. His other hand rests on my hip, and his thumb rubs back and forth over the exposed skin just above my waistband.

"Mmm," I purr, melting into his muscular arms as he ends the kiss and tugs me into his lap, wrapping me up tight. We're both quiet for a minute, just enjoying the moment.

"You scared the hell out of me," Blake whispers, his lips brushing against my hair as he speaks. His breath tickles my scalp and sends a shiver through me. My body is so responsive to his every touch.

"Right back at ya," I quip, trying to lighten the mood, but he's having none of it. Leaning back, he takes my hands in his and holds them against his chest.

"No, Zoe. I thought you were going to die. Either from the poison or at the hand of Jenna, if I didn't get her away from you. I didn't know how sick I was going to get, whether I'd be able to help you or protect you." He squeezes those smoky grey eyes tight and his chest rises as he struggles to stay composed. Our connection is even stronger, and I can feel his swirling emotions: relief, anger, and guilt. And fear. "And then Tyson. How did I not know he was here? I'm so sorry."

"Blake. Tyson didn't hurt me. He frightened me, but he did that to make me shift sooner." Given he wants to exact some kind of revenge on Blake, I'm not his biggest fan. But he had the chance to kill me to get back at Blake, and he didn't. Tyson might have enjoyed tormenting him, but he didn't attack him while he was weak, either. Maybe there's a chance that they can resolve things peacefully. Tyson isn't going anywhere. He has unfinished business, but I have a feeling he's not in a rush to make his next move, either.

"He helped you?" Blake frowns, struggling to believe that the same man who pretended to threaten me helped me get to him.

"Blake, he scared me into shifting so I could help you. Okay, he could have helped you himself, but he did nothing wrong."

"He said he *tasted* you." Blake's voice is lethal, and the tendons in his neck and jaw bulge as his entire body tenses up, waiting for me to tell him what happened.

Oh shit.

"Tyson didn't bite me. He licked some of my blood off his finger, just to freak me out." Blake takes it exactly as I expected and his eyes glow silver as every muscle in his enormous body goes rigid and seems to grow before my eyes. His claws lengthen, and I see his teeth push down against his top lip. His fury flashes down the bond to me and it's overpowering. If Tyson was here, there isn't a doubt in my mind he'd kill him.

"Blake—" Reaching out, I try to stop him as he goes to stand. His wolf is driving him to move, to do something. He storms to the window and paces, fists clenching and unclenching. He wants to fight, to rage, to destroy something. "Blake. It was a drop of blood from a graze on my leg. He was trying to spook me, and it worked, but that was it."

"Zoe, he's a VAMPIRE! He enjoyed it, fucking loved it. You are my mate and he dared touch you. To taste what's *mine*. To have the fucking nerve to speak of claiming you for his own!"

Spinning on the spot to face me, his body is taut and the atmosphere in the room crackles with electric energy. Something has changed. His thoughts aren't on Tyson anymore. Blake's attention is focused one hundred percent on me. Butterflies flutter in my stomach and I squeeze my thighs together as I feel myself getting wet. The tension is unbearable, stretching between us as we both hold our breaths, neither of us able to take our eyes off the other.

"You're mine," he hisses, eyes blazing with possessiveness. I nod, and I have no idea who moves first, but we crash together, lips and hands everywhere. I'm on my knees near the end of the mattress as Blake leans down and takes me in a bruising kiss. My hands find their way to his hips and I whimper as my palms meet the smooth, warm skin of his stomach and drift over every dip and ridge of his abs. Moving higher, I touch his pecs and drag my hands down his sides, enjoying the tingles shooting down my fingertips and arms where we touch.

Blake's hands are in my hair, then down my back, opening the clasp of my bra as he moves. Gripping the hem of my t-shirt, he yanks it up and over my head, pausing for a second to admire me before diving back in. Tangling his hands in my hair, he pulls me to him, kissing me like a man possessed.

"Beautiful. *And mine*," he growls, and my pussy clenches, desperate for him to show us exactly what that means. "Nobody will ever touch you again, Zoe. I promise. I'll kill anyone that tries."

"Yours," I agree, nodding enthusiastically. His possessiveness does something funny to my insides, and my need for him rises even higher. He's mine too, and it's time for it to be official.

My hands fumble to get his boxers off. The sight of his dark, happy trail, leading from his belly button down his taut abdomen before disappearing, has my core clenching.

He's magnificent, all tanned toned skin and lean muscle as he takes over and shoves down his boxers in one go and steps out of them. Blake never takes his eyes off me as he places a knee on the bed, coming back to eye level with me. His thick, long cock stands to attention between us, already leaking pre-cum from the broad head. But his focus is entirely on me.

Without saying a word, he topples me back on the mattress where I am completely naked in front of him. His hands caress my ankles and up my calves as he raises his eyes to meet mine.

"Are you sure, Zoe? This is it. No turning back." His deep voice is grave. This is my last chance. What happens next will tie us together forever. Nervous anticipation floods through me. I want this. I've never wanted anything more. His expression is serious, but his eyes are full of fire. And I want him to burn me alive.

"Do it, Blake. Make me yours." I arch my back as my arousal has me squirming. My body aches to have him inside me. I need him like I need air. He still looks every bit as intense, but a victorious smirk pulls at his lips. His hand closes around one of my ankles and he tugs me toward him suddenly, pulling me down the bed and parting my legs so they're on either side of his thighs. I gasp at the unexpected movement, but my body loves it, loves his display of strength and dominance.

He lowers his massive body down over me, holding his weight off me with one arm. Blake takes his time and lets his other hand trail a scorching path along my thigh, over my hip, and up my side. His eyes follow its progress, taking me in, and I can feel his pride and adoration. It shines in his eyes when he finally settles himself above me, leaning down to kiss along my jaw, nipping my neck playfully while he wraps his hand around my throat carefully, keeping me still. His touch is reverent, not threatening, and I lift my hips, seeking more contact. My patience is gone.

When I feel his heavy cock notch itself at my entrance, I groan, my eyes rolling back in my head. I try to push up against him, desperate to join with him and feel him in me. He growls as I get an inch of him into me, but with his hand around my neck, that's as much as I can move. I struggle beneath him, circling and rolling my hips to get more friction, more movement, more of him. I crave him.

"Naughty," he murmurs against my ear, and I freeze, a whimper escaping me, feeling wanton and reckless. He presses his lips to that spot just below my ear and I melt.

"Blake," I beg as he thrusts slightly, only giving me another inch of him before he pulls back until he's almost out of me again. Grabbing his ass, I pull him back, refusing to let him leave my body, needing that connection. He smiles against my skin as he continues to drive me higher with teasing licks and kisses to the sensitive column of my neck.

"You're going to be mine, angel. I love you, and I'm going to show you that every day for the rest of our lives together."

Shifting again, my stomach tightens and my pussy clenches around him, trying to pull him deeper into me.

"I love you, too," I whisper, tilting my head to give him better access. As soon as the words pass my lips, he thrusts deep inside me, filling me to the hilt and I cry out in ecstasy as he sinks his canines into my neck at the same time. An orgasm crashes over me and my body arches, my taut nipples and aching breasts pressing against his chest as I cling to him. His teeth are still in my neck and I call out his name, wave after wave of pleasure washing over me. My toes curl and every inch of my body buzzes and tingles.

"Fuck, Zoe." Blake groans. "Fuck, that's so good!" As my nails extend without me realising and dig into his back, breaking the skin, his control snaps and he finally moves, pulling back and then thrusting powerfully again. And again. It's rough and primal, hot and sweaty. His strokes are strong and sure, and his hand around my neck is all that stops me from being pushed further up the bed with each frantic thrust. His thrusts get harder and faster as the bond between us snaps into place with dizzying force. All of his emotions flood through me and I call out his name as the strength of his feeling for me, his love and devotion, fills me. God, I love this man.

Throwing one leg around his hip, I deepen the angle and with each thrust he rolls his hips, grinding his pelvis against my clit. I can't speak as he brings me higher again with each stroke and I feel another climax building.

"Blake, Blake." My pleas are frantic and needy as I tug at his hair. Knowing what I need, he removes his mouth from my neck and takes my lips in a searing kiss. The metallic taste of my blood in his mouth sends my wolf crazy. Warmth begins to spread from my fingers and toes as Blake eeks every bit of pleasure from me he can, wringing me dry as I feel his own release building.

Suddenly, though, there's panic. And I have to dig my heels into his ass to keep him from withdrawing from my body. My wolf snarls at him in my head.

Blake: Zoe, maybe we need more careful. You could get...

I appreciate his concern, but I want nothing more than to feel him come inside me. I need it. Locking one leg around his, I flip us and he looks up at me in shock as I straddle him now. He goes to sit up but I push him back, placing my hands on his firm chest as I roll my hips. Groaning, he falls back, one arm slung over his eyes.

"Are you sure? You might regret this," he whispers. I growl at the insinuation that I would ever regret making a pup with him and he shifts his arm to smirk at me. I doubt anyone growls at him. Ever. "Cute."

The nerve of him. I'll show him "cute".

Raising up, I push back down on his rock-hard cock, moaning in pleasure as he fills me, touching a magical spot deep inside when I tilt my hips.

"Fuck," he groans, his grip on my ass bruising as I wipe the smile from his face. I continue to drive him wild, bouncing on his thick cock and enjoying myself thoroughly as he's forced to give over control and let me set the pace.

Reaching back, I stroke his sac and perineum lightly. He jerks, cursing again and gritting his teeth. But when I roll his balls in the palm of my hand, continuing to pump up and down on him, he loses it. His enormous hands hold me down tight against him, locking me in place as he pushes up to meet me, shouting my name. His dick pulses inside me and stream after stream of hot cum fills me up.

Collapsing down onto his chest, my hands grip his shoulders. Blake pants, his chest heaving. He wraps his arms around me and holds me close, allowing me to catch my breath on top of him.

We're in our own little sweaty bubble of happiness. I've never been as content and I can feel his joy in marking me at last.

"This is the best day of my life," Blake whispers. "Thank you." He presses his lips to the top of my head and rubs his nose in my hair, breathing deeply.

"My mate."

I sigh and snuggle closer, not wanting to move an inch. Like he can read my mind, he rolls us onto our sides, still connected, facing each other. We lie there, staring into each other's eyes, nose to nose. Neither of us needs to say anything. We can tell we're both enjoying this moment, the wonder of being so close, so connected. It's incredible.

"I could stay here forever." Blake finally says, reaching up to run a knuckle down my cheek and along my jaw before dipping his head to kiss me softly. I sigh and close my eyes, savouring his touch and the lingering feel of his lips on mine.

"No can do." I shake my head, and an adorable frown appears between his eyes. He's not impressed, like a child that's been told he can't have his new toy.

"We've got a wedding to go to."

CHAPTER 41

BLAKE

Oh, no. Leah's wedding. I had completely forgotten.

Obviously, I'm thrilled for Rex and Leah, but all I want to do is lock myself away with my new mate and stay in our little bubble for as long as possible. To ignore all thoughts of family, friends, and work.

I can't resist looking at my mark on Zoe's shoulder, the red puncture wounds already closing with her new healing powers. My wolf preens, delighted in knowing that any male who comes close will know not only that she is taken, but exactly who she is taken by.

Me.

They'd have to be an idiot to touch her.

Without marking her, I'm not sure how well I'd have fared at a wedding in another pack's territory with unmated males all around. I have superb control of my temper, but the sight of her dancing with Cooper's playboy brother Nathan, or even his charming beta Ethan, would have been a significant test of it. Knowing she wears my claim calms my wolf.

As a new wolf, this will be incredibly hard for Zoe. She might be laid back, but her wolf is young and immature. She won't be one bit happy to see unmarked females anywhere near me. A lesser man would be thrilled at the prospect, but not me. Well, not much anyway.

"Hmm. Do you think it's a good idea to go?" I ask, shifting us so the length of her body is pressed against me. In a heartbeat, I'm hard again, my twitching cock pushing against her soft tummy and relishing the heat instantly building between us.

Zoe's eyes flash to mine, indignant at the suggestion that she ever miss her own sister's wedding. I have to smother a grin. Her wolf is a feisty little thing. I'll have to watch myself until she settles down.

"Of course, I'm going. Why wouldn't I?"

Searching for a way to put this diplomatically, I grip her ass and rock her against me, loving the feel of her soft flesh in my hands. Trying to distract her this way will make me feel better at least, even if it doesn't work on her.

"You've been through a lot, Zoe. Max told your sisters about the poisoning, and that you're okay now. But they don't know about your wolf. I knew you wouldn't want that bit of news to overshadow Leah's big day."

Zoe frowns and her lips twist as she considers what I'm saying. She knows I'm right. She would hate to steal the limelight from Leah.

"You can do your bossy alpha thing and make them all keep it a secret till afterward." She looks quite cheerful at the prospect of using my alpha command to keep everyone quiet.

"I thought you hated when I did that."

"To me, or Max. But this is different," she argues. She blushes, and I can sense her guilt at forcing silence on an entire pack for her own benefit. "It's for Leah."

"Angel, if that's what you want. I'll do it. Hell, you could probably do it yourself if you want now that you're Luna."

Zoe's eyes fly open in shock as if this is the first time she's thought of her new position.

"I can't be Luna. I don't know anything about wolves." She's shaking her head in disbelief, but I smile and nuzzle her neck.

Zoe will be the perfect Luna. She might not have the same networking and schmoozing experience as Hayley, but she works hard. She's clever, kind, and brave. And she'll keep me on my toes.

"Luna Zoe Steel," I murmur, quite liking the sound of that. From the way Zoe rubs herself against me, groaning at the friction on her clit, I'm guessing she likes it too.

"What about the other she-wolves?" I dare and a cute rumble starts in Zoe's chest as soon as the words leave my mouth.

"There will be no other she-wolves," she declares, reaching down to stroke her hand up my thigh, fingers dancing dangerously close to my cock and I'm suddenly a little nervous about pushing her any further when her claws are so close to the family jewels.

"At the wedding, angel. Do you think you'll be able to cope with being around other she-wolves? Talking to me, maybe flirting with me."

Zoe grabs my hair roughly in two hands and takes my mouth in a possessive kiss, showing me exactly what she thinks of that idea. Her tongue tangles with mine and she tugs my lip between her teeth as she rolls us until I'm flat on my back and she's lying naked along my front.

"We're mates and I'm marked. No she-wolves will go near you. They wouldn't dare." Her voice is certain, but then her face falls into a cute little puzzled frown. "Would they?

"They would, I'm afraid, Zoe. Rank is a powerful aphrodisiac for wolves. They might smell you on me, but you're going to be off doing your wedding duties…"

I shrug and smirk as she narrows her eyes at me, knowing full well that I'm winding her up, but there is more than a grain of truth in it. She'll struggle to stay in control and could shift on the spot without meaning to if her emotions get the better of her. There's little point in telling Cooper's pack to keep her transformation quiet if she turns into a white wolf in the middle of the ceremony.

"And obviously being the Alpha of all alphas, that makes you the hottest commodity around," she whispers with an edge to her voice, leaning down over me so that her hair tickles my chest and her breath on my ear sends shivers down my spine. "Lucky me."

She strokes her hands across my pecs and down my stomach, lower and lower, exploring my body and getting tantalisingly close to my cock again, which strains to get to her, craving her touch. With one hand, she trails a finger down the side of my neck, and I freeze when she touches the sensitive spot where her mark would go and pauses.

"I suppose I could save myself this torture by pressing my teeth into your skin right here, biting you, and leaving my mark. Letting everyone know you're mine."

"Only if you want to," I say hesitantly, making sure she knows it's her choice, and she laughs lightly. It's a sound I'll never tire of hearing, although I'd prefer if it wasn't at my expense.

"Only if I want to," she clarifies, and I can hear the smile in her voice.

"Of course. Whatever you want, angel. No pressure."

And I mean it, even if every cell in my body is screaming out for her to sink her fangs into my neck, to claim me as I've done to her. To make me hers. I want everyone to know I've found my mate. To know that I have that happiness in my life, but also to make our bond as strong as it can possibly be.

Zoe hums dubiously as she kisses my collarbone, the hollow of my throat, and up to my Adam's apple, which is working hard in anticipation of what I hope is coming next. When she sits up and straddles me, her hips are raised, and I get a perfect view of her pink glistening lips. I can't help but be amazed that this is the woman the fates gifted to me. She was worth every second I waited. She's perfect.

"So, you wouldn't mind if I left it? If I was the only one marked?" she asks, rolling her hips. I can feel and scent her arousal where her pussy touches my bare skin, ready for me once again. Through gritted teeth, I lie, trying not to force something she's not ready for.

"It's up to you."

Zoe nods, her gaze burning into mine, and she shifts on my pelvis, her core inching closer to where I want it, where I could grab her and thrust up into her in one swift movement. I fist the sheets beside me with lengthened claws, desperate not to give in to my wolf and lose control. She's taunting me and we both know it.

"If you tell me what you really want, maybe I'll give it to you," she teases with a glint in her eye, and I lose it. No more games. No more tiptoeing around.

Zoe screams as I grab her by the waist and turn her in mid-air. She lands face down, her cheek pressed to the mattress as I cover her from behind. My chest against her warm back and my cock resting against her ass feels amazing. Zoe's breathing is shallow, she pants quietly as she recovers from the shock. Her heart is racing, beating hard, and I can feel her excitement and exhilaration through the bond. She loves it.

"Zoe, if you want to mark me, I'd be honoured. To feel your teeth in my neck, for you to taste my blood as that tight pussy of yours milks my cock, squeezing me over and over again as I fill you with my seed. Maybe plant a pup in your belly," I whisper against her neck, giving her mark a nip and eliciting a full-body shudder and moan from my mate. "But it is your choice. And I won't push you.But if you keep teasing me, I'll fuck that naughtiness right out of you. "

"Blake," Zoe whimpers, her eyes falling closed as she clenches her thighs, now slick with her desire. She arches, the dip in her back becoming more pronounced, and pushes her ass against me. She's less fond of the teasing now that it's the other way around.

Shoving a knee between her toned, tanned thighs, I part her legs just enough to let me notch my length at her entrance. Catching her hands in mine, I stretch them out above her head, pinning them against the mattress. My mouth waters at the sight of her waiting beneath me. With my weight over her back, she can barely move. Her long, lithe body displayed beautifully for me. Zoe squirms impatiently and her juicy backside wiggles deliciously.

I push forward, entering her slowly, her pussy is unbelievably tight in this position, and she moans at the sensation of fullness. Every muscle in my body that was tightly coiled relaxes as I feel her pleasure propelled back to me through the bond. Slowly at first, I drive her higher and higher with every powerful snap of my hips.

Each time she cries my name, my chest swells with pride that I can satisfy my mate and bring her such pleasure. With one arm, I scoop her up under the stomach so she's on her knees. Keeping my forearm on her back to keep her shoulder down, I pick up the speed. Licking my fingers, I reach around to stroke her clit, causing her to gasp and tense. Her hand stretches back to grab my ass, keeping me close to her. Her pussy grips my cock like a vise, as if her body is refusing to let me pull out. Keeping me inside her as much as I want to stay there.

"Fuck, angel." I trail my fingers down her spine tenderly and goosebumps appear in their wake. Pulling her upright to me, my arm around her stomach keeps her steady as I pound up and into her. She tips her head back and rests her head against my shoulder, repeatedly mumbling my name and a string of incoherent curses.

"Blake, I'm going to... I'm..." She doesn't get to finish that sentence as a wave of pleasure washes over her features, her climax taking her by surprise and racking her slim body.

Goddess. My balls tighten with the breathy little moans she makes as she comes down from her high. She loops her arms back around my neck as she sighs contentedly, while I resume my thrusts, holding on by a thread. Zoe reaches down to where we joined and places her fingers on each side of me, touching where I enter her with each push in and out of her body.

"Zoe," I moan, my eyes rolling into the back of my head as I chase my own release. With my eyelids shut, I don't see her tilt her head, and it's only when I feel her soft lips on my skin and the points of her teeth scratch my skin that I realise she's turned her head to get access to my neck.

"Blake, there's no way I'm not putting my mark on your body. You're mine, just like I'm yours," she whispers, such tenderness in her voice that I melt. As I thrust into her hard for the last time, pinning her to me with a painfully tight grip on her hips, she strikes. The feeling of her taking me, owning me with her bite, sends a thunderous jolt of pleasure through me and I roar. Jet after jet of my cum fills her, and I keep her pressed back against me, trapping her there so she gets every last drop.

"Woah," Zoe whispers, as she buries her face in my neck, kissing my mark tenderly before turning to face forward, her chin falling to her chest in a mixture of sheer bliss and exhaustion. The power of the bond strengthening further is dizzying and I release her, the two of us collapsing onto the crisp white sheets underneath us.

In seconds, Zoe's breathing changes. The events of the last week have to have sapped all of her energy. She's doing so well, considering. Refusing to separate us and allow any of my seed to leave her luscious body, I tilt us so we're on our sides, her back to my front, her head lying on my arm and my chin resting against the top of her head. Heaven.

"Sleep, Zoe, sleep. We have a busy couple of days, and I still have something to show you."

CHAPTER 42

ZOE

Folding the white sheet of paper with Sharon's barely legible scrawl in two, I rest my head against the back of the porch swing and kick my feet. Blake's masculine scent reaches me before I hear him. Even with my vastly improved senses, he's still impressively quiet when he moves. His weight as he sits beside me causes the swing to shake, but he steadies it before using his foot to resume the gentle rocking motion.

His lips are soft against my temple as he throws one arm around my shoulders and pulls me gently to him, letting me lean on him and soak in his strength. He radiates calm and I try to absorb it because it's the exact opposite of how I feel right now.

"Blake, what am I supposed to do now?" I whisper, my voice coming out strangled as I swallow back a sob. The reality of what's happened and what it means for my future is sinking in. My life will be nothing like I thought it would be. Not that it's a bad thing, but it's a lot to take in. I need to learn how to live as a wolf and have a role within the pack, two things I know nothing about.

"Is that why the animals didn't like me?" I ask, and Blake frowns as a lone tear rolls down my cheek. Thinking of my last visit to the clinic, the dogs were quiet and submissive. I thought it was because Max was close by, but actually, it was me they were scared of. For some reason, this is the most upsetting thing of all to me.

"It's temporary, Zoe. I promise you. Once you get better control of your wolf's emotions, it will get easier."

"They were afraid of you that first night, too," I counter, but he smirks at me.

"I wasn't exactly in control of myself, angel. I was too worried about you."

He brushes my long hair back from my shoulder and kisses the exposed skin there.

"It'll be okay. Doc is happy to stay on for a while longer. He told Max he hated retirement and is thrilled to be back working, minus the hassle of doing all the admin."

That sounds about right. Doc loved the job, but the management of the clinic was making him weary. I'm glad he's there. Everyone knows him already and he has slipped in seamlessly to cover for me. But work is only the tip of the iceberg. Reading Sharon's letter has made this bigger than just me.

Blake will understand the details within it better than I, but Sharon discovered my biological grandfather was an alpha wolf, assumed dead long before he met my grandmother and had a pup. My mother.

The grandfather that *I* knew was actually a close friend of hers, who was happy to marry her, both to distract from his own sexuality and to help her raise a child that he knew he would never have himself. A single mother didn't have things easy back then either, so they came to an arrangement and decided to raise my mum together as his own.

Sharon has no way of knowing if my mother suspects that he wasn't her real father. How am I supposed to drop a bombshell like that on her?

Not all human and shifter offspring can shift, which seems to be the case with Mum. Regardless of whether or not she ever shifted, she passed on the wolf DNA. Blake's bite seems to have awakened the dormant gene, kick-starting my transformation. Sharon's not sure if it worked because he's such a powerful wolf, or because he's my mate. There's no way of knowing whether the same would happen to Hayley and Leah if their mates bit them in the same way. Although, given Hayley and I are identical twins, the likelihood seems high that, at least, she would.

"Hey." Brushing his thumb across my cheek, he wipes away my tears and kisses my damp cheek. "I know it's scary and daunting, but we'll get through it together. Let's just focus on getting to Leah's wedding and having a good time. We'll deal with the rest after."

Lacing my fingers with his, I sink into him and feel the tension leave my body as he plays with my hair, wrapping a strand around his finger and then releasing it. Dragging his fingers from my scalp down to the ends.

"Do you think you're up to going back to the pack?" he asks hesitantly. "If not, that's fine. I can get Max to bring some of my stuff here and—"

"No. I'd really like to go back. It is going to be my home, after all." Other than Jenna, I adored everyone I met there.

I feel his delight and relief at my words. The bond has been feeding me his emotions all morning. Worry for me, anxiety about what Sharon's discoveries mean for my family. What does all this means for my work? Pride at being mated and marked; despite what he said, carrying my mark means a lot to him. His joy that I'm now a wolf, too, quickly followed by the guilt that he's secretly thrilled about that development. It's been making my head spin. For once, it's nice to just feel his unadulterated happiness.

"Home," he murmurs, pulling me onto his lap and wrapping me up in his strong arms. There is a lot of uncertainty in my life, but not where this man is concerned. He's the best thing that's ever happened to me and I know that now we're together, I have everything I need.

BLAKE

Hearing Zoe call the packhouse "home" settles my nerves completely, and the next twenty-four hours, thankfully, go by smoothly. The pack welcomed her with open arms, even if they were a little stunned at her change. Word would spread quickly, and we need to have a conversation with her sisters and their mates before it reaches them through the gossip mill.

Everything else we will deal with when we get back. Because there is a lot to do. With all the resources at my disposal, I can find out about Zoe's family. Get answers to any questions she has and make sure she has plenty of time and support in developing her shifter side.

I'm worried about her safety too. I won't be with her every second of the day. Zoe will need to be able to defend herself to ensure Tyson never gets near her again, let alone taste her. I will never forgive him for that transgression and he knows it. It was a declaration of war, from one brother to another.

All thoughts of Tyson disappear instantly as Zoe emerges from the bedroom that Kim, Cooper's assistant, has put us in for the night. She looks stunning. A quick glance at my watch doesn't go unnoticed and Zoe chuckles as she saunters closer, hips swaying seductively just to torture me.

"We haven't got time for that," she teases, before spreading her palms across my chest and inside my suit jacket. Her dress is bright red, satin, and slinky, with a thigh-high split on one side that shows off her tanned legs as she walks. My pants feel uncomfortably tight and my fingers itch to hike up that dress and see whether she has anything on underneath.

"Fuck angel," I groan, letting my hands slide down her toned arms to her hands, enjoying the feel of her silky skin. "They won't miss us if we're a bit late." Pulling her to me, I press my face into her neck and sigh. Zoe smells like heaven and I long to drag her to bed. Again.

"They absolutely would." Zoe's laugh turns into a moan as I

nip her ear and tug it between my lips. My breath on her bare skin sends a shiver through her and goosebumps rise in its wake.

"I'm the Alpha. They might miss us, but they won't say anything," I murmur, amending my statement and Zoe scoffs.

"Have you *met* Marie Jones?"

Good point. Nobody wants to get on Marie's bad side. After I didn't turn up to Cooper and Hayley's wedding, she sent me a calendar for my next birthday present with this date not so subtly ringed in red. Straightening, I groan in frustration as I cup her face and press a chaste kiss to her lips.

"Fine. Let's go." I can't resist giving her ass a squeeze as she walks by me and she giggles, swatting my hands away, but I don't miss the slight flush to her cheeks. Goddess, I can't wait to get her back upstairs later on. The low back on the dress is sexy as hell, and I know all I need to do is sweep those straps off her shoulders and it'll fall straight to the floor.

Walking her to Rex's apartment, which has been commandeered as pamper central for the day, I'm about to try to tempt her back to our room when the door flies open. With wild hair and only one shoe on, Leah comes racing out with a deafening screech and pulls Zoe into her arms. She hasn't seen her since the barn when I stole her away. No doubt she was worried but has been giving us some space.

"Oh, my god. Oh, my god!" she squeals when she sees Zoe's mark, grabbing her by the hand and ripping her away from me. Zoe digs her heels into the carpet and comes to a halt, now far too strong for Leah to move her if she doesn't want to go. Turning to face me, she looks uncertain. Leah looks back and forth between us, rolling her eyes.

"Zoe, relax. He'll be fine for an hour or two without you. Blake, congrats. I'm sure you want to go find the boys now."

I know when I'm being dismissed. Sneaking one last lingering kiss with Zoe, I turn on my heel and stride towards Cooper's alpha suite where I can scent the brothers have gathered.

Normally, I'm their boss. Now they're family. This is going to be strange.

I'm so distracted by the change in dynamic of our relationship, I don't immediately register the silence that falls when I enter the room. When I lift my eyes to Rex's, he growls, low and threatening.

What the hell?

"Stop," I bark out the order immediately, letting a blast of my authority hit everyone in the room. An equally pissed-off-looking Cooper reluctantly submits to my command and tilts his head. This isn't quite the welcome I was expecting. As my new brother-in-laws glare at me, I understand what's wrong. All their eyes are fixed firmly on my neck. The collar of my shirt hides my mark from view, but they can smell the change in my scent and they know it's there. And it doesn't make any sense.

"Who the fuck gave you that?" Rex snarls.

CHAPTER 43

BLAKE

"Watch your tone," I warn, keeping my voice low, calm, and deadly serious. My hands are deep in my pockets to maintain the illusion of being relaxed, whereas in reality, my wolf has been on edge since we arrived on someone else's pack territory. Being on my land was okay. I can control everything that happens to a certain degree. Zoe's wolf is juvenile and unpredictable. Arriving late ensured the only people we've met so far are Zoe's family. While they are all human, I still need to make sure nobody does anything to trigger Zoe, and that her change doesn't become the focus of the day.

Cooper, Rex, and Nathan all move as one around the kitchen island, creating a wall of angry, protective brothers in front of me. They look imposing, but we've all sparred together at various alpha training camps and although I might not be significantly bigger than them in size, they are well aware of my superior strength. Not that they are likely thinking clearly right now. They consider Zoe part of their pack and are upset on her behalf. But she's not theirs. She's mine.

Cooper takes another step toward me just as the heavy footsteps of Marcus enter the room, the door banging against the wall as he pushes in. Marcus is the local sheriff, a burly bear shifter, who's mated to Cooper's little sister.

"What the *hell*?" he booms out, taking a big sniff and pausing in front of me. Instead of going to stand with his mate's brothers, he laughs, loud and raucous, clamping a giant paw-like hand on my shoulder and giving me a gentle shake.

"Congratulations. I don't know what is going on, but I'm delighted for you. You wolves, there's never a dull moment around here."

Shaking my hand with his other, he turns to look at the rest of the Jones men, who are standing like statues, looks of confusion plastered on their faces, replacing the fury from a few seconds earlier.

"What's wrong with *them*?" he asks, cocking a thumb over his shoulder at their serious expressions. Marcus looks like he hasn't a care in the world, despite the simmering tension in the room. It must come with being a giant grizzly that can take down pretty much anyone or anything.

"Their sense of smell isn't as sensitive as yours, Marcus. They can't quite work out who marked me." I'm speaking to Marcus, but I don't take my eyes off Cooper, who looks like he's struggling to control his wolf. His brown eyes glow amber. Cooper's wife is Zoe's identical twin. It's understandable he wants to look out for her.

"What?" He pivots so he is standing by my side, arms crossed over his broad chest. "Cooper, you can't be serious. You can't smell that?"

Marcus's disbelief and amused tone make Cooper pause and his gaze flicks to the big man who has a broad smile on his face, enjoying this immensely. Rex takes a deep breath through his nose and his eyes widen as he looks at Cooper in shock.

He's worked it out.

"No. No way," he states, shaking his head. Cooper takes another sniff before stepping back, stunned. This has implications for both of them.

"It can't be… how? That's not possible." Both men look somewhere between terrified and intrigued. Rex, in particular, has a glint in his eye. I've met Leah a couple of times. She's already quite a handful. He'll have his work cut out if she gets a wolf, too.

"It very much *is* possible. And I'll explain it all. But first, Cooper, I need you to order your pack not to say anything to Zoe or her sisters. This is Leah's big day, and we don't want it overshadowed by this news."

I could have issued the order myself, and I will if I have to, but I'm trying to be respectful by coming to him first.

Reluctantly, he takes a deep breath and his eyes glaze over as he issues his alpha command. Nobody is to mention the fact that Zoe has a wolf. At least not yet.

"Beer?" Marcus is leaning into the fridge, helping himself to a bottle. Nodding, I walk over to the island and sit down, just as he places a bottle on the counter in front of me.

"You might need one for this," I warn Cooper. "You too, Rex, but Leah might not be too happy about that." Rex scoffs and slides onto the stool beside me, palm outstretched toward Marcus, who places a cold bottle into it with a smirk. Rex looks resigned, accepting that some kind of madness is coming his way, but choosing to roll with it. Cooper, less so. He doesn't sit but places his hands on the cool surface to calm himself.

"Zoe has developed a wolf," I state simply. Cooper drops his head, knowing it was coming, but still not ready to hear it. Rex is slack-jawed, waiting for me to continue.

"We thought it wasn't possible, but it turns out the council and elders have allowed that untruth to be passed from generation to generation to stop wolves trying to turn their human mates, or any other humans, for that matter." I pause, waiting for questions, but Cooper still refuses to look at me, the tension in his shoulders obvious as he continues to stare at the countertop.

"I bit Zoe in wolf form, by accident, under the influence of the drugs Jenna was slipping to me. Apparently, the Walkers have a pretty powerful wolf in their family tree. The bite reawakened some dormant genes, with a little help from a witch."

Rex groans and downs the rest of his beer in one go, banging the bottle back down and pushing up from the table. Nathan has stayed unusually quiet. Given that he is unmated, and that they're no threat to his family, I suppose he's not that concerned anymore.

"Do we have to tell them? Leah is going to be all over this. She's definitely going to want one."

"We don't know yet. I'm still doing some investigating, but it's possible. For Hayley, it's pretty much guaranteed."

All eyes shift to Cooper, who hasn't moved.

"I thought it was because she's pregnant," he mutters, finally lifting his eyes and looking around the room. "She's stronger, can hear better, see better. I thought it was temporary from the pup because of our alpha bloodline, but maybe…?"

He turns to me for answers that I don't have. Yet.

"And maybe it is. We're assuming the bite triggered it, but maybe there's more than one way. We need to learn more. Zoe needs to tell the girls. After the wedding, obviously, and there are some questions she'll need to ask their mother."

I don't mention the fact that the sources of information we need might be a slightly suspicious witch and my psychopathic vampire step-brother who's hellbent on revenge and taking my pack. That might be more than they can handle at the moment.

"So, we all just have to act normal, like it's not even remotely odd that Zoe's now a wolf?" Nathan grabs a sandwich Marie left for us and shoves it into his mouth.

"Exactly."

"That's all fine in theory but has anyone told Mum?" Nathan poses the question that should have been first in my mind. Marie. As the former Luna of the pack and Cooper's mother, she won't be happy about being ordered to stay quiet. Will it even work?

She's an alpha female herself and has always done things her own way.

The colour drains from Cooper and Rex as they consider that. Cooper stands straight.

"I'll go talk to Dad, fill him in and make sure he keeps an eye on her."

Nathan scoffs and rolls his eyes, clearly not convinced that's going to be enough to keep Marie from blurting out the news.

As Cooper slips out into the hallway, Rex turns to stare at me again, his gaze lingering on the collar of my crisp, white shirt. Or rather, at what he knows is underneath. A small smile tugs at the corner of his mouth.

"If she gets a wolf, Leah can mark me back?"

Knowing how much I wanted Zoe to mark me, I can only imagine how excited he is at this prospect.

"Yes, she can. If she wants."

"Oh, she'll want." He absent-mindedly rubs his neck, and I can't hide my smirk. Looks like she tried it already.

"Goddess," Nathan swears, looking at this watch and snagging the empty bottles, depositing them into the utility room. "Have some sympathy for the lonely, unmated male amongst you."

Rex laughs heartily at that.

"Lonely? I don't think so. You forget I hear all the comings and goings from your apartment."

"Stuck for company, no. But that's not the same, is it?" Nathan asks, and Rex looks momentarily stunned. Ignoring his brother's curious glances, Nathan gestures with his hand for us to get a move on.

"Come on. Time to go. Rex, you don't want to risk pissing Leah off. She might decide to mark you on your… when she gets her wolf." He tips his head at Rex's crotch with raised eyebrows and a grimace.

Rex rolls his eyes, but he hops to it all the same. Marcus and I relax and watch the brothers getting ready to leave in silence. I like the big man. You know where you stand with him.

"I can understand the council's concern," Marcus finally says, and I nod. He's right. "I'm going to need you to keep me in the loop."

It's not a request. The last thing we need is for unmated wolves or rogues to think they can run around biting humans to turn them. And even though from someone else I might take offence at being told what to do, I don't feel the same with Marcus. He's practically family now and I know he only wants the best for his town.

"I will." Putting my hand out, he shakes it before smiling warmly behind his thick black beard. The smile turns into a laugh, long and loud as he shakes his head at me.

"You know this isn't going to work, don't you? This is going to be priceless."

There are too many people. Too many variables. He's right. It'll be a miracle if we get through the day without this secret getting out. But I'll try, for Zoe's sake.

CHAPTER 44

ZOE

Leah looks stunning. Her wild blonde curls hang loose around her shoulders and she's wearing a simple long, white silk dress with just a thin, gold bracelet on her wrist that I know Rex bought her for her birthday. Today will not be fancy. It's just a BBQ and buffet outside in the packhouse gardens with close friends and family. Try as Leah and Rex might, they could not convince Marie to do a casual dress code. Agreeing to no ties for the men was about as far as she would stretch, and, secretly, I think Leah is happy now that they let Marie get her way.

"You're glowing," Leah whispers with a cheeky wink as I kneel to help do the straps on her gold shoes.

"Quiet, you. That's how rumours start."

She chuckles and pulls me into a long hug as I stand up straight again, pushing my wavy hair back from my shoulders.

"Must be all the hot alpha sex. I'm so happy for you two." She squeezes my hand and grins. "It would have been so hard to keep all this a secret from you. I would never have lasted!"

Leah gestures around us at the packhouse, and I know what she's talking about. It would be hard keeping such a massive part of your life hidden from the people you love. Hayley shoots her a look but rolls her eyes affectionately when Leah refuses to look one bit sorry.

I was a little hurt when I found out that the two of them had this whole other side of their lives that I knew nothing about. Maybe not hurt, because I completely understood why it would have to be kept secret, so maybe it was jealousy. Although, I'm confident that as soon as babies arrived, the secrets would have broken. Surely having a vet in the family would have come in handy with wild shifter pups on the loose.

Leah takes a sip of her champagne, closing her eyes for a second and looking serene as she soaks up the moment. I doubt there has ever been a more laid-back bride.

"So, I hear you have a new man?" Mum appears beside me and pulls me into a tight embrace. "How am I the last to hear about everything with you three nowadays?"

"It was all a bit of a whirlwind, Mum, but Blake's great. And you'll meet him today." She glances at my other sisters, looking for confirmation of my assessment, and they nod enthusiastically. If Leah didn't like Blake, she wouldn't be shy about saying it, so I appreciate the support. There's no going back now, whether my parents like him or not.

"Fine. But you girls are making your father nervous with all these announcements. Can you wait a little while before you run down the aisle? And your brother is freaking out. He's driving me insane."

Mum pats her sleek blonde bob, looking beautiful, if a little uncomfortable, all glammed up for the day. Though her question was aimed at me, she thankfully doesn't wait for an answer. As soon as she spots Marie at the door, she sneaks out to meet her and they gossip away like old friends.

"Who wants to tell her?" Leah jokes, twisting her face into a grimace as she watches our mother chatting away with the former Luna. Knowing what I know, I can't help looking at her differently. Is her wolf just beneath the surface like mine was? If she had met a shifter instead of Dad, is it possible that she would have shifted, too?

"You okay?" Hayley touches my arm to drag me out of my daze and I smile weakly at her. There is no way of lying to your twin. Hayley knows me better than I know myself.

"It's a lot. And there's still some stuff I need to tell you. Not today, obviously, but soon."

"I'm not going anywhere. You can tell me anything, right? I know this has all been scary for you with everything that's happened, but you're mated now. It's going to get easier."

I smile, because what else can I do? Hayley takes that as my agreement and turns, offering me her back so I can slide the zip up on her dress. She's also in red, but a stretchy floor-length wrap dress that shows off her bump to perfection. It also hides the fact that she's wearing flip-flops, the only thing her swollen feet will fit into these days.

Finally, the photographer herds everyone downstairs and when we reach the seating outside, I notice the curious glances I'm getting from the rest of Hayley's pack. Instantly, my wolf's hackles raise. She's not enjoying the attention.

Blake: Relax, angel. Breathe.

His calming voice soothes me instantly, but I still feel uncomfortable under their scrutiny. This is all so new to me.

Zoe: But why are they staring? Cooper told them already, didn't he?

Blake: He did, but angel, I don't think that's why they're staring. You look incredible. They're all thinking the same as I am. How the hell am I lucky enough to be mated to you?

My steps falter as he sends me a mental image of him standing behind me, his chest pressed to my back as his hand drifts up the slit of my dress and dips between my thighs. Jesus. My legs turn to jelly and I don't trust them for a second as I try to regain my composure, aware that I'm in a room full of wolves who can tell exactly how aroused I am.

Zoe: Stop that! I can't think straight.

He laughs quietly as I clear my throat and continue to the

front, refusing to meet his eye now that I'm all hot and bothered. Hayley takes one look at me and swivels, fixing Blake with a warning glare. She already has that stern mom look down to a tee.

Once I'm in position, I lift my head and spot him staring at me, his eyes burning into mine with an intensity that takes my breath away. Those dark grey eyes are smouldering and everyone else fades away like we're all alone, ready to reignite the fire between us. When I feel Hayley's hand gripping the back of my dress and a sharp tug, I break eye contact and look down at her. She continues to stare straight ahead, a perfect fake smile plastered on her face, but hisses at me through gritted teeth.

"If you take one step from that spot, I'll tackle you to the ground, 100 months pregnant or not."

I blink rapidly and realise she's right; I was about to walk straight to him without even thinking about it. He has me hypnotised. When I glance at Blake, he's pouting. Clearly, Hayley is ruining all his fun.

The music starts and I watch Rex closely. He doesn't look nervous; he looks excited. So excited that he doesn't wait for Leah to reach the altar, but turns and stares proudly at her as she practically runs into his arms. Laughter goes up around the guests as Dad follows behind, reaching Rex and nodding silently to him as they shake hands. My father's eyes are shining as he hands over his youngest daughter. Mom's right. This is all probably too much, too soon for him. He's losing all his girls in one year.

The ceremony is simple and sweet, and before we know it, Leah cheers as they are announced husband and wife. Rex picks Leah up and kisses the life out of her in front of the entire pack, who whoops and hollers, clapping and cheering for the already mated couple. Dad groans, putting one hand over his eyes while mum pats his leg, reassuring him that everything will be okay.

Immediately after the service we stand around and chat, soft music playing in the background as dusk settles across the large lawn. Marie has outdone herself, with the pretty flowers, the casual seating, and the drinks. It's exactly what Leah would want, even if she probably didn't want anyone to go to as much trouble as this.

As I find myself caught exchanging pleasantries with Cooper's assistant, who looked after us so well when we visited before, for Hayley's hen, Blake catches my eye. He has a mischievous look on his face as he tips his head in my parents' direction and moves. Oh, god.

Making my excuses, I try to power walk as elegantly as I can to intercept him, but those long strides and my high heels have me beaten. While he confidently introduces himself, I can see my mother subtly checking him out. In his perfectly pressed suit and crisp white shirt, he's probably the last person she would have picked out as my date. That his hair is neatly styled and he's completely clean-shaven, will also throw her for a loop. My type before was more rugged; a bearded cowboy over the dashing businessman. Now, I'm all about the rolled-up shirtsleeves over tanned forearms, the way he loosens his tie after a hard day, and how he opens the button on his jacket with one hand when he sits. They do funny things to me and he has no problem taking advantage of them.

When I reach his side, Blake angles his body slightly to allow me enough room to stand beside him, slipping an arm around my waist and resting his hand gently on my hip. He presses a tender kiss to my head as he continues to charm my dad, talking about house and oil prices; all the things that my retired father loves to complain about to anyone who'll listen. I lean into Blake and feel my nerves ebb away. He knew I was anxious about introducing them to each other, so he did it for me, and I love him for it. My father will appreciate the bravery and confidence in coming to him under his own steam.

"You must come over for dinner soon." My mum places her hand on his forearm and Blake smiles genuinely at her, covering her hand with his and squeezing gently. She's smitten. Feeding boys has always been the sign that she has adopted them as one of her own. Rumour has it that Ethan, Cooper's former beta, still regularly calls in for tea and cake after visiting just once with Hayley.

"I would love that."

My mother beams because, like me, she can tell he really means it. Losing his own mum so young has to have been tough. It might be nice for him to have my parents in his life. Dad is a very level-headed person who says it like it is and Mum will smother you with kindness. Everybody needs people like that in their corner.

The band starts up and as the happy couple takes to the dancefloor; I wrap my arms around Blake's waist, pressing my cheek to his chest as we sway on the spot. Nathan should really be my partner, but there's no way in hell Blake will let him take me out dancing when we're so newly mated. Plus, it's Nathan. He doesn't seem that bothered by my absence as he drags a woman watching the first dance out into the middle and dazzles her with his moves.

"That went well. They loved you," I murmur, as Blake's hand stroking down my hair and back lulls me into a dopey haze. "I love you."

Blake tips my face up to his before kissing me, soft and sensual, and I can feel myself perking up under his attention. When his hands on my hips tug me a little closer, I can feel I'm not the only one. I'm aware of a presence beside us, so I lean back, pinching Blake's waist to get his attention. We turn at the same time and come face to face with Marie.

Shit.

"I need to know everything," she states bluntly, eyes wide with fascination. Behind her, Hayley frowns as Marie's demand catches her attention. She slips out of Cooper's grasp as the song ends and waddles straight over.

"Know everything about what?" Hayley turns her curious expression to me. Faced with the two feisty Lunas, my palms get clammy so I clasp them in front of me. Jonathan Jones appears from nowhere and, with a saucy wink, he pulls his wife into his arms and kisses her.

"I missed you, darling. Dance with me?"

Gossip temporarily forgotten, Marie waves over her shoulder as she allows herself to be led away.

"Come on, leave them alone. It's a miracle they got out of bed long enough to be here." Cooper whispers against Hayley's ear and, eventually, she relents with a small smile. Her shoulders droop and she leans back into him.

"Fine." Her features soften as Cooper takes her hand with a brief nod to Blake and turns to go. But he's not expecting Hayley to lurch forward and grab Blake by the front of his shirt to yank him down to her. Surprised by her strength and not willing to fight a pregnant lady, Blake allows himself to be manoeuvred. I groan as she shoves her nose against the collar and breathes. Her eyes flash, sparks of gold lighting up as realisation hits her.

"Nooooo!" Hayley hisses in disbelief, mouth hanging open as she looks back and forth between us. Anyone standing nearby cleverly edges away, wanting to be nowhere near this conversation. "What? How? And you!"

She twists to face Cooper and pokes him hard in the gut. He winces and rubs the spot with one hand, holding the other up in surrender. Hayley is stronger than she realises. I can't help wondering whether it's her power or the pups that are causing these changes in her.

"Shh. You can yell at me later, Hayley, but first, let's take this inside." Cooper gestures away from the dance floor and toward the pack house. After one more poisonous look, Hayley leads the way, glancing back every few steps to hit him with another huff and scowl.

When we reach the rear of the house, Cooper opens the patio doors and we slip inside, following him to his office on the ground floor. Pouring strong drinks for the three of us, Cooper looks reluctant to begin this conversation. And he shouldn't have to. It's my news, my transformation, our family tree. I suck in a deep breath and open my mouth to speak just as Cooper's door clatters against the wall behind it. A very nosy bride and a furious groom stand on the threshold, staring at our little foursome sitting around Cooper's desk like we're attending a meeting.

"Want to tell me what's going on?"

CHAPTER 45

BLAKE

There's absolute silence as Leah flounces into the room and perches herself on the edge of Cooper's desk, a glass of champagne still dangling from her fingertips. While Hayley looks furious, Leah's eyes dance with mirth and curiosity.

"Come on, out with it," she repeats when nobody says a word. Zoe shifts uncomfortably in her seat. Reaching out to wrap an arm around her shoulder, I pull her closer to me. She lifts her beautiful pale grey eyes to mine, and I nod encouragingly. She has nothing to worry about here.

"I marked Blake."

Okay, so we're starting at the end first. Hayley's eyes widen as Zoe confirms what she immediately suspected. Leah's head swivels back and forth between Zoe and Hayley, not truly believing what she's hearing.

"How? I tried, and it didn't work!" She looks so annoyed about it that I can't help laughing. Rex groans and puts a hand over his face. "What? I did. And nothing."

"That's because you're not a shifter," Zoe whispers, and Hayley turns, grabbing both her arms in shock.

"But neither are you…" Leah starts but trails off, her brow

knitting together as the alternative dawns on her. "No. No. Really?"

Zoe gives a tiny nod and Leah leaps to her feet, eyes wide and hands clasped together in front of her chest in delight.

"You have a wolf. Ohhh, I want one!" She bounces on her toes, radiating excitement. She doesn't seem one bit concerned about how or why Zoe has a wolf. Spinning on her heel, she leaps at Rex, who catches her in mid-air. His reflexes are impressive. This clearly happens a lot.

"How?" Hayley asks the obvious question, turning slightly in her seat to put her back to Cooper, who's clearly in the doghouse for keeping secrets, even if it was just for a few hours. Silently, Zoe produces Sharon's letter from her tiny purse and hands it over. Leah moves to stand behind Hayley and they read it together, glancing up occasionally at certain parts to see if this is for real. Cooper and Rex move around beside them, eager to find out as much as they can. Even they don't know all the details yet.

"Mom," Hayley whispers, looking up at Zoe, whose eyes shine brightly with unshed tears. I know this is the part that scares her the most, filling her in on who her real father is and what it has meant for her children. More than anything, Zoe wants to avoid worrying her mother unnecessarily, but there's no way around it. For a while, at least.

"Oh god, what about Chase?" Leah buries her face in her hands. "I'm not telling him. No way. You're the one with the wolf."

"If he gets a wolf and becomes even bossier, we'll never be able to listen to him. He's unbearable already," Hayley cringes. I need to find out more about their brother. It sounds like he's already pretty alpha without realising why. If he can't control himself and his urges, he could easily end up in trouble. Enlisting in the military might have provided a release for all that aggression, but it's temporary. It won't be enough to satisfy a trapped alpha wolf forever. He needs to know how to direct it into something positive.

Zoe smiles and I see the tension in her shoulders ease as her sisters process the information she's just given them. They've had a strange few months already, finding out about shifters and packs. I suppose nothing shocks them much anymore. Leah knocks back the rest of her champagne and walks over to Rex, gazing up at him adoringly.

"So… what you're telling me is that there's no way I'm going to turn into a wolf today?" Leah asks, not taking her eyes off Rex, who wraps his arms around her waist and pulls her close. They're adorable. Leah is normally such a firecracker, joking and messing all the time. But she shows her softer side around her new husband, and it's so good to see.

"Not today," I confirm. "Maybe never."

I feel like I have to reiterate this part because she seems far too excited. Hayley, on the other hand, is a sure bet. Zoe has one, so Hayley could bring hers out. If she wants to, that is.

"And Zoe's going to be okay?" She directs that one at me with a slightly dangerous glint in her eye.

"Absolutely," I agree, hoping that's true, that this all isn't too much for her. Goddess, when this is over I'm taking my woman on the best holiday ever. We both need it.

"Absolutely," Zoe purrs, hugging me and resting her head against my chest. That feels so good. Having her close to me, but also her faith in me, in us.

"Well then, let's get back to the party, and we'll sort this all out another day."

"Here, here," Rex concurs, picking his bride up and tossing her over his shoulder before marching out the door.

Blake: That went well

Zoe: For us. Rex will never hear the end of it.

I don't doubt that.

We follow them back out to the celebrations, Cooper and Hayley holding hands this time, but still having a serious conversation.

"I ordered him not to say a word." Stopping, I turn to Hayley, needing to explain myself. "I didn't want to take away from Leah's day, but that wasn't fair to you. You're partners. And I'm sorry."

Hayley eyes me carefully and then sighs.

"Thank you." Finally, she smiles and rubs her bump, stretching out her back. "I suppose I might be crankier than normal."

Cooper laughs and swings around, thumping me on the arm. Apparently, it's alright for her to say it, but not for him to agree. I'll have to remember these rules for when Zoe is pregnant, provided the Goddess sees fit to bless us with them. Cooper pulls her to him, and she pretends to struggle, finally grinning despite herself when he manages to place a kiss on her cheek.

She looks so like Zoe, but completely different at the same time. The different coloured eyes make them easy to tell apart up close, but it's also their nature. Hayley is more guarded, more reserved, until you get to know her. Zoe is an open book. She wears her heart on her sleeve and is who she is.

And who she is, is everything to me.

I think back to when I first met her and she was so brave, shooting me when she thought I was an intruder. And again, when she faced Tyson and Jenna. She might not be as comfortable being the centre of attention as Hayley, but she has other qualities that are going to make her a superb Luna. We're going to make a great team.

As I spin her around on the dancefloor and pull her into my arms for a sensual kiss, I can't wait to get home and start our life together.

ZOE

Blake whirls me around the dancefloor, and I can't stop smiling. I'm so relieved that my sisters know and I can relax. A problem shared is a problem halved and all that.

"Blake, my shoes are killing me. No more!" I complain,

laughing as he spins me away from him and then back against his rock-hard body. I slide my hands across the thin material of his shirt, feeling every dip and muscle. This man is so hot. A sudden urge to lick him washes over me and I have to compose myself. My wolf is determined to put on a show for anyone who wants to see whose man this is. Me, not so much. The mark will do.

"I'm sure I can think of a way to get you off those feet." With a wink, he turns and directs me away from the rest of the dancing guests. His front pressed against my back as we make our way through the crowds, his hand is resting lightly on my hip. As he rubs his thumb in a circle across the material, my blood heats. My wolf's desire for him rises quickly and suddenly, I have no desire to find a comfy chair. I want a dark corner somewhere instead so he can ravish me.

Inside, we find an empty living room and Blake closes the door behind him with a soft click that sends a shiver down my spine. I walk over to the minibar in the corner and pour us both a drink, but before I can even hand one to him, he's there, warm chest searing my exposed back. His hands drift slowly down my arms, edging lower and lower over the delicate fabric of my red dress. Deftly, he gathers the silk in his fingers and lifts it, exposing even more of my thigh through the slit down one side.

Caressing my sensitive flesh, I whimper. Pressing soft kisses to my back and shoulder, he lifts my hair carefully to give himself better access.

"I love you, Zoe," he murmurs, lips brushing against my neck as his fingers stroke across the sensitive creases at the tops of my thighs. My legs nearly buckle when he slips one finger under the lace edge and across my drenched pussy.

"I love you too," I whimper as he pushes one finger deep inside me, then two. He curls them, sweeping them across that magic spot inside. I lift onto my toes, placing my palms flat on the sideboard and arching so he has better access. His eyes meet mine in the mirror over the bar and my breathing quickens. Blake works me over quickly, knowing exactly what to do to drive me crazy, and I'm already on the edge.

"Blake, I love you. Fuck me. Take me." His eyes blaze silver, glowing in the dim light of the room. "Fuck me hard, Blake."

"Damn it." This wasn't in his plan, but he's as powerless to resist our new bond as I am. I hear his belt open and then he's hitching my dress up over my ass. His hands squeeze and explore, before the brief bite in my hip tells me he's ripped my flimsy underwear right off.

His thick length nudges at my entrance and I throw my head back to rest on his shoulder, our eyes locked in the mirror as he pushes inside. I rock forward on each thrust as he picks up a fast pace, pounding into me and making me feel every inch of him. The glasses in the cupboard rattle, but I don't care who might hear us. I just need him inside me.

"Goddess, you're so sexy." His voice in my ear and his breath on my skin drive me wild enough to push back against him on each stroke, desperate to feel more of him.

"Is that good, angel?" I nod enthusiastically, but then his other hand is strumming my clit and my head spins. Calling out, I feel myself rocketing toward my climax. Tingles spread out from my fingers and toes. I'm so close.

"Yes, Blake. Yes. Oh, god," I mutter incoherently as I reach between my legs and press his hand harder against my clit. Blake groans. He loves the fact that I'm taking what I want.

"Bite me." My voice comes out barely above a whisper, but he doesn't need to be told twice. I watch, completely aroused, as his canines lengthen, and he sinks them into the soft flesh of my neck, connecting us in two places. Instantly, my orgasm takes me and I cry his name, clamping down on his dick and pulsing my release with each wave. With one final hard thrust, he stiffens, grunting as he comes and filling me with his seed. Stream after stream pulses into me as he continues to give short thrusts with each aftershock to keep my pleasure going.

As we come down from our high, he drags his lips across my

skin, mumbling how much he adores me, how much he treasures me. I sigh contentedly as he pulls out and turns me, wrapping me up in his massive arms before carefully cleaning me up with his handkerchief and straightening my dress for me.

"Come on, angel. Time for bed." He kneels to help me step out of my shoes, slipping my torn panties into his pocket, before looping my sandals over one finger and lifting me with ease. With one gentle kiss to my nose, he turns and strides out of the room, heading quickly for the stairs.

"Where are we going?" My voice is slurred from tiredness rather than alcohol.

"It's a surprise. I hope you've got a passport, Zoe." I grin and kick my legs excitedly. That's exactly what I need. Reaching up, I run my fingers through his hair and down the back of his neck. It's been years since I've gone anywhere other than wherever my sisters were living for a quick break. No drama, just good food and good company sounds amazing. And I won't find any better company than this man.

"Where are we going?"

"Anywhere you want, angel. Anywhere at all."

EPILOGUE

BLAKE

As I emerge from the sea, feeling calm and refreshed, my eyes immediately search for my mate. She's lying back on a sun lounger, a wide-brimmed hat and sunglasses on, but I can tell through the bond that she's watching me and that she's enjoying the view. The sand is hot under my feet and the sun is warm on my back as I stride across the beach toward her. Her skin is glowing with the slight tan she's picked up, and her bright white bikini shows it off to perfection. With her long legs stretched out in front of her and a cocktail in one hand, she looks like the poster girl for holiday relaxation.

Her phone buzzes and she flips it over where she had it face down on the table beside her and she laughs.

"It's Max again," she murmurs against my lips as I lean over her, watching intently as drops of water fall from my hair and drip down her breasts and toned stomach. Maybe I'll lick them off. She tips my chin up to drag my attention away from her tight little body and to her face. She's speaking, but I'm staring at her lips now, and can't stop myself from cutting her off with a searing kiss.

"Blake," she chastises softly, even though she kisses me back. I ignore her complaints as I cup the back of her head and deepen the kiss, sweeping my tongue into her mouth and playfully nipping at her bottom lip. "You can't ignore him forever. What if it's important?"

"He can handle it," I say, one hundred percent convinced he can, in fact, handle just about anything that might come up. Everything except Tyson, that is. Sighing, I rest one knee on the edge of her lounger and reach for the phone. My hand drifts up her thigh, trailing lightly over her glistening skin, slick from suntan lotion, and she inhales sharply.

"We both know what this is about and he's just being a big baby." Sulking, I return his call and flop down beside my gorgeous mate, twirling one blonde wave around my finger while I wait for my Beta to answer the phone.

"About time!" Max grunts, annoyance clear in his voice. It's hard not to laugh.

"You called me two minutes ago. And I'm on my honeymoon. I have much, *much* better things to be doing." Zoe giggles when I stare directly at her as I say those words, and I loop my arm around her waist, bringing her to me for another taste of her pink, full lips. I can't get enough of her.

"Blake, you can't do this to me. They are driving me insane. Sharon would be bad enough, but Mandy too?" Max groans loudly and I can picture him flopping down on the old sofa in my office, feet up on the coffee table as he despairs at what to do with two women who are immune to his charms. They have completely decimated his macho persona.

"It's temporary."

Zoe's eyes light up in amusement as she listens to my beta plead for mercy against the two feisty women staying in the pack house while we're away. Sharon is pouring through the old manuscripts and books kept in my pack's library, searching for more information about the possibility of other human and alpha matings; anything that might help Zoe's family.

Mandy has stepped in to run the packhouse, even though I told her to enjoy the two weeks off while we're away. Instead of taking the opportunity to tour the pack and settle in, she got straight to work, much to Max's irritation, because he's the one now fielding all of her questions.

"When are you coming back?" Max sounds desperate.

"Not sure yet. We're having the best time. I'll be doing this more often," I warn him. We're heading home in two days, but I'm having too much fun to tell him that. A bang in the background tells me that's not the answer he was hoping for.

"Don't forget, I still have that photo of you fast asleep in Zoe's clinic. If you're not home within the week, I can't be held responsible for where that might end up."

Zoe laughs, loud and carefree, and I raise my eyebrow at her. Does she think that's funny?

"Fine, I'll be back within a week. But Max, seriously? You can't handle having some housemates? Frankly, I'm disappointed." I can't resist turning the knife.

"That witch, we have no idea what she can do. Even though she denies it, I know it's her. She acts all sweet, but she's not one bit... And then Mandy, with question after question..." Max rambles on, venting his frustrations, but I toss the phone aside and haul Zoe over me. She comes willingly, straddling my thighs, and sits back, stroking her hands over my chest, which is still wet from the sea.

"Did they find him?" Zoe's tone is casual, but I know better. Her grandfather's whereabouts, or even whether he's still alive, are weighing heavily on her. She'd like to know all she can before she tells her mother about her biological father's identity. But he has managed to stay hidden for this long. He has been very careful if the council and his enemies never tracked him down.

"Not yet." I won't give up hope, and Max is going to have to suck it up until we understand what happened and why. "We will though, I promise."

Zoe's love wraps around me as she looks into my eyes, a tender smile playing across her lips.

"So, Sharon's going to stick around for a while?"

There's laughter in her voice, and I can tell she's enjoying Max's misery as much as I am. While I maintain a healthy suspicion of the witch, Zoe seems to have bonded with her and she's happy there will be some familiar faces around the house when we return.

"She is." I grin, and Zoe throws her head back, laughing again. Poor Max. We'll be back in soon to rescue him, but I'll let him stew for a little while before I tell him that.

Zoe has hired Doc full-time at the clinic and he's enjoying being back to work without the responsibility of running the place. It's a good compromise. Zoe can work at the pack clinic, and when she develops better control over her wolf, she can ease back into working at her own clinic and decide from there. Selfishly, I'm delighted that she'll be closer to me. New mates don't like to be away from each other, but I could work out of the cabin a few days a week if I had to. Anything to avoid spending even one night apart.

Deciding there is plenty of time to worry about all that once we get back to the real world, I grip Zoe under her thighs and stand. She automatically wraps her legs around my waist, kissing my neck and nibbling on my ear. Our private suite opens up right onto the beach and I make it through the open patio doors in record time.

I launch her onto the giant bed and she lands on her back with a shriek, laughing as she braces herself to stop from rolling off the side.

"Blake!"

"Goddess, I love that I don't have to worry about hurting you anymore."

I crawl up the bed and she giggles as I tug on those tiny strings holding those three little triangles in place.

"You're beautiful."

I kiss my way up the inside of her ankle, calf, and knee, and I'm just about to reach heaven when her phone goes off on the bedside locker. Zoe reaches for it and I growl.

"No." Not meaning for it to come out so gruff, I balance it out with a delicate kiss to her pussy, and she squirms, placing her foot firmly on my shoulder to stop me from getting any closer.

"You know I have to."

She smiles indulgently at me and ruffles my hair as she leans over and picks it up. I feel like snatching it and flinging it against the wall.

"Oh, my god. It's happening? We're on our way!"

Zoe's smile is huge as she jumps from the bed and rushes into the massive walk-in wardrobe in our suite. Her phone is perched between her ear and her shoulder as she hops up and down on one foot, trying to get the other through one leg of her panties.

With a reluctant groan, I roll off the mattress and make my way over, kneeling in front of her so she can use me to balance and holding them for her so she can slip her legs through the holes. Sliding them up over her hips, I skim my hands up her thighs and let them linger on her waist. Zoe ends the call and drops the phone onto a chair before flinging her arms around my neck and kissing me hard. She's not making it easy to leave our bed behind.

"She's having the baby."

"I gathered that."

"Thank you for helping me."

She smiles shyly at me and it's adorable. I pick her up and swing her around. Zoe laughs in delight as I set her down gently and grab her ass, giving it a hard squeeze.

"You're welcome. It's good practice for when you'll be too big to put them on yourself." I press a kiss to her nose as she blushes, looking cuter than a button. "Come on. Let's go meet my nephew."

"Or niece."

I nod, not wanting to argue with her or ruin the surprise. But I know these things. I don't know whether it's my better-than-average sense of smell or a gut feeling, but I always get it right. Just like when I decided to wait one more month for my mate.

And it was the best decision I ever made.

THE END

To see what happens next, order The Hunt now.
Read on to get a sneak peek at Chapter 1.

If you'd like to read a bonus scene from this book, written from Tyson's point of view, download it at:
https://bookhip.com/SGQBNKA

If you want to go back and read how Zoe's twin Hayley and her sister Leah met their hunky shifters, read the *Shifters of Grey Ridge* series, starting with **The Alpha's Saviour**.

THE STEEL PACK ALPHAS

THE HUNT

REECE BARDEN

CHAPTER 1

MAX

"Stop flipping cursing!"

Zoe hisses at me across the kitchen island and pointedly nods toward our new house guests, Mandy and her teenage son, Noah, who are looking anywhere but at us. Blake's broad back remains turned away from me while he fixes his mates something to eat and continues to wait on her hand and foot. I don't blame him. They've had a rough time. But now that we know he never had moon madness, there is no reason for this insanity. Am I the only person who hasn't lost their mind?

"She can't be trusted. She turned Zoe into a wolf without telling either of you!"

My alpha's growl is low and quiet out of respect for our newest pack members, but its force is no less powerful as I feel its weight on my shoulders. Gritting my teeth, I remain standing tall out of pure stubbornness. I might only be half bear but that character trait came through loud and clear. Blake could force me to submit, but that means upping the ante in front of Noah and he won't make them uncomfortable.

"You don't need to remind me of what my mate went through, Max. Believe me. I will have nightmares about it for the rest of my days."

Zoe reaches out a hand to touch his hip gently, reassuring him she is here and well. Still, he does not turn, forcing me to keep up the argument all by myself. Palms up, I face Zoe, pleading with her to think rationally about this.

"Zoe. You can't be happy about this. She could have warned you about Tyson."

Zoe is like a sister to me now that she is mated to Blake. They are family. I can't bear to see them inviting even more trouble into their home. And that's what Sharon is, trouble with a capital T.

"Yes, but she made sure I could defend myself. And then gave me more information about my family than I ever have hoped to find on my own."

"But why does she have to live here?!"

Reaching up, I drag my two hands through my hair and give it a tug before throwing my hands up in the air. Frustration rolls through me, and I feel like I'm about to explode. This doesn't make any sense to me.

"I don't even know what to say. This is crazy!"

Light footsteps cross the hall and Sharon's scent reaches me as she strolls through the door, looking relaxed and at ease, like this has been her home forever. My nose wrinkles slightly and I try not to inhale her scent too deeply. Whatever perfume that witch wears, or spells she has been working on, makes her scent unpleasant to be around. The rest of the pack doesn't seem to notice it, but my nose is more sensitive and I try not to be obvious as I edge away.

"Something bothering you, Max?" she asks, sliding onto a stool at the island and bringing those bright violet eyes up to mine in challenge. She's tiny but fierce, I'll give her that. She has her pale grey hair pulled back in a tight bun and it makes her bright eye colour even more jarring.

"You shouldn't be here, witch, and you know it."

The words fly from my mouth before I can stop them, but I stand by what I said. She can't be trusted. Nobody from the council can, if you ask me. Plus, I'll have to live with her irritating scent all over the house.

"Max!" Zoe hisses, shocked at my rudeness.

"It's okay," Sharon says calmly, and the even tone of her voice sends my temper through the roof. She looks all reasonable while I'm the overly dramatic one.

"It's not okay. Not one fucking thing about this is okay."

Leaning my forearms on the back of the stool, I sigh, and for the first time in my life, I doubt my alpha's judgement on this one. He's not even listening to me and I eye the witch suspiciously.

Could she be why? Who knows what kind of ways she could be influencing him?

Blake sighs and finally turns around, placing his palms down on the pale marble countertop and looking at me with exasperation, like a parent trying to placate a naughty toddler.

"I get it, Max. You're not happy, but my decision is final. Sharon will stay with the pack to help us find out as much about Zoe's grandfather as we can, and she can help protect us against Tyson if he tries anything."

When I huff in disgust, he hits me with a glare that's cutting enough to make me keep my mouth shut.

"I will do anything I can do to keep my mate and my territory safe!"

His voice gets louder and angrier and the atmosphere in the room crackles with tension. I could point out that if she wanted to help protect us against Tyson, she could have done that by telling us he was still alive. But I'm already pushing it as it is.

"YOU are going to do nothing," I comment, pointing a finger in his direction, and then swinging it around to Zoe because I know she could also be a loose cannon. Doing what she's asked to do doesn't seem to be a strong suit of hers.

"What do you mean?" Blake blinks at me as if I've completely lost it.

"I mean... you're newly mated, to a white wolf who could be

some kind of long-lost fucking princess, and you're Tyson's primary target. There is absolutely no way either of you are going to be the ones traipsing around the forest trying to find the man who wants you dead."

"I can't believe I'm saying this, but he's right."

Sharon doesn't look at me. She's focusing on Zoe, who is probably the only person who can talk Blake out of going after Tyson. As I watch, a slow, self-satisfied smirk pulls at one side of Blake's mouth, then the other, until he has a broad smile on his and I have a worried frown on mine. Somehow, I know I've made a mistake, but for the life of me, I can't work out what.

"Excellent point. In that case, I want you and Sharon to find him. Together."

The only thing that makes his announcement slightly less awful is that Sharon looks equally horrified at the idea of working with me. She gives me a once over and shakes her head like she can't believe she's stuck with me either. We don't agree on much, but I share her sentiment exactly.

This is going to be a nightmare.

ABOUT THE AUTHOR

Reece Barden is a romance author, currently working on her romance series, The Shifters of Grey Ridge and the Steel Pack Alphas.

She loves creating steamy shifter stories about hot, growly alpha men and the strong women who both love and torment them.

She writes for people just like her who love a little light-hearted fun with their naughty heroes and edge of your seat storylines.

KEEP IN TOUCH

To keep up to date on new releases, cover reveals and the general chaos inside my brain:

- Join my mailing list at www.reecebarden.com
- Sign up to Reece's Racy Readers on Facebook, or
- Follow me on Instagram @reece.barden.

For exclusive access to chapters as I write, as well as bonus content and new stories, join my pack on Patreon.

OTHER BOOKS BY REECE BARDEN

Shifters of Grey Ridge Series

The Alpha's Saviour

The Alpha's Inferno

The Alpha's Revival

The Alpha's Regret

Steel Pack Alphas Series

The Chase

The Hunt

Printed in Great Britain
by Amazon